REKINDLED LOVE

On reaching the stable, Sterling slid the door open and stepped aside for Miranda to lead the way inside. She went to hang the lantern on a peg protruding from one of the thick, oak beams.

"I can find my way back without it. You'll need it to saddle Zeus. Remember to blow out the flame when you leave."

He reached out as she made to pass.

She stopped as his hand came to rest on her shoulder.

"I enjoyed the evening very much, Miranda."

Her chin came up slowly. "As did I, sir."

The look in her eyes tore through his heart.

"Good Lord, I've missed you," he blurted out.

Surprise and confusion swept across her pale face. As she started to speak, he lowered his head and took her lips in a gentle kiss.

She went rigid with shock, then slowly relaxed into his arms. His fingers entwined themselves in her silky hair, pulling her closer. To his elation, her mouth softened under the pressure from his—for a few ethereal moments she was returning the kiss. . . .

The Major's Mistake

Andrea Pickens

A SIGNET BOOK

SIGNET
Published by New American Library, a division of
Penguin Putnam Inc., 375 Hudson Street,
New York, New York 10014, U.S.A.
Penguin Books Ltd, 27 Wrights Lane,
London W8 5TZ, England
Penguin Books Australia Ltd, Ringwood,
Victoria, Australia
Penguin Books Canada Ltd, 10 Alcorn Avenue,
Toronto, Ontario, Canada M4V 3B2
Penguin Books (N.Z.) Ltd, 182–190 Wairau Road,
Auckland 10, New Zealand

Penguin Books Ltd, Registered Offices:
Harmondsworth, Middlesex, England

First published by Signet, an imprint of New American Library,
a division of Penguin Putnam Inc.

First Printing, August 2000
10 9 8 7 6 5 4 3 2 1

 REGISTERED TRADEMARK—MARCA REGISTRADA

Printed in the United States of America

PUBLISHER'S NOTE
This is a work of fiction. Names, characters, places, and incidents either are
the product of the author's imagination or are used fictitiously, and any
resemblance to actual persons, living or dead, business establishments, events,
or locales is entirely coincidental.

BOOKS ARE AVAILABLE AT QUANTITY DISCOUNTS WHEN USED TO PROMOTE
PRODUCTS OR SERVICES. FOR INFORMATION PLEASE WRITE TO PREMIUM
MARKETING DIVISION, PENGUIN PUTNAM INC., 375 HUDSON STREET, NEW YORK,
NEW YORK 10014.

Prologue

The young lady started at the touch of a hand on her shoulder and turned quickly from the shelf of books she was perusing. "Lord Averill," she said with some surprise, trying to keep her voice from betraying how less than pleased she was to find who had joined her in the dimly lit library. "I should not have thought you to possess an interest in books."

The gentleman leaned negligently against the carved oak moldings, a slight smiled playing on his lips. "None whatsoever," he replied softly. "I prefer my entertainment to be of flesh and blood, not ink and paper. Don't you?"

She ignored his comment and tried to step around him, but he shifted his position to block her way. "You know, Lady Miranda, you have a rare spirit for a female. That rather intrigues me."

"I care very little what intrigues you, Lord Averill. Now, if you would kindly stand aside."

"Yes, full of fire, aren't you? A shame it is wasted on your new husband. Grosvenor is a mere raw youth, as you have no doubt discovered."

Her voice became even colder. "Sir, I will not listen to such talk. Julian and I have the very best of relationships—"

"Ah, love." His tone mocked her. "Undying devotion

to each other? Faithful as two turtledoves? What a bird-witted concept, to be sure."

"I don't doubt that you sneer at such sentiments. It has become clear to me that you have little understanding of any real feeling and care for naught but your own amusement."

Averill's eyes narrowed, but the cold smile remained on his face. "You are nearly as naive as your husband, my dear Miranda. You will soon learn that everyone of the *ton* indulges in amusement. Trust me, you would find it most enjoyable." His voice lowered to a silky whisper. "There is no need to fear anyone might know. Julian is occupied at billiards with Wheatley, Renfrew, and our host. Several of the ladies have retired early, and the other couples are busy at whist in the drawing room. This part of the house is quite deserted."

Lady Miranda's mouth pursed in disgust. "I have no idea what Julian and the rest of his group of friends see in you, sir, but rest assured that while they may look to you for an example of how a man about town carries himself, I most certainly do not. Now, out of my way, if you please."

His hand stayed her step. "Yes, those green cubs have looked up to me since our days at Oxford, and still do." He gave a harsh laugh. "Why, you don't really think that Julian hasn't followed my advice—he's established a charming little *chère amie* in a small town house not far from your own residence so that he may indulge in other tastes when his regular fare becomes a bit . . . bland."

She drew in a sharp breath. "I don't believe you, sir. I have more faith in my husband than to be tricked by your lies."

Averill moved even closer, trapping her against the wall of books. "Actually, you're right, he's too much of a callow boy to know how an experienced gentleman should take his pleasure. But come, let me show you—a spirited filly like you needs an expert rider."

She made a sound of disgust.

His mouth came down toward hers.

Lady Miranda twisted her head and slapped out at his face, catching him a hard blow on the cheek.

Averill paused for a moment, drawing his fingers lightly over the spreading red welt. "You shall be very, very sorry you did that," he growled. "Too good for me? I'll see you pay dearly for your pride." With that, he pushed her up against the bookcase, pinning her arms behind her with his body. Before she could utter a sound, his mouth was upon hers, bruising her lips, forcing them apart while his hands pulled at her gown, working at the buttons and dragging the bodice down to her waist. After roughly fondling her breasts, he moved his palm up to cover her mouth while he nuzzled at her neck, leaving several raw marks on the delicate skin.

"Let that be a lesson to you," he said close to her ear, his hand still preventing any sound from her lips. "I could take more, but I shall leave it at that. And I suggest you don't say anything of this to anyone, most especially our dear Julian." His mouth curled in a smug smile. "You know what a stickler he is for family honor—you wouldn't want to be the cause of a scandal in front of Lord Greyson's other houseguests." Lady Miranda slowly stopped struggling and was very still. He let his hand fall away. "You had better wait here for a time and . . . compose yourself. Anyone seeing you now would be well aware what you have been up to."

She gave a gasp of horror mingled with seething anger as she covered her chest with her arms. "Get out, you cur," she managed to choke out. "For Julian's sake I shall remain silent for now. He seems to find you an admirable sort, though, God knows why. But things may soon change. Stay well away from me for the rest of our stay here, or else nothing will stop me from telling Julian what a filthy beast you truly are. And once we are back in Town, I never wish to lay eyes on you again."

"Oh, don't worry, Lady Miranda, I shall see to that," he said to himself as he sauntered from the room.

*   *   *

After brushing a crease from his sleeve and straightening his cravat in the small cheval glass in the foyer, Averill strolled into the billiard room and poured himself a glass of brandy. He tossed back several swallows then moved to stand beside one of the players, a tall, dark-haired young gentleman whose broad shoulders and long limbs showed more promise than sinew.

"I say, Grosvenor," he murmured after the other man had sent a polished ball skidding across the slate. "Let Wheatley continue on in your stead. I need to have a word with you." His voice fell even lower. "In private."

Julian Grosvenor's brow furrowed, but he handed over the cue and followed his friend over to a small alcove set off to one side of the massive table.

Averill cleared his throat in feigned awkwardness. "Not a pleasant thing I have to say, Julian. But seeing you are a good friend, I couldn't live with myself as a gentleman if I didn't speak up. I know you well enough to know how much you value your honor, what with your family name and future title to consider." He paused as the other man looked even more perplexed. "And well I know you'd never wish to be made a laughing stock of before Society." An exaggerated sigh followed. "It's your new wife, Julian. I hadn't wanted to say anything to you, hoping that marriage might change things. But apparently her feelings are still . . . engaged elsewhere. Very engaged."

Grosvenor paled. "What are you saying, Averill?"

"I fear Lady Miranda has been playing you for a fool, my friend."

"I . . . I don't believe it! Miranda would never—"

"Wouldn't she?" cut in Averill. "Are you so sure of yourself to think she has eyes for no other. After all, she is a beautiful young lady with no dearth of admirers."

The young man's jaw clenched.

"Perhaps you should venture to the library. I went

looking for a book to take up to my bedchamber and—
well, you may see things for yourself."

"The library . . ." repeated Grosvenor in a slightly
dazed voice. It suddenly hardened. "With whom?"

Averill lifted his shoulders. "It was too dark to see."

There was only a fraction of hesitation before Grosvenor abruptly spun on his heel and headed for the hallway, his boots beating a furious tattoo on the polished
parquet. Averill followed not far behind, an expression
of smug satisfaction on his features as he watched the
young man wrench the library door open.

A single branch of candles was set on the far side of
the ornate desk. Standing before the mullioned window,
Lady Miranda was attempting to pin back the worst of
her disheveled curls. The front of her gown was still sadly
askew, with one rosy nipple quite visible above the wrinkled silk, and the flickering flames seemed to lick at the
red mark of passion on her neck.

"Good God."

She whirled around. "Julian!" Choking back a sob, she
started toward him.

He took two steps backward.

"Julian! You wouldn't believe—" She froze on seeing
Averill's shadowy face behind his shoulder.

"No," he said roughly. "I wouldn't, not if I hadn't seen
it with my own eyes."

"I'm sorry, Grosvenor. Truly I am. But you had to
know," murmured his friend.

"Who, Miranda?" demanded Grosvenor in a hoarse
whisper. "For God's sake, who was it?"

Stunned, she could only stare at him in utter disbelief
for several moments before finding her voice for a reply.
"You think I—" Her eyes flooded with raw hurt. Without thinking of the import of what she was saying, she
cried, "Why don't you ask Lord Averill?"

"Good God," he repeated faintly, nearly reeling from
the shock of his assumptions. He fell back several more

paces, then the pain on his smooth features hardened into rigid anger.

Without further words, he reached out and slammed the door shut on her.

A quarter of an hour later, a caped figure stumbled toward the darkened stables. Minutes later, the clatter of galloping hooves sounded over the cobbled courtyard as a large grey stallion was spurred toward London.

Grosvenor swore violently as he paced rather unsteadily before the mullioned windows of his town house study. His hand ran over his unshaven cheek, then raked through his tangled locks. Suppressing the urge to heave the small oval miniature sitting on the table, along with any other object that lay close at hand, into the crackling fire, he slumped into one of the leather wing chairs near the hearth and poured himself yet another glass of brandy.

After what seemed like an age, he rose abruptly and went to his desk. His shaking fingers took up a pen and began scribbling a detailed set of orders to his man of affairs.

Within a week he should have his commission as a major and be on his way to the Peninsula.

The divorce would of course take somewhat longer.

Chapter One

April 1808

The bramble caught on the hem of Miranda's gown. As she bent to release it, she noted with some consternation that a thorn had caused a tiny tear in the worn fabric. Her lips compressed. Another bit of darning. Pretty soon there would be precious little of the original dress left, but it couldn't be helped. She couldn't afford a new one.

With a small sigh, she picked up a basket filled with assorted herbs and roots and made her way back to the narrow dirt cart path. "Justin," she called. "Come, love, it's time to return home."

"Yes, Mama." A shock of tousled dark hair appeared at the edge of an overgrown field, barely visible above the tall grasses. As the little boy hurried toward her, it was evident that something was cradled very carefully in his chubby hands.

"Look!" he cried as soon as he was close enough to reveal his treasure. A rather large toad was struggling to escape from the boy's grasp. "Isn't he grand?"

She smiled. "Oh, indeed he is," she replied as she regarded the multitude of warts and the wide mouth gaping at her. "Pray, what do you plan to do with him?"

"I'm sure Angus will help me build a box so that I may keep him along with the others."

She made a mental inventory of the current residents of her son's room—four field mice, a baby sparrow with

a broken wing, a jar of tadpoles, and a praying mantis—
and wondered just how many more creatures the household could tolerate. Given the toad's appearance, he
would not be the most welcome addition. But on taking
in the boy's eager expression, she hadn't the heart to
say no.

"Very well, love. But do remember, we cannot turn
Aunt Sophia's house into a menagerie. Mr. Toad will
have be the last addition for a time." As if indignant
over the lukewarm reaction to his presence, the creature
made another lunge for freedom. "Oh, do be careful not
to squeeze him too hard," she added.

"I know that, Mama," answered Justin with just a
touch of impatience, and to be sure, he was handling the
toad with great care for his age. "But you see, I have an
even better way to carry him home." With that, he undid
the top button of his shirt and slid the toad inside.

Miranda repressed a laugh and took her son's hand.
"Very clever young man, but let us make sure that Miss
MacKenzie is well out of your room before you make
ready for your bath." The woman who served the role of
both governess and nursemaid in their small household,
though extremely tolerant in every other area, had shown
herself to be more than a little squeamish when it came
to Justin's pets—Miranda wasn't sure this latest one
wouldn't bring on a fit of vapors if it simply popped out
of her son's shirt without warning.

"A bath?" cried Justin with dismay.

She looked at the dark smudges on his cheeks, the bits
of hay and leaves sticking out of his dark hair, and the
mud encrusted on the knees of his pantaloons, and
merely raised an eyebrow.

"Oh, all right," he sighed. Then his expression brightened. "Perhaps the toad would like to come in, too."

"It is a toad, not a frog," she reminded him. "And no,
he may not. Soap would not be as agreeable to his skin
as it is to that of little boys."

Justin made a face, but his spirits were not long dampened by the prospects of immersion in a tub of hot, sudsy water. In a moment or two, he was back to telling her about the different sorts of butterflies he had seen near a clump of heather. For the rest of the short walk back to their home, Miranda was content to listen to his enthusiastic chattering. Once again, she gave thanks that her son was of a naturally cheerful disposition. He didn't seem to be suffering from the dearth of playmates his own age or the lack of expensive toys or ponies or. . . .

Her jaw tightened and her blue eyes clouded for a moment. Money didn't guarantee happiness, she reminded herself.

They passed along by a stretch of weathered stone fence, overgrown with climbing vines. On the other side a large flock of sheep grazed amid a patchwork of thistles and rough grass. The northern light dappled their shaggy coats as grey clouds scudded in front of the setting sun. Rain was likely before long, she thought, shifting her basket to the other arm. It was well that they would reach home before the chilling drops caught them out.

In the distance an elderly shepherd raised his arm in greeting, waving it vigorously to catch her attention. "Gud day te ye, Mrs. Ransford," he called. Moving more quickly than might have been imagined possible, he caught up with them where a rickety wooden gate gave access onto the cart path.

"I be wanting to thank 'e fer the poultice ye fixed. Did wonders fer me aching leg, as ye can see."

"I am glad to hear it, Mr. Calhoun. I shall be happy to leave another batch at your cottage, then."

"Yer a kind soul, ye are, to give a care about an old goat like me. Now, best step lively." He pointed his crook to the sky. "Afore ye and the wee bairn get wet."

Thanking him for the warning, she took up Justin's hand and hurried their steps down the rutted path.

Rose Cottage sat in a small dell, protected on one side from the winds whistling down from the moors by a stand of ancient live oak. In front of it was a small, well-tended garden, the soft colors from the climbing roses just beginning to peek out from the new buds. Miranda pushed open the heavy oak and stepped into the welcoming warmth. Though not a large abode, it radiated a comforting coziness. The furniture and drapes, though simple, were done in a cheerful mix of muted floral chintzes and stripes. The pine paneling throughout the rooms, mellowed to a rich honey shade over the years, was redolent of beeswax and lemon oil, and a generous fire crackled in each of the hearths. Earthenware crocks filled with fresh-cut greens and fragrant herbs graced both the dining table and the sideboard of the parlor. From the kitchen the aroma of fresh-baked bread wafted through the air.

"Shall I take your basket into Cook?" asked Justin with an eagerness that indicated his hope that scones or shortbread might also be emerging from the ovens.

Repressing the twitch of her lips, she handed it over. "I should be very grateful."

He grasped it in his small hands and struggled to conceal the effort it took to lift it even several inches from the ground. She refrained from offering any help, knowing how much it pleased him to be able to help her, and merely watched with a fond expression as he managed to lug it across the stone floor of the entryway and into the hallway. Then with a small sigh, she brushed a few remaining wisps of straw from her faded skirts and entered the small sitting room to the left of the stairs.

"Did you find everything you needed, my dear?" The speaker looked up from the mending in her lap. Though advanced in years, her face still retained the classic features that had made her a diamond of the first water in her day. Her once raven hair, now entirely silver, was as thick as in her youth, and age had not dulled the vibrancy of her sea-green eyes, or the look of keen intelligence that lurked in their depths. "I feared that you and Justin might be caught unaware by the storm blowing down off

Ben Lomond. You must be chilled to the bone in any case. Come sit by the fire, and I'll ring for some tea."

"It is still early in the season, but I did manage to find some goldenseal. I should have felt badly had I not been able to locate all the ingredients. Mrs. Fraser is feeling even more poorly than she did last week, and I know this potion will help her." Miranda took a chair near the hearth and stretched out her hands toward the flames as she repressed a slight shiver. "Tea would be lovely, Aunt Sophia."

Sophia, Lady Thornton's face took on an expression of concern. "You must have a care, Miranda, that you do not push yourself too hard and take ill as well. You are not responsible for every ache and cough in the entire shire."

"But it is so hard to say no when I can help them with the knowledge I have gained."

"I know, my dear, and have nothing but admiration for the good works you do. But I still worry." Her brows came together slightly. "And I wish you would let me provide you with a new gown and a warm cloak and gloves—"

Miranda's slender hands knotted together in her lap. "You already do so much for us," she answered in a low voice. "I must accept your generosity in providing a roof over our heads and food on the table, but I will not take a penny of yours for anything else. You have little enough to spare—I can see to the needs of Justin and myself."

Lady Thornton gave a sigh of exasperation. "As if you and Justin are a burden to me! I can well afford to keep my family in comfort if not in luxury. And well I know that every farthing of your meager income is spent on your son, not on yourself."

"I have little need of anything," she replied doggedly. "What does it matter whether my gown is new or worn?"

"It matters to me. Because I do not wish to see my dear niece in rags."

Miranda's chin rose a fraction. "You are not responsible for my predicament—why, I don't even have a claim to call you aunt or to appeal to your charity except by . . . marriage."

Two spots of color rose to Lady Thornton's cheeks. "I will pretend I did not hear that."

Miranda bit her lip in anguish. Her head turned away toward the fire as she struggled to repress the tears welling in her eyes. "I didn't mean to sound so ungrateful. You know you are dearer to me than anyone—"

Their conversation was interrupted by the entrance of an elderly maid carrying a tray with the tea and an assortment of cakes. She was followed by Justin, telltale crumbs of fresh shortbread clinging to his ruddy cheeks.

"I am not sure toads like shortbread," he announced as he peeked down into his shirt.

Miranda could hardly keep a straight face, despite the emotions stirred by the previous exchange of words. "Well, perhaps it is an acquired taste. And perhaps Mr. Toad should not learn to like it, lest he feel deprived once he returns to the wild."

Lady Thornton smiled as well. She was well used to her young relative's fascination with both flora and fauna. "I need not ask what is making the muslin of your shirt twitch in such a manner."

"Would you like to see him?" asked Justin eagerly.

"I believe Aunt Sophia knows what a toad looks like," said his mother dryly.

"Oh, very well." His hand surreptitiously took up a slice of rich Dundee cake studded with raisins. "May I go show Angus, then? He could help me make a box and fix it with some nice dirt and leaves."

"Yes, you may. But you mustn't be too long. Supper will be ready soon, and then there is a bath awaiting before bedtime."

"Yes, Mama." The little boy's shoulders sagged in resignation as he abandoned the fleeting hope that his mother had forgotten about the promised soap and water.

"And that's quite enough sweets for now."

His hand shot back from the tray. "Yes, Mama."

As soon as he was gone from the room, both of the ladies couldn't help but exchange amused smiles.

"I vow, my life would be sadly flat without the two of you here, so let me never hear another word about you being a burden to me," said Lady Thornton as she poured them both a cup of tea.

"Oh, Aunt Sophia, I'm so sorry if I—"

"You needn't say anything more on the matter. I didn't mean to overset you. Of course I know your determination to deal with the consequences of . . . the past." Lady Thornton pushed at the gold spectacles perched on the bridge of her nose and cleared her throat. "While you know I have always admired your courage, I cannot help at times to think you allow . . . pride to cloud your better judgment."

Miranda's head jerked up, and she looked for a moment as if to speak. Then she bit her lip and began to stir her tea.

"But let us talk of other things," her aunt said quietly. "Did you see Mr. MacAllister in the south fields? He wanted to ask your opinion on. . . ."

The conversation steered to less turbulent topics as they discussed the latest news from the surrounding farms and a few bits of local gossip. Though Lady Thornton kept up a cheerful countenance and a constant stream of pithy comments, Miranda knew her well enough to sense something was amiss. Finally she set aside her plate, the cakes untouched.

"Aunt Sophia, what is wrong?"

The older lady stopped midsentence. Instead of answering right away, she rose and went over to the writing desk by the wall and took up a folded letter. Without a word, she handed it to her niece.

Miranda skimmed the contents, then looked up, her eyes betraying a flare of emotion.

Lady Thornton met her niece's troubled gaze. "I grew up at Talney Hall. I hadn't expected my brother to leave it to me, but as it wasn't part of the entail, and he knew what fond memories I have of it. . . ." She trailed off for a moment. "I know how loath you are to set foot in England, my dear. If you are entirely opposed to it, I shall not consider taking up residence there. However, at some point, you are going to have to address Justin's future."

Miranda's jaw tightened perceptibly.

"It is true that Highcroft Manor is close by," she added in a voice barely above a whisper. "But it is a minor estate that I have never known Julian to visit. Why, I doubt he even knows he owns it. Besides, he is only lately returned from Portugal, and after so many years of absence, I doubt he shall wish to stir far from London for quite some time."

At the mention of that name, Miranda paled considerably. Her fingers clenched the creased paper, causing a slight crackle.

A sad little sigh escaped Lady Thornton's lips. "I only ask that you think on it—"

"That isn't necessary," replied Miranda. She gave a harsh laugh. "You are no doubt right. London has entirely too many attractions for him to think of quitting it for some time."

Her aunt's lined face took on a look of pinched concern. "Miranda—"

"No, really. When do you wish to leave?"

"Do not rush your decision, my dear. I only meant to broach the idea—"

Miranda cut her off with a determined shake of her head. "It would be selfish in the extreme for me to deny you this." She cut off another attempt at protest from her relative with a quick gesture of her hand. "And you are quite right about Justin. Obviously he must return to

England at some point, and perhaps it's best done while he is young." She fell silent for a moment as she stared at the lines of script that had so swiftly altered her life. "In any case, after seven years, a new scandal must certainly have come to the fore." Her mouth quirked in an attempt at a smile. "Surely no one will care overly about a cast-off wife, even if they discover who I am."

"Miranda," repeated Lady Thornton, her voice was full of anguish.

"No, truly, it is all right. I believe I am ready to face it. At least, as you say, there is little chance of having to encounter his lordship until . . . much later."

"You are sure?"

She nodded, wishing she felt nearly as certain as her words would indicate.

The contents of the glass were downed in one swallow, then quickly refilled from the crystal decanter on the polished mahogany sideboard. The tall, lean figure then limped to the oversized leather wing chair by the fire and took a seat with a grunt of relief. He unknotted the elegant cravat at his throat, tossed it aside, and stretched his long legs out toward the dancing flames. His eyes fell shut as he raked one hand through his raven locks. With an audible sigh, he closed his eyes and took another long draught of the aged French brandy.

The library door opened quietly, and a wiry little man made his way across the thick Aubusson carpet with hardly a sound. His brows came together slightly at the sight of the other man's exhausted face.

"Tough night, guv?"

Julian Grosvenor, the Marquess of Sterling, rubbed wearily at his aching forehead. "I had forgotten how interminable these evenings are, what with a gamut of prosing bores at my club, the simpering hosts and ballrooms packed with predatory. . . ." He gave a humorless laugh. "I swear, Sykes, at times it seems that facing Boney's troops was less of an ordeal than a Season in Town."

The other man grinned as he removed the discarded cravat and bent to move a small hassock in place under the marquess's left boot. "That bad, is it? Well, I should be well glad I don't have to endure the terrible hardship of swilling champagne with the toffs and dancing until dawn with all them beautiful ladies. A rough life indeed, guv."

That coaxed a low chuckle from Sterling.

Seeing that the fine lines of stress etched around the marquess's eyes were beginning to relax, Sykes went on. "Surely you have no complaints of where you end up. 'Pon my word, I ain't never seen a more ravishing ladybird than that opera dancer of yours. Half the gentlemen of the *ton* would give a fortune to trade places with you."

Sterling showed no surprise at the frank manner of his former batman. He pulled a face as he gave another short laugh. "A fortune is exactly what they would give! I fear the ravishing Madame St. Honore is also becoming rather too demanding." His mouth tightened. "Despite the fact that she doesn't shrink from the sight of my disfigurement." He finished off the rest of the brandy in one swift gulp. "Pour me another, will you, Sykes? And one for yourself."

The other man regarded the marquess for a moment. "Ain't you had enough for tonight? Why not let me help you up to bed. You've been hitting the bottle rather heavily these past few weeks, and we've seen what it can do to a man. Can't be doing you any good."

Sterling stared into the fire. "No doubt you are right," he answered after a moment. His eyes pressed closed. "Now, be so good as to fill my glass."

Sykes took it without a word and splashed a small amount of spirits into it, then fixed one for himself. He cleared his throat as he handed over the brandy. "Well, perhaps a female presence will be a civilizing influence in this house—though I imagine there will be some changes. I doubt some fine lady would tolerate the likes of me as a titled gentleman's valet."

Sterling's head jerked around. "What the devil is that supposed to mean?"

"Servants talk, guv. Word has it that an engagement between your august self and this Season's Incomparable, the lovely Miss Wiltshire, is not far off." He paused for a fraction. "The betting books list the odds at over two to one for those wagering a yes."

A string of oaths exploded from Sterling's lips, followed by further imprecations concerning scheming mamas and obsequious papas with pockets to let. "Why, the lady in question cannot repress a shudder at the sight of my dragging step, no matter what charming manners her parents have tried to drum into her head." He took a deep breath and added with some vehemence, "You may be assured I have no plans to fall into the parson's mousetrap any time soon."

"Now that you've come into the title, don't you have to think about setting up a nursery?"

"I'm not about to stick my spoon in the wall just yet," muttered Sterling. "I have plenty of time to . . . deal with that issue."

Sykes eyed him with a certain curiosity, but refrained from any comment.

"Have you ever been to the Lake District?" asked the marquess abruptly.

"Can't say that I have, guv."

"I am considering a visit there to one of my properties."

The former soldier rubbed at his jaw to hide his surprise. "Now, why do we want to go and do that for? From what I hear tell, nothing much up there but hills and sheep and . . . lakes, I suppose."

"Precisely."

"Well, it's a hell of a trek if what you're looking for is a bit of peace and quiet. Why don't we just retire to Crestwood if you wish to avoid Society for a time?"

Sterling shook his head. He forbore to add that his primary estate still held too many bittersweet memories

for him to take any comfort there. "It's time I paid more
attention to the rest of my holdings. I mean to take my
responsibilities seriously. Since my father's death three
years ago and my accession to the title, I've barely spent
more than a fortnight in England . . . until now." He
gestured toward his desk. "There is a pile of correspondence from bailiffs of estates I didn't even know I
owned."

"Can't we pick one a tad closer to the comforts of
Town?" groused Sykes. "I'd have thought you'd had
enough of roughing it after all them years on the Peninsula. I know, I damn well have," he added under his
breath.

"The farther, the better," muttered Sterling. "You
don't have to go along, you know. You are welcome to
stay here in Sterling House and have run of the place
while I'm gone."

Sykes gave a snort of disgust to show what he thought
of that suggestion. "Oh, aye. I'm just the sort of paltry
fellow to shrink from a little discomfort and let you go
haring off on your own. Or perhaps, now that we're in
England, you'd rather hire some fancy fellow as more
befitting your station."

Sterling's mouth quirked in a rueful smile. "What, and
miss your deferential manner and polite conversation?"

The other man grinned, then shook his head in resignation. "Well, at least it's useful you being a fancy lord
and all. I imagine we won't have to be sleeping in a
bloody stable, like old times."

Miranda wrote out yet another recipe and placed it in a
pile with the others. That should do it, she thought with
grim satisfaction. She could not recall anyone else whom
she had forgotten. The draughts, tisanes, poultices, and
broths were all spelled out. For those who could not
read, the vicar would no doubt be happy to help. A wave
of sadness came over her as she fiddled with the end of
her pen. She had been of some use here and had gained

no little affection from her neighbors, a taciturn and reserved folk not given to taking outsiders to their heart.
It was hard to give that up.

Her sleeve came up to brush at her cheek. Well, she
would just have to start anew. She had done so before,
under far more daunting circumstances, she reminded
herself. This time it wouldn't be nearly so difficult. After
all, she was much older now—and wiser. Her eyes drifted
over the familiar surroundings, the nicks in the beaded
moldings, the rough texture of the whitewashed plaster,
the grain of the polished oak floor. Yes, it was sad to
leave, but she had to admit that even had she the means
to stay behind, she could never abandon the redoubtable
older lady whose staunch support had, at times, been the
only thing that kept her from sliding into the blackest
despair.

She began carefully folding each sheet of paper and
lettering a name on the blank surface. She would deliver
all of them this afternoon, along with a final good-bye.
So engrossed was she in her thoughts that she wasn't
aware her aunt had entered the room until a voice spoke
up close to her ear.

"Perhaps you should simply publish a book of remedies, and save your hand from falling off," said Lady
Thornton lightly as she surveyed the stack of papers.

Miranda essayed a smile. "Well, now that they shall
know all my secrets, I'll no longer be needed."

Her aunt's arm came around her shoulder. "My dear,
you will always be needed. You have done much good
here. Of that you should take great satisfaction."

She nodded pensively. "In many ways, my life has
been much more rewarding than . . . it might have been.
Truly," she added, noting the look in her aunt's eyes. "I
am well aware that I could easily have become used to
a frivolous existence, thinking of naught but my own
pleasures and the latest fashions, the next ball or the
latest bit of gossip." Her lips creased in a ghost of a
smile. "I know at times I am stubborn and unwilling to

compromise. Perhaps those traits have landed me in a briar patch of my own making, but I believe I am a better person for having struggled with the thorns. I may be cut and bruised a bit, but am stronger and hopefully a bit wiser.''

Lady Thornton couldn't refrain from wrapping her in a tight hug. "My dearest Miranda,'' she whispered. "I don't think I have ever been prouder of you.''

It was a few moments before either of them could speak. Then Lady Thornton fumbled for a handkerchief in the pocket of her gown and blew her nose rather loudly. "Well, I saw Angus is waiting with the gig. Best be off so that you'll be back before dark.''

Miranda nodded, not trusting her voice. She took up the pile of papers and tucked them under her arm, bestowing a quick peck of her aunt's cheek as she left the room.

The gig was indeed waiting outside, the shaggy Highland pony harnessed in its traces nearly dwarfed by the tall, burly man who stood holding its bridle. At the sound of the door falling shut, he turned, a hearty smile spreading across his broad face. His beefy hand ran through his unruly blond locks as he dipped his head in greeting.

"Hello, Angus. I'm sorry to trouble you, but I shall never be able to make all the visits I would like if I go on foot.''

He reached out and took the willow basket from her hands. "Tain't no trouble at all, Lady Miranda. I wish you would let me take ye more often. It's not right fer a wee slip o' a lassie like you te be trudging over these rough hills with such a heavy load. Wear yerself right down te the bone, ye do.''

Miranda tucked her head to hide a smile. With her tall, willowy form, she couldn't remember ever having been referred to as a wee slip. But then again, to Angus, most everyone looked rather small. "I thank you for your concern, but I enjoy walking. I have grown to love the moors and the wild beauty of the locks and the colors of the heather and gorse."

He helped her into the gig and spread a coarse woolen blanket over her lap. "Ye's never dressed warm enough, either." With a shake of the reins, he urged the pony into a brisk trot. "If ye like it here, why do ye have to go down . . . there?" A jerk of his massive head indicated the direction of the English border.

"Because Lady Sophia has inherited her childhood home and wishes to live there once again." Her voice tightened. "And remember, my son is English. He must, at some time, learn his heritage."

Angus nodded slowly. "Well, I suppose those be fair enough reasons." He slanted her a sideways glance as he guided the gig around a tight corner. "But I can see ye ain't overly happy about it."

She picked at a bit of chaff caught on the blanket. "My feelings are not important. After all the kindness she has shown to me, it is the very least I can do for my aunt."

"Aye, then." His eyes narrowed. "Well, all of us know there ain't a disloyal bone in yer body, m'lady."

The color rose to Miranda's cheeks.

"I'm sorry if I've said something te put ye to blush. It's—"

"No, it's quite all right." She took a deep breath and sought to deflect the conversation away from herself. "But what of you, Angus? You should not feel in the least obliged to uproot yourself from here. You have more than repaid any debt you might feel you owe to us." Miranda paused as she recalled the night nearly five years ago when she had spied the half-starved young man poaching rabbits in the neighboring squire's wood. Hunger had driven him to be careless, and the gameskeeper was quick to have him at gunpoint. She had acted without even thinking. The evidence disappeared into her basket before the two men returned to the traps. Without any real proof, and with her assertions that the stranger was their new groom, merely helping her forage for herbs, the squire was forced to let the matter drop.

"Well, seeing as I ain't from around here, it don't make too much difference to me. Jem feels the same." He grinned. "And the way I figure it, England is a whole lot closer than the South Seas, where by all rights is where I should be, save fer ye, Lady Miranda."

She couldn't hide her look of relief. "Any debt you might feel you owed me has been paid long ago, but I am most happy to hear your decision. We should have missed you, especially Justin. You have been extremely kind to him—believe me, I know how trying a boy of that age can be at times."

"Oh, nay, he's a good bairn, he is. No trouble at all." A sudden chuckle erupted from his throat. "But what are ye going to do with all them creatures he's got collected? Be a mite difficult to take them along."

Miranda laughed as well. "Indeed, I convinced him that Mr. Toad and the rest of his menagerie will be much happier forgoing a long carriage journey. And I have promised that he may find a number of new friends when we reach England."

The gig stopped in front of a stone crofter's cottage, and Miranda climbed down to deliver a recipe for warding off chillbains as well as a fond good-bye to a wizened little woman with several skinny grandchildren clinging to her woolen skirts.

She was heading off to a new life and leaving the past behind her.

Or was she?

As the last strains of the waltz died away, Sterling moved even deeper into the shadows cast by the arrangement of potted palms and took another long swallow of champagne. He watched the elegantly dressed crowd ebb across the polished parquet to exchange partners as well as the latest tidbits of gossip. The vast ballroom, aglow with the light of a myriad of candles glinting off the costly silks and jewels, echoed with the trill of laughter and the notes of the violins and cellos adjusting their tune to the next melody. A mood of heady gaiety seemed to float in the air, along with the lush scent of mixed roses and wisteria.

So why, he wondered, did it all leave him feeling rather flat.

"Good lord, Julian, your expression is nearly as black as that fine set of evening clothes you're wearing. Don't Weston's creations feel a damn sight more comfortable than sweat-stained regimentals?" The gentleman who appeared at the marquess's side took a sip from his own glass as he surveyed the crowd. "I would have thought you would be enjoying the delights civilization has to offer now that you are back."

Sterling pulled a face. "You call matchmaking mamas and breathless chits fresh from the schoolroom a delight?"

Lord Atwater gave a chuckle. "Ah, is that what has driven you into hiding? My title is neither so august nor my pockets so plump that I would know of such things."

"Well, you may take satisfaction from the fact you are doing something useful, Fitzwilliam." He gestured toward the swirling dancers. "I cannot help but find the interests of most of those present so. . . ." Sterling's voice trailed off as his mouth compressed into a tight line. "How goes it at the Home Office?" he asked abruptly. "At least with you, I can expect to have an intelligent conversation."

His friend shot him a look of concern before answering. "Do not take what I am about to say amiss, my friend, but I do not like the note of cynicism I hear in your words. During the time we were together under Wellington, I always admired your good sense, as well as your courage." He drew in a breath. He knew vaguely of his friend's past and searched for a careful way to say what he had in mind. "Now that you are back to take your place in Society, I should hope you are too intelligent to allow yourself to become . . . bitter toward the world."

Sterling gave a sigh. "Sorry. I suppose I am a bit out of sorts tonight."

Atwater dropped his gaze. "Is your leg causing you much pain?" he asked quietly.

"No more than can be expected." As a footman passed in front of them with a tray of champagne, the marquess exchanged his empty glass for a full one. "And I promise I am not about to sink into a fit of sullens, moaning about life like that idiot in Lord Byron's new work. Come, now, let us discuss something more interesting than the past. I should like to hear about what you are doing."

Atwater glanced to ensure that no one else was within earshot. "Actually," he said in a low voice, "I am dealing with a rather serious matter of late. News has just arrived concerning the recent unrest in the north. We are not entirely sure yet, but it may be being instigated by an agent of France. Apparently Bonaparte believes that if he can encourage any sort of uprising, especially one that may spread into Scotland, it would severely hamper our war efforts. Unfortunately, he is right." His hand tightened around his glass. "And whoever is responsible for fomenting the actual trouble has proven damn elusive. He wreaks a nasty havoc, but manages to disappear before we can move in the militia, only to surface not long after in some other place. I've just received word that there have been suspicious doings around Hingham that may indicate he is ready to strike yet again."

Sterling's brow creased. "What do you intend to do to stop him?"

His friend looked grim. "I am not sure yet. The one man I trust to handle such an important mission is away—"

"You say the trouble is around Hingham?"

Atwater nodded.

"Send me."

"What!"

"As a matter of fact, I have just been planning a visit there—my bags are already packed. Think on it. I have a large estate nearby and therefore have a perfectly plausible reason for being there. I shall be able to look into things without attracting undue suspicion."

"The arrival of a marquess will hardly go unnoticed," remarked the other man dryly.

Sterling played his trump card. "That may be so, but you remember my batman, Sykes?"

"Indeed, I do."

"Well, he is now my valet. He will be along, too. Between the two of us, you may rest assured we will get to the bottom of what is going on."

Atwater stared at the tiny bubbles in his glass. "I'm well aware of your prowess in the field. But do you truly wish to undertake such dirty work when you are so recently returned from the rigors of war? I need not tell you it may be . . . dangerous."

Sterling fixed him with a withering look.

"Very well. Come by at nine tomorrow morning, and I will fill you in on all the details." He cleared his throat. "You have solved my dilemma, Julian. I'm immensely grateful. However, I can't help but feel a bit guilty for dragging you away from the height of the Season after all the years you have been away."

"Not at all, Fitz. In fact you are doing me an immense favor." Sterling raised his glass in toast. "Here is to overcoming the challenge ahead."

Chapter Two

Sterling reined his mount to a halt on top of the ridge and paused to take in the view. It was certainly worthy of all the countless stanzas of poetry penned in its praises. The sun was sinking slowly into a feathering of clouds, and the diffusion of light cast a soft yellow glow over the still surface of the lake. In the distance, the craggy cliffs and steep hills of yew mixed with pine took on a flat, ethereal quality in the gathering shadows.

The big bay stallion tossed his head and gave a whinny of impatience. Sterling lingered a moment longer, then turned the animal back down the narrow trail. He did not regret in the least his decision to quit Town. Somehow the balls did not seem nearly so glittering nor the conversations quite so entertaining as they had in his youth. The *ton*—the gentlemen in their impeccably tailored evening clothes and the ladies in their silks and jewels—were no longer as perfect as he had remembered, merely ordinary people with the same strengths and frailties as the rest of humanity.

Perhaps the grueling years of military action on the Peninsula had changed more than just his physical appearance, he mused. Hunger, thirst, fear, suffering, the prospect of death—all had the effect of making the artifices of Polite Society seem so very trivial. After such experiences, it was hard to listen to eligible young ladies carefully schooled to chatter on about nothing more substantial than the weather or the latest fashion. Even worse were those who hung on his every word, assiduously nodding in agreement to any opinion he voiced. At times, he felt he could have announced he was going to strap on wings and fly to the moon, and no one would have dared dissent. After all, he was a marquess, and he was wealthy. And eligible. The combination gave him rein to have whatever it was he wanted in life. He let out a weary sigh. Maybe while he was here, he would begin to figure out just what that was.

The trail threaded down through a stand of live oak, thick with an undergrowth of brambles and bushes. As he rounded a tight bend, still deep in thought, his mount came up short, shying sharply enough to nearly send him tumbling from the saddle. With a few choice words, Sterling settled the animal and urged him forward. The horse still refused, and the marquess was forced to dismount to lead the animal forward. Then he saw what the problem was.

Half hidden by an outcropping of rock, a young woman was kneeing in the middle of the rough path, gently lifting an injured crow into a large willow basket set down by her side. "A moment," she called, without turning around. She carefully arranged a bundle of cut herbs to keep the broken wing from jostling against the woven vines before getting to her feet and brushing back a loose strand of dark hair.

"I am sorry for startling your horse—" Miranda froze in mid-sentence, and the basket nearly slipped from her numb fingers. For a few moments she could only stare in shock, then whispered a single exclamation.

"You!"

Sterling was equally speechless. His body went rigid as he regarded her face, thinner than he remembered it, but no less lovely.

Without another word, she whirled around and slipped away into the trees.

Sterling stood staring at the swaying boughs long after the figure was gone. It wasn't possible! He had thought that she lived far to the north, in Scotland, with his redoubtable great-aunt. His hands grew tight around the leather reins. What was she doing here, of all places?

A cold knot formed deep within him. Had she left his aunt's home, perhaps to . . . marry? He tried to take a deep breath, but his chest felt as if an iron band was encircling it. Why should it matter? he chided himself. After all, it would be strange if she had not taken a husband, despite the cloud of scandal hanging over her. She was a beautiful woman, and many men would be willing to overlook a . . . transgression of the past. As if in sympathy with his mental state, his leg buckled slightly with the strain of standing. He shifted his weight and leaned against his stallion's flank for support.

His jaw set on edge. He told himself that if he had any sense at all, he would set off for London at first light and inform Atwater that he must find another man for the job. Staying here could only serve to open up painful wounds, and Lord knew, he had enough of those already without having to deal with ones from the past. With an audible grunt of distress, he forced himself into the saddle and continued the ride on to his estate. Far out across the lake, a mass of storm clouds blew down from the high hills, casting an ominous black shadow over the still waters. But not nearly as black as the Marquess of Sterling's mood.

Sykes shook his head as he took in the pinched face, haggard from lack of sleep, and the awkward limp, more pronounced than usual. "What in the devil is so important that you have to go haring off again on horseback this morning, guv? You look like hell, if I may say so. Whatever it is, let it wait until later. Come on back to the library and finish attending to your correspondence. I'll stir up a nice fire and fetch some tea."

Sterling ignored his valet and signaled for the groom to lead his stallion over.

The other man muttered something under his breath that included the words "stubborn" and "ass."

"I appreciate your concern, Sykes, but I'm not yet a total invalid." There was an edge to the marquess's words. "I believe I can manage a simple ride." Without further words, he set his foot in the stirrup and, after only the slightest hesitation, mounted the big horse.

Sykes's lips tightened as he watched the marquess trot off. He couldn't help but wonder what errand one of the young grooms had been engaged in this past morning. Whatever message he had brought back, it certainly had his employer in a rare mood. After another few moments, he gave a resigned sigh and turned back toward the manor house.

As soon as he reached the lane leading into the village, Sterling set his horse into a easy canter. The information had been easy to attain. Of course his neighbor, the garrulous Squire Lakeland, had been able to tell him something of the neighboring gentry. The name of Lady Thornton appeared somewhere in the middle of the list, along with the information that the lady had recently arrived to take up residence at the small property she had inherited. Why, the squire even vaguely remembered the lady from years ago, though, of course he was not nearly as old as she was. At least gossips had some use, Sterling thought with a grimace. He hadn't bothered to read the rest of the long and prosy missive, which detailed the histories and pedigrees of the other nearby residents.

So Aunt Sophia was here. Another grimace passed over his face. How ironic that he had chosen his most isolated holding, imagining that he was escaping from the concerns of his present, only to stumble into the shadows of the past. He urged the big bay into a faster pace. Duty as well as affection demanded that he pay a call on his aging relative, but he knew if he were entirely honest with himself, he would have to admit that something much deeper was spurring him onward. During the grueling military campaigns, he had learned it was best not to shy away from one's fears but to face the enemy head-on. Perhaps now, older and wiser, he might finally vanquish what hold the past had over him, along with the nightmares that plagued his sleep for seven long years.

The directions were simple enough. He turned his mount into a narrow drive lined with neatly pruned elms. It wound up through a copse of yew and oak, then opened into an open expanse of meadow and walled gardens. Up ahead was a small stable and barn while farther on, an ivy-covered limestone manor house, modest in size and adornments, sat surrounded by a profusion of rosebushes, its light color aglow in the afternoon sun. As he drew near to the stable, he slowed the stallion to a walk. In his haste to arrive, he realized he had given precious little thought to how exactly he meant to proceed.

A figure came out from the shadows of the potting shed. She was wearing the same ill-fitting garment as last night, and her long dark hair was pulled back in the same simple way, though a few more tendrils had escaped to brush against her alabaster cheek. As the sight of him, she stopped dead in her tracks and clutched the large copper vat she was carrying close to her chest.

"I wish to pay my respects to Aunt Sophia." His voice sounded cold and brittle, even to his own ears.

Her lips curled slightly. "Your wishes are of no concern to me, my lord. And in any case, you would hardly find her here but up at the manor house." She turned and began walking away toward the stable.

Sterling drew in his breath. He hadn't meant to start out so badly. For some reason, rather than ride on, he guided his horse at an angle to cut off Miranda's retreat.

"Sophia is not at home." There was a fraction of a pause. "But of course," she added with some asperity, "you needn't take *my* word for it." With that, she quickly ducked around the dancing stallion and disappeared through the tack room door.

He slid down from the saddle and stood for a moment, not quite sure what it was he meant to do. If his aunt was away, there was no reason for him to linger, and yet his feet were strangely reluctant to move. He let his gaze wander over the place, and indeed, there did not appear to be anyone else stirring. Feeling rather foolish to be standing like some nodcock in the deserted stable yard, he forced himself to turn back to the saddle, when all of a sudden, a high-pitched yelp caused his head to jerk around.

A small boy darted out from one of the stalls. Head bent low, he ran in zigzag steps in the direction of Sterling and his horse. So intent was he on pursuing something that was slithering through the dust with astonishing quickness that he didn't spy the visitors until he was nearly upon the two of them.

"Grab it!" he cried, making a last ditch dive to catch the creature's tail.

The stallion shied violently. It took a moment for the marquess to bring the skittish animal under control, and by that time, the large corn snake had raced between his boots and was lost to sight among the tall grasses at the edge of the paddock.

The boy gave up the chase and fixed Sterling with a baleful look that made clear his disappointment, both with his own efforts and those of the gentleman before him. "If you had been quicker, you might have got it," he said rather pointedly, brushing at a large streak of dirt down the middle of his jacket. "It went right by your feet." A pronounced sigh followed. "I have always wanted just such a colorful snake, but I guess I shall have to ask Angus to catch one for me."

Sterling repressed his amusement at being scolded by a child barely out of leading strings. "My sincere apologies, lad, but had I let go of the reins, my horse might have bolted and caused you some harm."

The loss of the snake appeared quickly forgiven as the boy stared up with undisguised admiration at the magnificent bay towering above his small form. "What a real top o' the trees horse—" The words cut off as a guilt expression stole over his face. "Oh! Mama says I'm not to repeat certain expressions I hear in the stable."

Sterling's lips twitched again. "I don't think she need be informed of this little slip, especially since he is, as you say, truly top o' the trees. He served me well on the Peninsula."

The little boy's eyes widened even more. "You were in the army? Oh, how grand! Jem is forever telling me about all the battles and what heroes our men are. Were you a general like Wellington?"

The marquess couldn't help but chuckle. "I'm afraid not. Just a lowly major, lad."

He mulled that over for a moment before deciding he was still suitably impressed. "I suppose a major is not too shabby," he allowed.

"I shall try to measure up to such high praise," murmured Sterling dryly.

The lad's gaze was still riveted on the marquess's mount. "I've never seen such a big stallion. May I pet him?"

"Just a moment." Sterling took careful hold of his mount's bridle. "He can be skittish with strangers," he explained. "Now you may touch him, if you like."

The little boy's fingers brushed against the horse's nose, and he gave a delighted giggle as the tongue flicked out and left them wet and sticky. After wiping them on the front of his jacket, he ventured to reach up and scratch behind the ears. To the marquess's surprise, the high-strung animal tolerated the attention with an uncharacteristic docility. As the boy spoke in low tones to the stallion, Sterling regarded him with some curiosity, wondering just how he belonged here. His clothing was simple but of good quality and cut. It seemed most unlikely he was the child of a mere washerwoman or hired—

His thoughts were interrupted by yet another question. "What's his name, Major? And may I have a ride on him?"

"His name is Zeus. As to the ride, I suppose it would do no harm to take you up for a short time."

"Oh, thank you." The boy gave a wide grin as he continued to stroke the velvety tip of the stallion's nose. "That's a very fine name. He is big and powerful, just like Zeus in the stories."

"You know the Greek myths?"

He nodded. "My mama reads them to me at night. And I am learning about all the English Kings from Miss MacKenzie, and my letters and sums as well. I can even write my name," he added proudly. Bending over, he traced some large letters in the dirt with his finger. "See?"

"Justin," read the marquess. "That's a fine name, too. He held out his hand. "I'm Sterling."

Justin shook it gravely. "That's a funny name. Even funnier than Angus."

"That is not my Christian name. It's my—well, it's my title."

"I like Major better." Justin's eyes went from the toes of the marquess's polished Hessians to the immaculate riding coat and silk cravat to the curly brimmed beaver hat. "Are you a real gentleman, then?"

"Well, yes, I suppose I am."

"Oh, I've never met a real gentleman before." The boy paused for a moment. "What kind of gentleman?"

"I am a marquess, lad."

"A marquess?" repeated Justin slowly. "Do you have a grand castle with turrets and towers and dungeons. Is it near here?"

Sterling laughed. "No, my main estate is far away, and even that might prove a sad disappointment to you. No ghosts, no chains, no drawbridge."

The boy did indeed look slightly disappointed. "Then, I should prefer to be a major—"

A call from inside the stalls interrupted his words. "Justin! Where have you gone off to?"

"I'm here, Mama. With Major. He said I might have a ride on his horse and—"

Miranda came outside and stopped short on catching sight of the little boy in conversation with the marquess. "Justin!" she repeated rather sharply. "Please go up to the house."

"But, Mama—"

"This instant, young man."

The boy shot a last longing look at the stallion and the marquess, then set off with a reluctant step, hands jammed into the pockets of his jacket.

Sterling stared at the retreating form, feeling a strange tangle of emotion begin to knot inside him. "I was not aware you had a child," he said tightly after some moments of silence. "Aunt Sophia never mentioned it in any of her letters. He must be nearly of an age to be . . ." As he spoke, his gaze darted down to take in her roughened fingers, devoid of any ring. Before she could make any reply, he blurted out, "Why didn't you marry whomever the father was, once you were free?"

An inscrutable expression passed over her face before she regained a measure of control. "Justin's father didn't want me for a wife."

The marquess's brow furrowed. "I thought—" Suddenly he stopped, and his throat became so tight he could scarcely speak. "What are you saying?"

Miranda drew in a deep breath and looked away. "It doesn't matter."

She started to follow her son, but his hand reached out to take her arm. "Oh, but I think it matters a great deal." His fingers clenched like a vise. "Sweet Jesus—am I . . . his father?"

Miranda went very pale, but made no answer.

"For God's sake, tell me. I have a right to know."

There were several long moments of silence before she answered, her voice barely more than a whisper. "Yes."

He swallowed hard. "You are . . . sure?"

She fixed him with a look of utter contempt. "It is *you*

who are the bastard, my lord, not my son. She tried to
pull free of his grasp, but he kept a firm hold. "Let go
of me!"

"No. We must talk—"

"I have nothing more to say to you."

"It is imperative we discuss his future—"

"Is something wrong, m'lady?" The hulking figure of
Angus came out from behind the stable door. His shirt-
sleeves were rolled up around his massive forearms, and
a large pitchfork was dangling from one hand. He took
a deliberate step closer to Miranda.

"His lordship was just taking his leave," she said. "If
he needs assistance, you may heave his well-tailored
rump into the saddle for him."

Angus narrowed his eyes. "Ach, with pleasure, m'lady."

Sterling slowly released his hold. There was little point
in pressing things any further at the moment—indeed,
his mind was still reeling from the stunning revelation
that he had a son. "Very well, I shall take my leave
for today. But rest assured, you have not seen the last
of me."

Miranda bit her lip, then with an abrupt turn, she hurried off toward the manor house.

Angus glowered at the marquess and took another step
closer. Sterling met the other man's eyes without a
waver. His lips set in a grim line as he thrust his boot
into the stirrup.

"Until later."

Miranda grabbed up a pair of worn stockings and
jammed them into the small canvas valise. With a ragged
sigh, she pulled open another drawer and began to take
out the rest of her meager belongings. So much for the
assurance that he never set foot in this area, she fumed.
She knew she should never have left Scotland. How dare
he appear to overturn her life once more! Well, she
wouldn't have it. Not yet.

They would come to grips with their son's future when

she decided it was time, not when *he* ordered her to do so.

The door to her bedchamber opened a crack, then Lady Thornton slipped in. "Miranda! What in heavens name are you doing?"

Miranda didn't answer, but opened the pine armoire and removed her only other gown.

"What is wrong, child?" continued her aunt. "You look as if you have seen a ghost."

She stopped in the midst of stuffing the faded muslin in with the other items. "I have."

Lady Thornton looked totally at a loss.

Miranda took a deep breath and sat down on the edge of her bed. "He's here."

The other lady gave a slight gasp. "Julian? Julian is here?" Her hand came to her throat. "You . . . saw him?"

She nodded, not daring to speak for a moment. "Last night. We met by chance while I was gathering herbs by the lake. Then he . . . he came here this morning while you were visiting Mrs. Trowbridge, and saw Justin. I had hoped that he might not think overly on the matter— but he was never a gudgeon, was he? Despite his other faults."

"Oh, Miranda." Lady Thornton sat down. "Does he know, then?"

She nodded again, unable to hide the pain in her eyes. "That is, if he believes me," she added with a trade of bitterness.

Her aunt reached over to touch her hand. "What were you planning to do?"

"Go back to Scotland!" Her voice broke in a near sob. "That is, if you will lend me the money. I swear, I shall pay it back. I . . . I shall go into service if I have to—"

"Calm yourself, my dear. It shall never come to that. If you are determined to return to Scotland, I shall of course come with you." She paused for a moment. "I only ask that you consider it carefully. Naturally you are extremely upset at the moment, but are you very sure this is the right decision? You know you will have to face it at some time. Perhaps it's best done now, when Justin is young."

Miranda brushed at a tear. "Oh, Aunt Sophia—I don't know!"

"Think on it tonight, at least," she counseled.

"Very well." Her eyes fell away to the tiny miniature of her son perched on the stand by her bed. "What would you do?" she asked for a long silence.

Lady Thornton shook her head sadly. "It is a choice only you can make, Miranda. But I have every confidence you will make the right one."

She put the note down and looked up over her spectacles at the tall liveried footman who stood rigidly in front of her desk. "You may tell his lordship that I shall expect him at two o'clock."

The man bowed and withdrew.

Lady Thornton regarded the bold script on the crested stationery. The formal request to see her came as no great surprise, and if truth be told, even though she sympathized with Miranda's feelings, she found herself looking forward to the meeting. A rather special bond had developed between herself and her nephew when he had been at that awkward age between boy and man. She and her husband had resided near Crestwood, and while the late marquess and his marchioness had chosen to ignore the existence of their firstborn in order to spend most of their time in Town, she had not.

The young man soon had running tame in their home, rather than sit in the splendid isolation of his family's estate. That he had been lonely was clear. That he had been a bright and sensitive lad was also more than apparent. They had shared countless hours discussing a broad range of topics. He had laughed at her interest in Scottish folk history, she had teased him about his infatuation with snakes, and they had seemed to take a great deal of pleasure from each other's company. When it had been time for him to go down to Oxford, she had felt almost as if she had been parting from the son she never had.

Lady Thornton looked down at the familiar handwriting. How quickly things could change. Her husband had been carried off by a bout of influenza, and soon after, she had announced that she was moving to the wilds of the Highlands to pursue her scholarly interests. Her family had reacted with shocked disbelief—only the young Julian had encouraged her to follow her dreams.

She had seen a bit of him in London before departing for the north. His studies finished, he had come to Town like all the other young men of the *ton.* But even though he was still the same intelligent, perceptive young man she had grown close to, she could not like the crowd he had taken up with. It had seemed to her they were a rather rackety bunch, with the leader the worst of the lot. Several years older than the rest, he had seemed to exercise an inordinate amount of influence over the others, encouraging more drinking and gambling and reckless behavior than was good for them.

The few hints of advice had been met with a stony face. They were his friends, he had replied, and that was all there was to it. She had kept her thoughts to herself after. He had had precious few friends growing up, so it was not to be wondered at that he should want to be part of a group. Still, she had worried and hoped he would outgrow them. When he had started courting Lady Miranda Hotchkiss, Lady Thornton had breathed a sigh of relief. Here was a young lady whose beauty was matched by her sharp mind and common sense. The two of them had sensed a mutual rapport during the few times they met, and Lady Thornton had felt her nephew could not have made a wiser choice.

A tear came unbidden to her eye. If only she had not been so far away when the trouble occurred. Perhaps things would have turned out differently if she had been there to offer some counsel.

Perhaps. But there was nothing to be done about the past. It was the present that she must address.

A discreet knock came at the door some time later, jarring her out of her reverie.

"Come in."

The tousled white head of her longtime servant appeared through the crack. "His lordship, the Marquess of Sterling to see you, my lady."

"Have him come in, Wells."

The tall, muscular man that stepped into the library bore only a passing resemblance to the untested youth she had last seen in London over seven years ago. The hair was still the same raven color, the eyes still the same interesting hue between turquoise and cerulean, but everything else was quite changed. His features had become stronger, more angular—if anything it had made him even more handsome, for there was a certain strength that radiated from the face, rather than mere good looks. The depth of his gaze also revealed someone who had seen more than a passing glance of the good and the evil in the world.

"Hello, Aunt Sophia."

"Hello, Julian."

He bent to bestow a light kiss on her cheek.

She continued to regard him in a long enough silence that his lips finally gave a twitch.

"Am I up for auction at Tat's?"

She made a show of adjusting her spectacles before finally speaking. "Well, it appears the army has done you some good—last time I saw you, I feared you were quite on your way to becoming a rather shallow prig."

He let out a low chuckle. "I may have changed, but you, thankfully, have not." There was a slight pause. "It is very good to see you."

"And you, my dear." Her brow furrowed in concern as he shifted his weight with an awkward shuffle. "Your leg—"

"It's nothing," he said quickly. "Merely something that flares up from time to time."

Lady Thornton gave a glimmer of a smile. "That is a condition with which, at my age, I am all too familiar. Come, then, let us sit by the fire." She rose a bit stiffly and indicated the comfortable sofa facing two matching wing chairs.

After exchanging further pleasantries, a bit of family gossip, and the latest news from London, the conversation trailed off into an uneasy silence. Sterling looked around the room for a moment, taking in the stacks of books, the modest furniture, the polished mantel set with a collection of small tartan boxes, before bringing his gaze around to meet that of his aunt's.

"I imagine you know why I am here."

She merely nodded.

He cleared his throat. "It appears that Justin is my son." His inflection made it more of a question than a statement.

Lady Thornton's expression didn't change. "I believe Miranda answered that question."

"Do you believe it true?"

Her chin rose. "I won't even grace that question with an answer."

Sterling's eyes dropped away in some embarrassment as he tugged at the corner of his waistcoat. "I had better become acquainted with the lad, then, and make some plans for his future. He should—"

"That shall be entirely up to Miranda."

"What!" he exclaimed. "You cannot mean to oppose my right to my heir. Why, I have only to appeal to the courts to have the lad removed to my custody entirely—"

Lady Thornton was on her feet in an instant. "How dare you march into our home and threaten such a thing!" She was nearly shouting. "No child could have a more loving and caring mother than Miranda has been to Justin. And you, who have known him not above ten minutes, have the arrogance to think you would provide him with a better upbringing?"

The marquess paled at the cold fury in her voice.

"What would you do? Ensconce him in the empty confines of Crestwood with some hired servant to look after him while you amuse yourself in Town with balls and other . . . entertainments?" she continued with scathing sarcasm. "A fine boyhood that would be, sir, as *you* can attest to."

"I—"

"I haven't finished yet," she snapped, wagging a thin finger under his nose. "You will give me your word as a gentleman here and now that you will *never* attempt to take Justin away from his mother."

Sterling's lips pressed together.

"In return, I will seek to convince Miranda that you should have the right to become acquainted with your son."

"And if I refuse?"

"Then we will return at once to Scotland, where as you well know, English courts have no jurisdiction. Think on it carefully, sir, if you wish to have any contact with Justin before he reaches manhood." The fire in her eye left little doubt as to whether her threat was an idle one.

Sterling's jaw tightened, and his head jerked around to stare into the fire. It seemed like an age before he gave her an answer.

"Very well," he said in a hoarse whisper. "You have my word."

She nodded with grim satisfaction. "So I understand you to mean you will not seek to remove Justin from his mother by any means, be it the courts or other means?"

"Yes."

Her breath came out in a long sigh. "Well, now that that is settled, I shall ask Miranda to come in so that we begin to work things out in a manner befitting rational adults."

She rose and left Sterling seething in self-righteous

anger, returning a short time later with Miranda, who
looked equally unhappy. The marquess couldn't help but
notice that she refused to look at him as she walked
stiffly to one of the wing chairs and took a seat. Even
on facing him, she kept her eyes averted, as if some detail
of the old Oriental carpet held a particular fascination.

"Miranda has agreed to discuss what arrangements
might be acceptable," began Lady Thornton. A glance
at the two young people showed only deep antagonism
and mistrust etched on both their faces. It was going to
take all of her considerable skills to bring about any sort
of mutual agreement. With an inward sigh, she continued. "Have either of you a suggestion for how to
proceed?"

Sterling's jaw tightened as he realized that despite his
demands, he had absolutely no idea of what he meant
to do with a little boy. Miranda merely shook her head.
"Perhaps you might have an idea," she said so softly that
her aunt could barely hear.

Lady Thornton considered her niece's words. "I do."
She turned to her nephew. "Julian, do you wish my
opinion?"

He gave a curt nod.

"It seems to me that a fair way to begin would be to
allow Julian to take Justin for, say, several afternoons a
week while he is in residence here—"

"I cannot agree to having Justin enter his lordship's
home. It might cause undue comment, and I won't have
my son exposed to any hint of scandal," cried Miranda.

"Then, perhaps we could agree that Julian will take
him, say, for a ride in the country. That surely can be
explained by saying my nephew is simply being kind to
a relative of mine."

"I suppose that would be acceptable," she murmured.

"I should like him three days—"

"One is quite—"

"It is not necessary for either of you to shout," broke
in Lady Thornton. "Let us try to act as civilized adults."

Both of them looked rather shamefaced as she fixed them with a stern look. "Two days is reasonable," she announced. "Shall we say . . . Monday and Thursday."

Neither of them voiced an argument, though the tension in the air was growing more palpable with each passing moment.

"His lessons are not to be disrupted, so it must be after his nuncheon—not before one o'clock. And he must be back for tea," said Miranda. "Furthermore, his lordship is on no account to tell Justin that he is his . . ." Her words faltered. "He's too young to understand."

That her wishes were entirely reasonable was beside the point. The events of the past few days had buffeted his emotions to the point where he was ready to lash out at any provocation. It was the last straw that she had the gall to act angry with *him*! After all, it was *he* who was the injured party.

"Anything else?" he demanded with scathing politeness. "Perhaps I might be permitted to buy my son some decent garments." His eyes raked over Miranda's worn gown, and a sneer crossed his lips. "What has happened to you, living up there in the wilds? You used to have impeccable taste—now you look . . . little better than a scullery maid."

Miranda turned absolutely ashen.

Before she could answer the marquess's cutting words, Lady Thornton quickly spoke up. "I believe we have finished discussing what concerns Justin, my dear. Pray, let me have a word in private with Julian."

Miranda's chin rose a fraction, and she stood up and left the room with a quiet dignity that no rags could disguise.

Sterling shifted uncomfortably in his seat, feeling that somehow, he had not shown to advantage. It was some moments before Lady Thornton spoke to him. This time, her tone was more one of sorrow than anger.

"Julian, have you any idea of what became of Miranda's dowry when you divorced her?"

The question took him by total surprise. "Why, er . . ."
His brows drew together. "No," he admitted. "I never
really thought on it. But what—"

"It sits in your banker's hands, along with the rest of
your considerable wealth."

He made to speak, but she held up her hand. "Have
you any idea what happened when she returned to her
parents?"

He shook his head.

"They disowned her—threw her into the street," she
replied bluntly. "As her own husband had denounced
her as little better than a whore, they refused to have
anything to do with her, saying she had disgraced the
family name and might as well be dead, for all they
cared."

Sterling's hand came up to rub at his temple.

"Aside from a small yearly income come down to her
through her grandmother—one, I might add, that would
scarcely purchase a pair of those elegant York tan gloves
you wear—she has nothing. I repeat, *nothing*. And every
paltry farthing she receives, she spends on Justin." Lady
Thornton folded her hands in her lap. "So whatever
anger and resentment you still harbor should not be
given voice in cruel sneers and petty taunts. I would have
thought that the suffering and hardships you have seen
in the course of war might have taught you to have a
modicum of compassion."

His eyes pressed shut. "I . . . never knew any of this."

"There is a great deal you didn't know," she said
softly.

"What is that supposed to mean?" When it became
clear she didn't mean to answer, he frowned slightly but
went on. "Surely you know I never intended that she
live in such poverty. I . . . I shall contact my man of
affairs immediately and arrange for a generous sum to
be put at her disposal."

Lady Thornton shook her head sadly. "I am not terribly plump in the pocket, my dear, but you don't suppose

I would willingly let Miranda want for anything. She will not accept any money or gifts of so-called luxuries from me. She most assuredly will not accept them from you."

His mouth compressed in a tight line, and he turned to stare at the flickering flames. "Why did you never write to me of—any of this?" he asked after some minutes.

"It was not my right to do so."

There was another lengthy silence before he got to his feet and made his good-bye. "Bloody hell," he muttered under his breath as he started for the door, walking with slow, deliberate steps to conceal the worst of his limp.

"My sentiments exactly," whispered Lady Thornton to herself.

Chapter Three

Sykes gave a tug at the girth and cinched it in another notch or two. "Riding out alone again, guv?" he inquired. "Must be finding something of interest out there," he added under his breath, making little attempt to hide his pique at not being invited along.

Sterling made a noncommittal sound as he tied a small package at the back of his saddle. "Perhaps you might wish to put that new hunter to the test this afternoon and let me know what you think. See if he takes the fences as well as Squire Paxon claims."

Sykes pulled a face, only slightly mollified by the generous offer. "Very well, seeing as I don't seem to be of any use to you in the field."

The marquess smiled slightly at his valet's bruised feelings. "I've told you, it is prudent to get people used to our presence here before we appear to be asking too many questions. You may rest assured that when the time is right to get with our mission, you will be involved. I am merely paying a social call—which I know you cannot abide." He mounted and set his spurs to the big stallion.

The aroma of freshly baked shortbread wafted out in their wake, leaving the other man even more puzzled than before. Well he knew that it was the marquess who could not abide the tedium of paying social calls, so he couldn't help but wonder just what had Sterling haring off in such a hurry. And with a package of cakes? He

scratched his chin, wondering whether he was cut out for
life among the swells.

There looked to be no one about the stable and barn.
Sterling reined to a halt, debating whether to wait here
for a bit or to simply ride on to the main house and
fetch the lad. Now that the moment had arrived, he felt
butterflies in his stomach. Surely facing a six-year-old
boy was not nearly as intimidating as storming a Spanish
artillery position, he reasoned to himself. Nevertheless,
his mouth was slightly dry and a trickle of sweat etched
a slow path down his spine at the prospect of taking his
own son in his arms for the first time.

Miranda stepped out from among the shadowed stalls.
"He is helping Angus fetch a lamb down from the upper
pasture," she said curtly, indicating a rocky path leading
behind the stone building and up a steep hill. "This way."
Without waiting for a reply, she turned and started off
at a brisk pace.

Sterling hesitated. Common sense warred with pride
as he eyed the treacherous footing. It would be difficult
going—

She stopped abruptly. "Are you coming?" she demanded. "Or are you afraid of getting a speck of mud
on Hoby's latest creations?" After a fraction of a moment, she added, "Or are you now so puffed up with
your own consequence on coming into the title that you
expect everyone to bow and scrape before you?"

He slid down from the saddle as she once again turned
her back on him and continued up the path. With gritted
teeth, he sought to follow at a reasonable pace. The
sweat was running freely now, pain knifing through his
scarred leg. If she wished to pay him back for humiliating
her the other day, she would be well rewarded at the
sight of his stumbling steps, so different from . . . before.
With a slight grimace, he looked up, only to find that
she was staring at his polished Hessians.

"Your leg . . ." she said softly.

His lips curled in a humorless smile. "Yes, as you can see, I'm quite crippled."

A flicker of emotion passed over her face as their eyes met for a brief moment, then she quickly looked away.

"Wait here. I'll get him." The edge was gone from her voice.

When she returned a short while later with Justin, Sterling had already returned to the stable yard and was leaning against the paddock fence to ease the strain on his injured limb.

"Major! Major!" cried Justin at the sight of him. He started to run forward. "Mama says I am to take a ride with you! Shall I show you the stream where two swans have built a nest and the bramble patch where a family of rabbits live?"

Sterling smiled. "I should like that very much."

"I have to ride Thistle, who is a slug, but perhaps I might finally have my gallop on Zeus?" continued the lad as he clattered to a breathless halt in front of the marquess.

Miranda caught up with her son. "Now, Justin," she said in a gentle reminder, "don't forget your manners. You wouldn't want the marquess to think you have been brought up in a barn."

The little boy looked slightly abashed. "Yes, Mama." He carefully straightened his jacket and executed a solemn bow. "Good afternoon, your lordship."

Sterling reached down and ruffled Justin's dark locks. "Major is just fine, lad. And I think Zeus would not object to showing off his paces for you."

Miranda kelt down beside the boy and with a worn handkerchief rubbed a smudge of dirt from his cheek. "Now, remember to be on your best behavior for the marquess. You mustn't wander off or pester him with too many questions—"

"I'll be very good, I promise, Mama."

She gave him a hard hug and pressed her lips to the

top of his head. As she slowly released him, her eyes met Sterling's.

"You may rest assured I shall have him back well before supper," he said quietly.

Miranda rose and brushed the dust from the skirts of her gown. "Why, here's Jem with Thistle," she announced.

A strapping young man not yet out of his teens led the shaggy little cart horse out from the stable. "Here ye are, Master Justin." He bobbed his head to Miranda. "Gud day te ye, Mrs. Ransford." His gaze shifted to Sterling, and his eyes narrowed slightly. Aside from that, he studiously ignored the other man's presence. "Come, now, bairn, shall I put ye up in the saddle?" With effortless ease, he reached down and tossed the lad up onto the horse's back.

Miranda moved to take the bridle. "Thank you, Jem," she said with a warm smile.

The groom dipped his head once again, and after a fond pat to the lad's head, ambled back toward the stable.

Sterling shifted slightly, uncomfortably aware of being very much the outsider in this little exchange. He searched for something to say.

"So, you know how to ride, lad?" It was rather lame, but the best he could manage under the circumstances.

Justin nodded vigorously. "My mama taught me."

"Then you must be very good, for your mama is an excellent—" His words cut off abruptly. He cleared his throat. "Well, shall we be off?"

As he untied Zeus from the fence, Miranda spoke in a low voice. "Please be aware that you must go at a slower pace than you are used to. He does not have a firm seat as of yet and might hurt himself if he fell off. And he mustn't go too close to the riverbank, for the bank is very steep and slippery, and the current quite strong. And—" She took a deep breath. "I fear you are not very used to small boys," she blurred out. "You must keep a careful watch, for they can get in all manner of mischief without trying in the least."

He gave a wry smile. "I imagine after handling a platoon of infantry, I might be up to managing a six-year-old lad."

She looked rather dubious, but released her hold on Thistle's bridle.

"Good-bye, Mama!" called Justin.

Miranda waved until he could no longer see her, then she turned and fled toward the house.

This was not so difficult, thought Sterling as he listened to the boy's eager chatter. He nearly chuckled out loud. Why, the lad needed little encouragement to keep up a running commentary on the choicest berry bushes, the tallest oak trees, and the best places to look for toads.

"Oh, shall we stop here?" exclaimed Justin. "Then I could show you the robin's nest. It has three blue eggs. But you have to promise to be very, very careful, so you don't scare away the mother."

"You have my word on it." Sterling dismounted, but before he could move toward Justin's horse, the boy slid down to the ground with a thump. "See?" he called. "I can get down all by myself!"

The marquess looked suitably impressed. "You are quite a bruising rider, lad."

Justin's face beamed with pleasure. "Well, I still need help up," he admitted. "But soon I'll be tall enough."

Sterling regarded the stirrup iron that hung about level with the little boy's forehead and repressed a chuckle. "Yes, I can see that."

Justin's attention then turned to a copse of mulberry bushes. "Come this way," he said in a low voice and motioned toward the far end. "It's over there." He began to pick his way through the briars and fallen twigs, careful to make as little noise as possible. The marquess set his teeth, determined not to show to disadvantage. After a slight hesitation, he followed with slow, deliberate steps, taking great pains to move as quietly as he could.

They gained the spot that Justin had indicated without mishap, and the boy slowly parted several of the large branches. "See?" he whispered. "Near the top."

Indeed, there was a nest of woven twigs and grass, with three pale blue eggs nestled in the middle.

"Very handsome," murmured Sterling.

"I thought you would like them." Justin continued to regard them for a moment with a proprietary fondness, then let the branches fall back. "We better go now."

As soon as they were well away from the bushes, his boyish exuberance reasserted itself, and he began to scamper off toward where the horses were browsing in the long grass. Just as suddenly he stopped and turned back toward the marquess.

"What happened to your leg?" he asked.

Sterling took a sharp breath. Would being a cripple sink him irreparably in his son's esteem? Well, there was nothing to do for it, he thought bitterly. His limp was never going to disappear, so perhaps it was best to have done with it.

"It was injured during the war," he replied.

Justin stared at him very solemnly for a moment. "Does it hurt?" he asked in a small voice.

"Sometimes." A rueful smile came to the marquess's lips. "I just can't move as fast as I used to."

The little boy waited for him to catch up. "I don't mind waiting." Then his eyes dropped to the ground. "Mama says it is unkind to comment aloud if people have something wrong with them, because it might make them feel bad." He kicked at a stray stone. "I forgot— I didn't make you feel bad, did I, Major?"

Sterling swallowed a lump in his throat. "No, lad, you needn't worry about that."

Justin let out a sigh of relief.

The marquess ruffled the boy's hair. "Come, let's find

Zeus. He is carrying something that may be of interest to you."

When they reached the big stallion, Sterling untied the package and carried it over to a rock outcropping that was large enough to afford him and the boy a seat. He undid the oilskin covering, and Justin's eyes lit up at the sight of the sweets.

"Oh, shortbread is my very favorite thing!"

The marquess passed him a large wedge and was amazed at the speed with which it disappeared.

"May I have another?"

Sterling couldn't help but feel pleased with himself for hitting upon such a good idea. Really, this matter of how to deal with a little boy wasn't half so difficult as he had imagined. "Why, have as many as you like," he replied heartily.

As the boy's hand crept out to snag another treat, the marquess began to ask him a few tentative questions about the sorts of things that interested boys of his age. It took little urging before Justin was chattering away, stopping only long enough for frequent nibbles. Sterling leaned back on his elbows and closed his eyes, letting the music of his son's high, clear voice wash over him, paying scant heed to the actual words. It was at once wonderful and frightening. The vagaries of war had tested his emotions in many ways, but they had never quite prepared him for this—

". . . Can we, Major?"

Sterling forced himself out of his musings. "Er, can we what?"

"Can we ride over to see the new lambs?"

"I don't see why not." He reached over to take up the leftover shortbread, and his brows rose slightly as the sight of the once generous pile reduced to naught but crumbs. With a shrug, he tucked the empty oilskin in his pocket and followed Justin's eager steps back to the horses. The sight of the lad trying a futile leap or two to reach the saddle pommel brought a smile to his lips.

"Here, now." His hands came around Justin's middle. "Up you go." For a brief moment, he savored the feel of his son in his arms—the sweet scent of lavender and little boy, the warmth of Justin's soft breath against his cheek—before lowering him into the saddle.

Justin waited patiently as the marquess slowly mounted Zeus, then indicated the direction they should take. Sterling kept up a series of questions, but it seemed that the answers were becoming briefer and briefer. In another few minutes they died out altogether. A furrow creased the marquess's brow as he searched for some other suitable subject to bring up. Horses. The lad seemed enamored of all animals, so perhaps he would care to hear about—

"Major," came a small voice. "I don't feel very well."

Sterling reined his stallion to a halt. "Why, what's the matter, lad?"

"My tummy hurts."

"Ah . . ." He regarded the upturned face. It did indeed look very pale. A stab of concern knifed through him. What could have happened in such a short time? "Perhaps I should bring you home."

Justin clutched at his saddle and nodded miserably.

Sterling took hold of the cart horse's bridle and urged his own mount into a brisk trot. It wasn't long, however, before he was brought up short by a loud sob. He turned to see the little boy in a pitiable state, hunched way over, his head nearly buried in his horse's mane. His own face paled as well. With awkward haste, he dismounted and took the lad in his arms. The small arms wound tightly around his neck as another sob burbled forth.

"Mama. I want Mama," he wailed.

"Steady, lad. I shall have you home in a trice."

His hand brushed against Justin's forehead, which felt hot and clammy to the touch. The marquess grew even more alarmed. Was it possible that the boy had been taken seriously ill? With a silent prayer to the heavens, he remounted and threw all caution to the wind, spurring his stallion into a gallop. The jarring pace caused his son to moan even louder. Sterling gritted his teeth and tried to suppress a rising wave of panic.

Dear Lord, he thought. Don't let the boy die now, when I have just found him.

The answer was hardly encouraging—Justin was suddenly, violently sick.

It seemed like ages before they reached the stone pillars marking the entrance to Lady Thornton's home. The stallion thundered up the winding drive and past the stable. Before the marquess had pulled the lathered animal to a stop by the front entrance, Miranda had already flung the door open.

"What have you done to him!" she cried, taking in the sight of Justin's pallid face, streaked with tears and vomit. Without waiting for an answer, she snatched him from Sterling's arms before he had a chance to dismount.

"He's ill—"

"I can see that!" she snapped. Her mind raced over the possibilities. There were any number of poisonous plants or berries for a curious little boy to come to mischief with. Her throat was seized with fear. "Plants! Did he eat some sort of plant?"

"I . . . I don't think so," stammered Sterling.

"Justin, darling. Tell Mama exactly what you ate," she said as she smoothed the hair off his brow.

"Shortbread," he croaked.

"Shortbread!" She turned back to the marquess, her gaze straying to the mess on his elegant riding jacket. "Pray, how much shortbread?"

He swallowed sheepishly. "Rather a lot."

Miranda let out her breath in visible relief. "What in heaven's name were you thinking of, my lord? Have you no more sense than to let a small child make himself sick with sweets?"

To his dismay, he found himself coloring slightly under her withering look.

"Come, love," she whispered to her son. "Let's put

you to bed. I promise you shall be feeling better very soon." With that, she turned on her heel without so much as another glance in Sterling's direction.

The door fell shut.

Sterling raked his hand through his windblown locks. Well, he had certainly managed to appear a complete idiot in everyone's eyes, including his own. He shook his head slowly. It was hardly an auspicious start—even his own son must think him a total ninny. His military training suggested that perhaps the best order of the day was to retreat with what little dignity was still intact. But despite the prospect of further humiliation, he dismounted and entered the manor house, determined to make sure Justin was indeed recovering. She might ring another stinging peal over his head, but what did it matter? It was abundantly clear she could hardly think any worse of him.

And yet, something seemed askew. After all, it was *he* who was the injured party. It was *he* who had the right to harbor a burning anger after all these years.

An elderly maid directed him toward the boy's chamber. After all the exertions of the day, it took a considerable effort to negotiate the stairs, and his step was dragging rather worse than usual as he made his way down the narrow hall. Miranda emerged from one of the rooms, a damp cloth and empty glass in her hands. In her haste she nearly collided with him as she turned for the stairs.

His left leg buckled slightly.

"Oh—" She drew back as if touched by a hot iron.

He regained his balance. "I . . . I wanted to make sure the lad was all right."

Her expression softened somewhat. "Yes, there's nothing wrong with him, now that he has rid himself of the source of the discomfort. I gave him a draught to soothe the ache, and he's fallen asleep." Without thinking, she brought the cloth up to dab at the soiled shoulder of his coat. "Have Mrs. Walters rinse that out for you. Otherwise it will stain."

He glanced down at her hand.

She pulled away abruptly, a tinge of color rising to her cheeks. The edge came back to her voice. "No doubt your valet would have a fit of apoplexy if you were to ruin one of Weston's creations."

"Actually, I doubt my valet would notice, much less care," he murmured.

The set of her lips indicated her skepticism. She made as if to go by. "If you will excuse me, my lord."

Sterling stepped aside, but his hand caught at her elbow. "I'm . . . I'm sorry," he said haltingly. "It was careless of me. I . . . realize I have much to learn. I shall be more attentive in the future."

Miranda could only stare at him. A spasm of surprise, and some other emotion, flickered across her face before she disengaged her arm. She looked as if to speak, then merely gave a curt nod and brushed past him.

At the bottom of the stairs, Sterling was met by the same elderly maid.

"Mrs. Ransford said as you are to give me your coat, your lordship, so that I can give it a good sponging." She was already reaching out toward him, so he reluctantly slipped the garment off and handed it over.

Mrs. Ransford, he thought with a prick of irritation. So that was what she called herself? Why the devil—

"Well, Julian, it appears that you have had an interesting afternoon."

Sterling turned to fix his aunt with a baleful look. "Well, I see it's taken little time for word to spread of what a complete cake I've made of myself."

"The cake, it would seem, was rather visible."

He managed a rueful smile. "I suppose I did present a rather laughable picture."

She smiled. "I'm glad to see you haven't lost your sense of humor, my dear. Don't be too hard on yourself—children have a way of creating havoc, despite the best-laid plans." She slipped her arm through his. "Come, let me pour you a glass of sherry while Maggie finishes with your coat. You look as if you could do with something a bit stronger than tea."

Miranda pushed away her empty cup. "If you could have seen Ju—his lordship's expression! It would have been quite funny, had not . . ." Her words trailed off, and her own face became more serious. "Well, perhaps I dare hope the experience has given him his fill of small children. It is hard to imagine that the marquess will care to subject himself to any more such unpleasant occurrences. No doubt he will soon tire of the novelty and return to London."

Lady Thornton's brow came together. "Miranda, I should not count on it. I got the distinct feeling that Julian is not about to forget about his son so easily."

Her niece shot up from her chair. "Justin is not *his* son—he is *my* son!" she cried. "It is *I* who have birthed him, who have nursed him through illness and sought to teach him to be an honorable person. Rank and fortune do not give his lordship the right to march in here and think to take command. I'm not one of his foot soldiers— or his wife, anymore."

"Calm yourself, my dear," said Lady Thornton gently. "We have Julian's promise that he means to do no such thing, and I believe that we may take him at his word. Despite whatever else you think, he is an honorable man."

Miranda's eyes dropped to the carpet. "I'm sorry, I didn't mean to imply that I questioned his integrity," she stammered. "It's just that it is still all so very . . . confusing."

"I know it is. But for Justin's sake, you and Julian are going to have to figure out a way to put aside the hurt and resentment of the past and deal with the present— and the future."

Miranda gave a heavy sigh. "I shall try."

But her face betrayed what she really thought about the chances of that ever happening.

This time the tear was a bit bigger. "Damnation," muttered Miranda rather loudly as she struggled to disengage the bramble from the thin material of her gown.

A chuckle came from behind the hedgerow. She whipped around to find a man of average height and wiry build already out of his saddle and coming toward her. "Perhaps I may be of some assistance."

She shrunk back.

His keen haze eyes didn't miss the slight movement. He stopped. "You needn't have any fear on my account. I simply mean to help." With that assurance, he continued on and knelt down by her side. Miranda couldn't help but notice that though his fingers were thick and scarred, their touch was surprisingly gentle. He had her free in a matter of moments.

"Is that yours?" He was pointing to the large willow basket filled with roots and cuttings that she had dropped amid the tangle of thorns. She nodded, and he reached over to extricate it as well. Taking her arm, he helped her back to the well-worn cart path.

Miranda smoothed the skirts of her worn gown in some embarrassment.

He seemed to sense the source of her discomfiture. "Briar patches are devilish things—and being stuck like that has brought out far worse language from me, I assure you, ma'am," he said with a grin.

Her lips gave a twitch despite her resolve to keep her distance. "That is very gentlemanly of you to say," she murmured.

He laughed. "Well, I certainly ain't no gentleman, as you can see, but I appreciate the sentiment." He held out his hand. "The name is Sykes. William Sykes."

She hesitated a fraction before taking it. "How do you do, Mr. Sykes."

He looked at her expectantly.

"I am Mrs. Ransford," she added with obvious reluctance.

Sykes tipped his cap. "A pleasure, Mrs. Ransford." He made no effort to return her basket. "Perhaps I might carry this for a way—it's a mite too heavy for a slip of a female like yourself to wrestle with."

Miranda's mouth compressed. "I'm quite used to it, you may be sure, sir. Besides, I shouldn't want to take up any more of your time than I already have." She hoped the iciness of her tone would put a damper on any further offers of help. But far from discouraging the man, her reply only elicited another grin.

"Oh, no trouble at all. I'm at loose ends this afternoon and would be happy to oblige. I'll just fetch my horse and walk with you for a bit." Before she could raise any further objection, he had already wrapped the reins of the big animal around one hand and fallen in step at her side. "Now, which way are you headed?"

She indicated the path to the right.

"Do you live near here?" he inquired as they began to walk along the path.

"Not far."

Sykes cleared his throat as it became clear that conversation was not going to be an easy thing. "Does your husband have a farm or— "

"I live with my aunt," she said rather sharply. "And my son," she added pointedly, as if that might discourage his interest.

One eyebrow came up in question, but he forbore to press the topic as it was obviously one that she wished to avoid. An awkward silence stretched over some minutes. Finally Miranda spoke up. "Forgive me. I don't mean to be rude, Mr. Sykes, but I'm afraid I'm simply not very sociable. I prefer to . . . keep to myself."

As he slanted a sideways glance at her lovely profile and wary eyes, he couldn't help but wonder why that was. There was certainly an air of mystery about the young lady—for lady she appeared to be, despite her

ragged clothes. "I don't mean to trespass where I'm not
wanted, ma'am," he answered quietly. "It's simply that,
well, I'm new in the area, and I thought I might make
some acquaintance of my neighbors."

She looked down at her scuffed half boots, feeling
rather churlish. Perhaps a bit of conversation was not
too much to ask. He did not appear to be like most men,
trying to press his attentions on her in the most obvious
of ways. A sigh escaped her lips. "Well, I fear I shall be
able to give you precious little in the way of information
as we have only recently come into the area."

"Where did you live before, if I am not prying?"

"In Scotland."

Sykes found that an interesting piece of news, but refrained from pressing the young lady any further on personal matters. Instead, his eyes fell to the contents of her
basket. "By the way, what is all this?" he asked with a
quizzical expression.

"Herbs and roots mostly, along with some barks and
moss."

"What are they for?" A twinkle came to his eye. "You
are not by any chance one of those Scottish witches who
toil over a cauldron—*Adder's fork and blind-worm's
sting, Lizard's leg and owlet's wing, For a charm of powerful trouble, Like a hell-broth boil and bubble.*"

Miranda couldn't hide her surprise. "You are familiar
with Shakespeare?"

"Aye. My employer is fond of reading. In our travels
we have passed many an hour with the Bard or Marlowe
to raise our spirits."

"It sounds as if you have an interesting employer."

"Oh, me and the guv suit each other pretty well. He's
fair, he's principled, he's even-tempered and not at all
toplofty, as many of the swells of his rank can be."

"He certainly sounds to be quite the perfect gentleman," she remarked dryly.

He grinned. "I must sound like a swooning female,
singing his lordship's praises, but Lord knows there's

enough of them sort in London, dangling after him now that he's the marquess. It's one of the reasons he is up here, to get a little space to breathe and get used to being back in England—you see, we've been off on the Peninsula for quite some time and—"

Miranda turned away quickly, but not before Sykes saw the color drain from her face. After a few more strides, she halted abruptly at the edge of a copse of beeches. "If you please, I shall take my basket now."

Sykes stopped as well, a look of puzzlement on his grizzled face that quickly changed into chagrin as it occurred to him that he might have unknowingly touched on a raw nerve. Many a husband had been a casualty of the war.

"Did I say—" he began.

"Good day, Mr. Sykes." The words were barely out of her mouth before she wrenched the basket out of his hands and hurried off into the shadows, leaving him utterly puzzled as to what he had said wrong.

The burly figure slid back off the rocky ledge into the shelter of several large boulders.

"It's that tall cove again, the one with the bad leg," he muttered to the other man huddled low to escape the biting wind.

His companion tugged his thick wool cap lower over his stringy locks. "What's a swell like him doing here around the border? Don't recall ever seen his face round these parts afore."

The other man took a surreptitious pull at the small flask cupped in his hand. "How often do the English landowners bother to show their pretty faces on the estates they milk dry?" he asked with a bitter laugh. "No doubt he's simply been forced to rusticate to the country for a time." His hand came up to wipe his lips. "However, we can't be too careful. We better let McTavish know about this."

Chapter Four

Justin carefully tilted the small pitcher and filled the earthenware bowl with milk. The fuzzy little ball of fur by his feet nearly knocked it over in its haste to lap up the frothy contents.

"What have you here?" Miranda knelt by her son's side.

"It's the runt," he explained. "The others all push him away when it's time for feeding. Cook said I might bring him this."

She gave his little shoulder a squeeze. "That's very thoughtful of you, my love."

"You have always told me I must help those who are less fortunate than me."

"That's quite right, and I'm glad to see that you are taking it to heart. Kindness and compassion are qualities that every gentleman should have."

"I shall remember that, Mama." He watched the scrawny kitten lap at the milk for a moment. "Mama, am I a gentleman?"

Miranda drew in her breath. "We shall discuss that when you are older."

Justin shifted slightly in the pile of straw. "The major is a grand gentleman." It was said more as a question.

"Yes. Indeed he is."

"He said I might ride on Zeus again." The boy's face took on a rapt expression. "The major is a great gun, isn't he!"

Miranda carefully schooled her features to reveal no

hint of her inner emotions. "You are quite right, Justin. The major is a great gun." She brushed a wisp of hay from his dark locks. "Now, you had better run along and help Angus saddle Thistle. His lordship will soon be here to take you riding. I shall make sure your newest protégé finishes his nuncheon." With a last little hug, she sent him on his way.

A figure stepped out of the shadows of the barn door.

"That was . . . good of you," said Sterling haltingly. "You didn't have to say what you did."

Miranda quickly rose. "I have no intention of coloring Justin's feelings toward you, sir. It is only right that a boy should respect and . . . love his father."

The marquess swallowed. "Given your sentiments, that is more than generous," he said in a low voice.

Her eyes dropped to watch the kitten nudging the empty bowl along the dirt floor, as if searching for a way to conjure up another helping. "I told you, my sentiments are irrelevant, my lord."

Sterling cleared his throat. "I should like your permission to give Justin a proper pony to ride. He is so fond of animals, and I thought that, well, that he would like it."

"I . . . I cannot afford the upkeep," she said in a tight voice. "If Aunt Sophia would be willing—"

"Of course I shall see to all the expenses," he said quickly.

Her hands twisted together as she considered the matter. "Seeing as it is for Justin," she said slowly. "I suppose that will be acceptable."

He murmured his thanks.

"But I mean to warn you, sir, I'll not allow you to make a habit of showering him with all manner of costly presents. He doesn't need to be spoiled to be happy."

He gave a curt nod.

"Justin is waiting—"

"Mrs. Ransford, Angus asked whether you be needing him to fetch you anything in the village this afternoon." The young groom came around the stalls and stopped short at the sight of the marquess in conversation with Miranda. "Oh! Master Justin said as you was here, but he didn't mention you had company." His hands unconsciously balled into fists at his side. "Do you need me for anything, ma'am?"

"No, that's quite all right, Jem. And you may tell Angus that I have no errands for him."

Jem shot a black look at the marquess before reluctantly taking himself off toward the paddock.

Miranda turned to go as well.

"Mrs. Ransford," repeated Sterling softly. "Just how is it that you choose to go by that name?"

She spun around. "I'll not have Justin subject to vicious taunts of being a bastard, so yes, I go by 'Missus.' As for Ransford, it was my grandmother's maiden name." Her chin rose a fraction. "I don't think she would begrudge me its use, as my own is no longer welcome to me."

Sterling's jaw tightened. "You might have kept Grosvenor," he said in a near whisper.

Her face betrayed a flicker of emotion, then just as quickly hardened into a stony mask. "I don't want it— nor am I entitled to it anymore, my lord," she replied coldly. "Now, if you will excuse me—"

"M . . . Miranda."

There, he had finally said it aloud, though it had echoed countless times in his thoughts over the years.

She froze at the sound of her name on his lips, her face going a ghostly pale.

"Despite what you may think, I . . . I never meant for you to suffer such . . ." His words caught in his throat as he groped for how to go on. "That is, Aunt Sophia only lately informed me of what your circumstances have been for these past seven years. I never knew." As he said it, he realized how inadequate it sounded. "I would like to see that you receive a yearly sum—"

"My circumstances are no longer any of your concern!" With that, she whirled and fled from the barn.

The kitten jumped back from the bowl as a string of low oaths exploded from the marquess's lips. They trailed off into an exasperated sigh as he raked his hand through his hair, then limped off to meet his son.

The one they called McTavish slipped into a seat at the back of the smoky tavern and signaled for the barmaid to bring him a tankard of ale. The two others at the small table scraped their chairs in a little closer.

Scofield spoke without preamble, his voice low so that no one else could overhear. "We've discovered he's a bloody marquess. And what's more, he was in the army until the injury to his leg forced him to sell out."

A look of grave concern crossed the face of his ginger-haired companion. "Think he has anything to do with the government?" he asked haltingly.

"Don't be such a lily-livered goose, Gibbs," growled Scofield, giving his companion a look of disgust. "I've sussed out that he's got a minor estate nearabouts, so there's nothing too suspicious about him paying a visit." As he spoke, his eyes sought assurance from the obvious leader.

McTavish was sitting with head bowed, a blank expression on his features as if unaware of the conversation taking place around him. But when he looked up, his flinty grey eyes were sharp enough to make the others flinch in their seats. "We can't afford to assume anything," he said. "He's to be watched. I want to know everything—where he goes, who he sees, when he uses his damn chamberpot!" He glanced around the room. "We'll meet again in four day's time, this time at the tavern in Dunham." He pushed aside his untouched ale. "When you have the answers, I'll decide what to do."

Sykes finished putting the final polish to the marquess's riding boots and looked around the master bedchamber. There was nothing left to do. The silver-backed brushes were neatly arranged on the dresser, the hacking coat and breeches were hung away in the armoire, the fire was freshly stirred, and the silk dressing gown was laid out on the carved four-poster bed for whenever its owner decided to retire.

The valet frowned as he considered that with each night, the hour that Sterling finally sought his bed was getting later and later. Far from improving the marquess's frame of mind, the sojourn to the country seemed to be only exacerbating his dark moods. It made no sense. Now that they had finally left the rigors of war behind them, it seemed his employer should finally begin to relax and enjoy life a bit. After all, he was in a position to do exactly that. It appeared he could have whatever he wanted, which made his odd edginess even more puzzling.

Sykes couldn't help rubbing at his jaw as he wondered whether some discovery concerning their mission here was causing the marquess some concern that he was keeping hidden. His eyes clouded over at the thought that after all they had been through together, Sterling might not care to be on quite the same footing as they had before. After all, the man was no longer a mere major but a titled lord.

With a final, vigorous rub, the ex-batman laid the boots aside and went downstairs.

Sterling's head came up with a jerk at the sound of the soft knock on the library door. "Come in," he growled.

Sykes entered, carrying a glass filled with an amber liquid in one hand. "It's late, guv. Thought perhaps your leg was acting up, so I brought you a draught of laudanum."

The marquess made a face as he turned from staring into the flickering fire. "You know I refuse to become dependent on that vile stuff. We've both seen how it can ruin a man."

"An occasional dose does no harm." He gave a pointed look at Sterling's drawn features. "If you don't let yourself get some sleep, you'll drive yourself into the ground."

"My leg is no worse than usual." Taking up the book that lay open in his lap, the marquess made a show of starting to read. "What makes you think I'm not sleeping."

"For one thing, I hear you crying out at night—the nightmares have come back, nearly as bad as right after you were first hurt," answered Sykes frankly. "If it isn't your leg, what is troubling you?"

"I don't know what you're talking about," snapped Sterling.

A faint flush stole to the valet's cheeks at the marquess's cold rebuff. He walked stiffly toward the hearth and stirred the logs to life with rather more force than necessary. After a few minutes of heavy silence, he essayed to find a less touchy topic of conversation.

"It seems we have an intriguing neighbor. Have you by any chance crossed paths with her during your rides?" He expected Sterling to respond with a modicum of curiosity, but his words were met with nothing more than the same ominous silence. Still, he went doggedly on. "I've seen her several times in the last week, even managed a bit of a chat with her before she took off like a skittish mare." He shook his head slowly. "Aye, there's some mystery about Mrs. Ransford, there is. Quite a beauty, too, despite the shabby dress—"

Sterling's fist slammed down on the side table. "I *never* want to hear the name of Mrs. Ransford on your lips, do you understand me? *Never!*"

Sykes slowly straightened from his crouch by the brass fireguard, his grizzled face rigid with wounded pride. "You know, guv, perhaps the time has come for us to go our separate ways. When we were soldiers, it was one thing—I warned you I didn't know anything about being some high-and-mighty gentleman's gentleman. You'd be better off hiring a fellow more used to the ways of the *ton,* because I doubt, at my advanced age, that I can learn to be a toad eater. It appears you want a . . . servant, guv, not someone like me anymore." His hands jammed in the pockets of his jacket. "So I'll just take myself off in the morning. Good night to you."

Sterling watched in mute shock as his longtime companion made his way out. The closing of the door echoed like a cannon shot through the near darkened library, causing the marquess to slump forward in his chair and bury his head in his hands.

It was quite late, and Sykes was nearly finished folding the last of his shirts when a slight rasping sound in the narrow hallway outside his room caught his ear. He paused for a moment, then returned to the task of packing his modest belongings into a traveling valise.

The sound ceased, then the door suddenly opened without a knock. Sterling limped in. "May I sit down?" he asked, gesturing at the simple iron bedstead.

Sykes nodded. "You needn't have climbed the stairs, guv. I would have said a proper good-bye in the morning." To hide his emotions, he turned and fumbled with several sheets of paper. "I've written out instructions for how best to treat your leg when it's acting up. There's also the ingredients for that special polish for your boots and—well, I imagine the new man will as like know a good deal more than me about that sort of thing."

Sterling's jaw twitched. "I was married once, you know. A long time ago," he said abruptly.

Sykes put the papers down. His brows drew together in surprise at the sudden turn of thought. "I . . . never knew that. You never brought it up." He swallowed hard. "I imagine it is a subject too painful to talk about. I mean, losing a loved one is not easy—"

The marquess looked up, a bleak expression etched on his features. "My wife did not die," he said in a near whisper.

Sykes looked even more confused.

"I was granted a divorce, by an act of Parliament."

There was a sharp intake of breath.

A humorless smile ghosted across Sterling's lips. "Yes, rather shocking, is it not?" His hands came up to rub at his temples. "I would take it as a great favor if you would pardon my harsh reaction of earlier tonight. You see, Mrs. Ransford—" He was speaking very deliberately, taking great care to control the tremor in his voice. "—Mrs. Ransford is my . . . former wife."

"Good Lord." Sykes blinked several times. "You had no notion, then, that she was living here?"

He shook his head. "She went to live with my great-aunt, Lady Thornton, in Scotland. It was only recently that Sophia inherited a small property in the area."

There was a long silence. "I'm sorry, guv," said Sykes quietly. "It is no wonder you've been in a rare taking lately. I mean, what with the stirring of old memories and such."

The marquess let out a ragged sigh. "That's not the worst of it. I have just learned I have . . . a son. He's six years old, and I never knew he existed."

The ex-batman's eyes flooded with companion. He remained silent, sensing that any words would be woefully inadequate. After several moments he simply walked to the bedside and placed his hand on Sterling's shoulder. "Come on, guv, let me help you downstairs. I think both of us could do with a liberal shot of brandy."

Miranda hefted the large basket. The weight was considerable, but there really was nothing to be done about it. The herder's widow was still abed with a high fever, and by the look of the eldest boy who had come to request her help—a lad not much older than Justin—the brood of children must not have had a decent meal in several days. She glanced up at the leaden skies and pulled the thin shawl a little more tightly around her shoulders. It was unfortunate that the cart horse was still nursing a strained left hock, but perhaps the rains would hold off until she had returned.

A raw gust rustled through the rosebushes. Lady Thornton came to the door, a look of concern crossing her face as she eyed the heavy load. "I'm sure that Angus or Jem would be happy to take that to Mrs. Smythe for you, my dear. I cannot like the idea of you trying to manage that basket for such a distance."

Miranda shook her head doggedly. "Both of them are in the middle of replacing a rotted timber in the hayloft, and I'll not make extra work for them. Besides, the poor woman is still very ill, and mayhap it would be best that I look in on her again."

Her aunt knew it was useless to argue when it came to the needs of others. "At least take my cloak. The day promises to become even nastier."

"I shall be quite fine, Aunt Sophia." Her fingers curled around the thick handle. "You know I don't mind a bit of a walk."

An hour later, her spirits had become considerably dampened. A light mizzle had blown through, spitting just enough rain to soak through her thin garments and chill her to the bone. Her arms felt like leaden weights from the strain of the basket, and her bare fingers were chafed and blistered from the rough willow. She set down her load for a moment and clasped her hands together, trying to rub some warmth back into them. It wasn't that much farther, she noted. She set her teeth and forced herself to start moving once again.

It was with great relief that a short time later she spotted the widow's small stone cottage nestled by a copse of elm not far off the road. But any hope of respite from the elements was dashed by the sight of the smokeless chimney and lack of any light emanating from the tiny windows. Indeed, it was nearly as cold and damp inside the stone structure as outside. With an inward sigh, Miranda put her basket down on the earthen floor and set to work.

After laying out a portion of the food she had brought for the five hungry children, she kindled just enough of a fire to heat some water. The sick woman lay on a narrow pallet by the far wall, her slight form wracked occasionally by fits of coughing. Miranda had brought along a crock of poultice, and on examination of her patient, applied a thick greenish paste to the widow's sunken chest. From a small burlap bag she chose several packets of herbs and brewed a strong-smelling tisane. With much gentle urging, the woman was coaxed into swallowing a small dose.

Miranda stepped back from the pallet and joined the children at the rough pine table, where they had already finished the pot of stew and loaf of freshly baked bread. She showed the eldest boy the herbal potion she had made. "Joseph, you must see that your mother drinks a glass of this once more before nightfall and twice during the night. Can you do that?"

He nodded solemnly.

She reached out and patted his skinny shoulder. "I know you can. And you must keep an eye on your brothers and sisters, for you are the man of the house, and see that they have their supper." She took out more packages from the basket and placed them in the small cupboard. "I will come again tomorrow."

"Will my mama get better?" he asked in a small voice.

Miranda swallowed hard. "I shall do everything in my power to see that she does."

Outside, the skies had become even greyer, a shade that matched her mood. The woman should recover this time, but the grinding poverty and constant fight to feed six mouths would eventually take their toll. She suddenly felt very weary. Very weary and very alone in the face of the overwhelming odds. Her eyes fell closed for a moment, and she felt the sting of tears against the lids. Was it worth the effort to fight against the vagaries of life? Just as quickly she gave a fierce shake of her head to banish such thoughts. Somehow she had managed to weather worse storms without being dashed to bits on the rocks. She wasn't about to let herself go adrift now.

With a determined set of her shoulders, she shifted the basket to the other hand and started for home.

As she trudged around yet another bend in the road, the sound of a carriage moving at a fast clip caught her ear. She moved off onto the grassy verge to allow a matched pair of greys to trot by in perfect stride. Justin would no doubt be in raptures over such magnificent animals, she thought as they passed. The elegant phaeton was no less impressive, though in truth, she was so tired she scarcely noticed. It was only when it pulled to a sudden halt that her eyes came up to meet the marquess's steely gaze.

His mouth quirked in a slight frown.

Miranda's own expression tightened as she realized what a sorry picture she must present. Still, he had no right to make his disgust of her so obvious. She quickly turned and began walking again, the pace of her steps fueled by anger and embarrassment. To her great surprise, the phaeton moved on only until it was abreast of her, then stopped once more.

"If you please, get in and I shall take you home," he said.

She kept going. "Thank you, but I prefer to walk."

Sterling was forced to drive forward. "Let us not brangle in public," he said sharply. With a nod of his head, he indicated a group of laborers in a nearby field who had stopped their work to observe what was going on. "If I am to visit Justin without creating gossip, it must be known that Sophia is my aunt," he added. "It would also help if we are seen to be on cordial terms."

Miranda could not argue with the sense of his logic. Her mouth thinned in an obstinate line, but she came over to the phaeton.

"Pray, don't bother," she snapped as he started to dismount to assist her. She climbed up beside him, taking a place as far from his person as the seat allowed.

He gave a flick of the reins, and the pair broke into an easy trot.

Rigid with wounded pride, Miranda turned slightly so as to stare out at the passing countryside. No doubt he was enjoying this, seeing her humbled so. A faint flush stole to her face. Well, let him, she told herself. His opinion mattered not a whit to her, not anymore. A stony silence reigned as the wheels rattled over the ruts and rocks. The wind had kicked up once again, causing her hands to clench together even more tightly in her lap, as if mere will could ward off the biting gusts. Despite all her efforts to the contrary, she began to shiver uncontrollably. Cold, exhausted, humiliated—she could only close her eyes and pray for the hellish miles to pass as quickly as possibly.

A soft, heavy warmth suddenly settled over her worn skirts. Her lids flew open to find the marquess's gloved hands tucking the thick merino carriage blanket up over her waist. Before she could utter a word of protest, he had already shrugged out of his elegant capped driving coat and draped it around her quaking shoulders.

"That's . . . that's quite unnecessary, my lord," she mumbled through chattering teeth.

He didn't answer but gently took one of her hands and uncurled it to reveal the chafed and raw skin. A muscle in his jaw twitched. In a trice he stripped off his expensive kid gloves and slipped them over her fingers.

A cutting rebuke died on her lips as he looked up at her. The expression in his piercing blue eyes was neither gloating nor smug but rather something infinitely more complex. Startled by what looked to be a tinge of concern, even sadness, she turned away in some confusion.

"You needn't go quite so far with the charade of friendship," she managed to say.

"Justin hardly needs to have his mother catch her death of cold." His hand came out to adjust the corner of the blanket. "What in the devil's name were you doing out in such weather, so far from home?" he demanded. To her surprise, his voice sounded almost angry.

"Mrs. Smythe, the widow, is ill, and her children have

not eaten more than a crust of bread in several days," she answered in a low voice. "She needed my help."

"Why didn't that hulking groom of yours drive you or—or take it himself?"

"Thistle has pulled up lame, and both Angus and Jem were needed at the barn. It could not wait."

It was a few minutes before he spoke again. "Were you able to do some good?"

She nodded. "I think so. But she is still not out of danger."

"When do you go again?"

"Tomorrow."

A frown creased his features as he looked first at the basket then at her hands. "If you name a time, I shall be happy to drive you there."

Miranda stiffened. "That won't be—"

An exasperated oath rent the air. "Fine. If you cannot tolerate my presence, I shall send Sykes with a horse you may use until Thistle is recovered."

"I fear that . . ."

"That is, I shall send a horse to Aunt Sophia," he added coldly. "What you choose to do with it is your own affair."

He lapsed into a moody silence for the rest of the journey, leaving Miranda to puzzle over his strange behavior. Why, he sounded almost . . . hurt over her rejection of his offer of help. She shook her head slightly. That made no sense. After all, it was *he* who could not abide her presence.

"Major! Major!"

Justin jumped off the wooden hogshead, nearly tangling himself in the long leather reins he was holding for Angus in his haste to greet Sterling.

"Here, now, bairn, have a care," growled the big groom as he steadied the lad, then returned to his work of mending the worn bridle.

Sterling didn't miss the black look thrown his way. He

shrugged as he reached down to ruffle the lad's dark hair. It was odd for the two stable hands to have taken him in such violent dislike, odder still that they had the temerity to show it. Well, he had more important things to concern himself with, he thought as he reached down to take Justin's small hand in his. There was a slight constriction in his throat at the touch of his son's soft little fingers and the sound of his voice chattering on about how the kitten had managed to overturn a pitcher of cream in the kitchen that morning, much to the Cook's wrath.

They walked out of the barn toward where the marquess's smart phaeton stood, its matched team jangling the gleaming harnesses in their haste to be off.

"Mama, Mama. We are going on a picnic!" The lad left off his story as Miranda rounded the corner, a basket of freshly gathered eggs on her arm. "Major says his Cook has fixed all sorts of good things to eat—"

"But rather a small portion of shortbread," added Sterling, unable to repress a slight grin.

Miranda found her own lips twitching. "How lovely. I'm sure you will have a very nice time."

Justin's face suddenly came alight. "Major, can Mama come with us?"

"Of course your mama would be welcome," murmured the marquess.

"Oh, I cannot," said Miranda quickly. "That is, there are errands I must attend to . . ." Her words trailed off as she watched the little boy's expression crumple into one of disappointment.

"Perhaps they might wait," suggested Sterling in a soft voice.

She bit her lip in uncertainty. It was so very hard to deny the unspoken plea in her son's eyes. "Well, I suppose just this once—"

"Hooray!"

"I shall have to deliver these eggs to the kitchen first,"

she warned. Looking down in dismay at her dusty gown, she swallowed hard. "And see to . . . a few other things."

"No hurry," said Sterling pleasantly. "I'm sure the horses will be more than happy to avail themselves of these lumps of sugar I have in my coat pocket. Just the right size for a lad's hand, I should imagine."

"Oh! May I really feed them?" cried Justin.

They strolled off together, leaving Miranda with no further chance to change her mind. She set off for the manor house, and after informing Cook that the stove would no longer be needed to brew a batch of peppermint tonic, went to fetch her only shawl. As she passed the large oval mirror in the hallway, she paused at the flash of her own reflection. Unconsciously, her hand came up and sought to rearrange the wisps of hair that had escaped from the simple bun at the nape of her neck. A twitch of her shoulders sought to rid her gown of the worst of its sags and wrinkles as a slight grimace crossed her face at the hopelessness of making the worn fabric look any less sorry.

Just as quickly, it changed into a self-mocking smile. She forced herself to take a hard look at reality. It mattered not a whit whether a tendril was loose or her garment hung like a sack, she reminded herself. The Marquess of Sterling was hardly going to notice anything about her humble person. After all, as one of the most eligible men in London, he was no doubt surrounded by the most elegant and lovely ladies of the *ton*, all vying for his attention. The only thought he might give to her was to take note of how low she had fallen.

But then, he had long since believed her sunk beneath reproach.

Still, came a small voice within her, she could cling to a modicum of pride. She would never let him see how hurt—

"Miranda?"

She spun around, a faint flush of embarrassment creeping over her at being caught studying her own image in the mirror.

Lady Thornton regarded the shawl in her niece's hands. "Are you going out, my dear? I had thought you meant to spend the afternoon in the kitchen. Have you discovered you are missing some ingredients?"

"No, it's not that," stammered Miranda. "I—that is, Justin begged that I accompany him on a picnic with . . . with his lordship. He was so eager that I come, I hadn't the heart to say no," she added quickly.

Any surprise the older lady might have felt was perfectly hidden. "Well, it looks like a very pleasant day for a picnic," she said in a neutral voice.

"Yes—yes, it does." Miranda studiously avoided her aunt's eyes. "Ah, I suppose I had better not keep the horses waiting any longer." With a nervous tug at her skirts, she excused herself and hurried out the door.

Lady Thornton stood deep in thought for several moments, staring first at the mirror then at the door through which her niece had fled.

"Hmmmm."

Chapter Five

Miranda found that Justin's bubbling enthusiasm made any other attempt at conversation unnecessary. With silent thanks for her son's loquacity, she leaned back against the soft leather of the phaeton and simply watched the countryside rush by. Even without slanting a sideways look in his direction, she was acutely aware of the marquess's presence, from his firm control of the spirited team to the occasional mellifluous laugh at some remark by the little boy. It was disturbing, yet oddly poignant, bringing back memories of when they had—

She shook her head to banish such disquieting thoughts. That was all well in the past.

The horses stopped at an opening in the hedgerow. A narrow path led up through a tumble of wild blackberries to a ridge overlooking rolling pastureland and a gravelly river that wound through the center of the narrow valley. As Lady Thornton had remarked, the day was nearly cloudless, the bright sun bringing a warmth to the air that hinted of the coming summer.

Two large hampers gave promise that Justin would not be disappointed in the array of treats in store for him. The marquess set them down on the grassy verge, then came around to help the other two down from the high perch.

Justin rushed over to the heavy baskets and took hold of one of the handles. "I'll help you, Major."

The effort to lift it nearly pitched him into the center of an apple tart.

Miranda tactfully held out a folded Merino blanket. "Perhaps you might carry this for me, love."

"And that way, you might also go ahead and pick out the best spot for us," added Sterling, seeing a hint of mutiny on the little boy's face at being denied the larger burden.

Instead, Justin fairly beamed with pleasure at being assigned such a grown-up task. "I'll find the very, very best spot," he promised. "And I'll even spread out the blanket all by myself." With that, he scampered off through the leafy gap.

As the marquess tended to the horses, Miranda took up one of the hampers herself, meaning to follow her son. It was with great surprise that she suddenly felt its weight lifted from her hand.

"You have lugged enough baskets for a time," he said quietly. "Allow me."

"But I'm quite used to it," she answered, reluctant to give it up.

His blue eyes seemed to take on a deeper intensity. "I've no doubt that you are—but not today."

For some reason she relinquished her hold without further argument. At his bidding she went on first, and though once or twice she heard his step falter over the rough stones, she kept her gaze riveted straight ahead.

Justin waved from beside an outcropping of rock. "Look!" he cried. "See how flat this is—it's just like a table."

"Why, how very clever of you," exclaimed Miranda as she gave him a hug. "I daresay there isn't a more perfect place than right here."

It took a few minutes for the marquess to reach them. There were beads of perspiration on his temples, though it was evident they had little to do with physical effort. His face was a shade paler, and the fine lines around his mouth drawn a little tighter. He put the hampers down on the rock, leaning rather heavily on its edge as well, to take some of the weight off his leg.

"Well done, lad," he said lightly, striving to hide his discomfort. "A splendid place for a picnic."

Miranda quickly began unpacking the varied contents. "If you will sit down, sir, I might begin to pass you the linens and silverware."

He didn't argue but lowered himself gingerly down onto the blanket. In a few minutes his color began to return, and the tension wracking his lanky frame seemed to ease a bit. His lips relaxed into an easy smile as Justin pointed out a circling hawk and began to speculate on just what might end up as its next meal.

"Well, we have no such worries about whether we shall suffer empty stomachs, have we?" quipped the marquess.

"Indeed not." Miranda had already unwrapped a roasted guinea hen, a pigeon pie, several thick slices of Yorkshire ham, along with a generous wedge of Stilton. "Did your Cook imagine she was feeding an entire regiment, sir?"

He grinned. "I mentioned there was a small boy involved. I'm afraid she also feels I'm a sad reflection of her culinary skills and hasn't given up trying to stuff me like a Strasbourg goose."

"You are indeed thinner—" Her words cut off abruptly. She turned and began carving the fowl with slow, deliberate strokes.

The awkward moment passed as Justin tugged on the marquess's sleeve and directed his attention to a rabbit that had ventured out of the shelter of the brambles to nibble at the tender shoots of grass. She finished with making up a plate for each of them, then took a seat on the blanket next to Justin. Despite her misgivings, the meal was not nearly as dreadful as she imagined. The boy's irrepressible spirits, coupled with the marquess's encouragements, ensured no lack of conversation. In fact, she fell to listening with half an ear, hearing more the sound of her son's clear soprano in concert with the rich baritone of his father than any mere words. It was lovely music, she thought, though it struck a deep chord of sadness within her.

There was a sudden stinging in her eyes. She turned her face toward the river and pressed her lids very tightly closed.

"Mama, I'm finished—may I have a piece of short-bread?"

She forced herself to smile. "Just one."

He made a face but accepted his limit with naught but a small sigh. "What's that?" he asked between bites, pointing to a long, thin package still wrapped in oilskin that lay behind the hampers.

Sterling slanted an apologetic glance at Miranda. "Ah, I haven't had a chance to ask your mother if you might take a look."

Her brows came together in question.

"It's a boat," he explained in a whisper. "There is a small stream nearby, and I thought. . . . However, I do not wish to overstep—"

"A boat is quite acceptable, your lordship." In a louder voice she said, "Justin, his lordship has brought you a present. Come bring it here and unwrap it, love."

The little boy carried it over and eagerly stripped the covering from a sleek wooden hull. His eyes lit up with awe at the sight of the brass fittings, varnished planking, and brightly painted keel.

"Oh, thank you ever so much, Major. It's smashing!" He turned to Miranda. "Mama, isn't it the grandest boat in the world?"

"Indeed it is."

"There is a mast and sails as well, waiting at home," added Sterling, nearly as pleased as Justin himself that the gift had been received so well.

"May I take it down to the stream?" Before Miranda could answer, he added, "I shall be very careful not to muddy my shoes or tear my jacket, I promise."

"I am more concerned that you do not end up in the water, my love, so mind where you step. And, yes, of course you may see how it takes to the water, but don't stray too far."

Justin tucked it under his arm with the greatest of care, and hurried off toward where a shallow stream twisted its way along the edge of the fields.

Sterling watched the boy's retreating form until his small head was barely visible above the tall grass and clumps of gorse. Save for an occasional cricket or the chirp of a robin, there was silence. Miranda's hands tightened in her lap—she hadn't considered that the two of them would be forced to spend any time alone. She stole a glance at the marquess, whose attention was still riveted on Justin. He had removed his coat, and his immaculate white linen shirt only emphasized the breadth of his muscled shoulders and taut planes of his chest. The fitted buckskins and polished Hessians were also of the finest quality and showed his form to perfection.

She looked quickly away. If anything, he was even more handsome than when she had first met him. The changes the years had wrought were, to her eyes, only for the better. The fine lines etched around his eyes softened the blind arrogance of youth, and the set of his lips somehow bespoke a firmer, wiser man. Her breath caught in her throat. She had no illusions of how she must appear—thinner, plainer, poorer. No doubt he must be congratulating himself of being well rid of her.

To make matters worse, she once again felt the prick of tears. She couldn't restrain a silent oath. Damnation, she knew it had been a mistake to come. A confused anger welled up inside her. Anger at herself for allowing self-pity to rear its head, anger at Sterling for reappearing in her life. After all, it was much easier to hate a phantom of her own imagination. With a jerk of her skirts, she made to get up.

"You have been a wonderful mother, Miranda."

His words, spoken softly, caught her totally off guard. She turned toward him in astonishment.

"What?"

He shifted uncomfortably on the blanket, but his eyes never wavered from hers.

"I said, you have raised him well."

There was a sharp intake of breath. "I . . . I never expected to hear you say anything good about me."

His brows came together for an instant. He looked as if to say something, then turned his gaze off toward the stream, where Justin was dancing along the shore, pushing at the bobbing hull with a long stick to free it from the rocky eddies. Finally, he gave a long sigh. "I wish I had known I had a son all those years I was on the Peninsula. It would have made . . . a difference."

His tone was not accusatory, merely one of regret.

Miranda twisted a bit of fabric in a hard knot. "It was not out of malice, sir," she said, her voice barely above a whisper. "Can you truly say you would have believed me if I had written of it?"

Sterling's face creased in thought, then his mouth pursed in a rueful grimace. "Touché." He leaned back on his elbows, the wind ruffling his long locks. "Tell me everything about him," he said abruptly. "Hell's teeth, I don't even know his birthday! Was it a . . . difficult birth? What was he like as a baby? When did he take his first step?" The questions were fairly tumbling out of his mouth.

She stared at him in wonder.

"Please," he added in a low voice.

Her eyes fell to the muted plaid of the blanket. "Yes," she began slowly. "It was a difficult birth. I nearly lost him. . . ."

How long she talked she wasn't sure. He interrupted often, eager for every detail of the little boy's life. She avoided any references to her own circumstances, but at times he paused to regard her with an odd look before asking of something else. Finally it seemed the subject was nigh exhausted.

"Well, my lord, there is really little more I can tell you about your son."

He grinned. "I know he loves frogs and hates brussels sprouts— "

"All little boys hate brussels sprouts."

The marquess feigned an injured expression. "*I* loved brussels sprouts when I was little."

Miranda quirked a tentative smile. "Oh, fustian, sir!"

"Well, maybe I didn't *love* them."

The sun had become quite warm, and as Sterling spoke, he reached down to undo the cuffs of his shirt and roll them back from his wrists.

"Oh, Ju—sir!" Miranda sucked in her breath as she stared at the jagged white scar cutting across his forearm. "Why, that is from a saber!"

"Naught but a scratch," he muttered, quickly turning back the soft linen.

Her eyes came up to meet his. "And your leg? Was that a saber, too?"

"Shrapnel," he answered curtly as he looked away. The laughter had drained from his face, and a faint color rose to his cheeks. "As you see, I'm hardly the man I once was." His lips twisted in a mocking smile. "Damaged goods."

Miranda was shocked to hear him speak thus. Never would she have imagined that he, with all the advantages of position and wealth, could feel unsure and even a bit afraid. And yet, all too well she recognized the raw vulnerability beneath the glib words. It betrayed a very different side of the Marquess of Sterling, one that she had hardly expected. Without thinking, she was moved to respond.

"It seems to me, my lord, that the man you once were has only changed for the better. The things you refer to are of no real importance at all."

He looked at her with an intensity in his deep blue

eyes that caused her own face to flame. She rose hastily to cover her embarrassment. What had prompted her to say such an idiotic thing, she wondered? No doubt he would think her a fool—or worse. "It's getting late. I must go check on Justin."

She rushed off, leaving the marquess trying to digest all that had been said.

Sykes reined his mount to an easy walk, letting the big chestnut hunter cool down from the gallop over the moors. He fell to whistling a lively marching tune as he contemplated the bright blue sky and the scudding clouds—

"Mr. Sykes?"

Miranda's tentative greeting jerked him out of his reverie. He drew to a halt and tipped his cap. "Why, good day to you, Mrs. . . ." There was a noticeable hesitation before he added, ". . . Ransford."

Her mouth set in a grim line. "It seems that his lordship has informed you of who I am."

He nodded.

"Well, I don't know who else he has seen fit to tell, but I would be grateful for your discretion, at least. I must live in these parts long after you and the marquess have returned to London."

Sykes slipped from his saddle to walk beside her. "I have never been known for loose lips, milady. And you may rest assured that his lordship has no intention of causing any unwanted talk."

"Ah, yes, naturally I appreciate his concern for my reputation." She immediately regretted her obvious sarcasm. "Forgive me," she murmured. "That was uncalled for."

He remained tactfully silent.

She cleared her throat and went on. "I had wanted to ask you about . . . the marquess's leg. Has he seen a good doctor?"

Sykes scratched at his chin. "Hates them," he answered. "Ever since that first night, when I had to hold the sawbones off with my pistol. Wanted to cut if off, they did. The guv won't have any truck with 'em—any of 'em."

Miranda's face paled. "Cut if off? My God." She walked on a few paces. "Are the tendons severed in his knee?"

"I don't rightly know about anything like that, ma'am. But I do know there are still a goodly amount of splinters left in there. I could see—" He stopped. "It's not something bears describing."

She bit her lip. "Does he take laudanum for the pain?"

"We try to avoid it—I imagine with your knowledge of such things, you're aware of what prolonged use does to a person."

She nodded. After another moment she dug into the pocket of her gown and withdrew a small vial filled with a brownish powder, which she thrust into his hand. "Two teaspoons in a glass of water. No more than three times a day. It may help, and has none of the side effects of opium."

Before he could utter a word, she quickened her steps and turned off onto a narrow dirt path that led into the woods.

The dark smudges under the marquess's eyes, coupled with the lines etched deeply at the corners of his mouth told Sykes that the evening was not a good one. Unaware of his valet's presence, Sterling attempted to shift his outstretched leg on the hassock, stifling a groan at the stab of pain that even such a slight movement caused. Beads of sweat broke out on his forehead, and his hand groped for the glass of brandy sitting next to him on the side table.

Sykes walked quietly to the fire and stirred the logs into a crackling blaze. "Bad tonight, it is, guv?"

Sterling took several long swallows of brandy. "Bring me the bottle," he said in a rather unsteady voice.

"No. I've a better idea."

"What the devil—"

Sykes had already left the library before the marquess finished speaking. He returned a short while later with a glass of steaming liquid whose color was not so very different from the spirits clasped in Sterling's hand. The marquess wrinkled his nose at the pungent, woodsy aroma that filled the air.

"What in the devil's name is that?" he demanded.

"Drink it."

Sterling's face took on a mulish expression. "I'll be damned if I will!"

"No ill effects, I promise. What do you have to lose?"

He eyed it with lingering suspicion. "Where did you get it?"

"Come on, now, trust me, guv." The marquess still hesitated. "Or would you rather I take hold of your jaw and dump it down your throat? It's your choice," he growled.

That drew a grudging bark of laughter from Sterling. "You would, wouldn't you?"

"Aye. Because I think it will help."

Sterling drained the contents and set the glass down with a thump. After a moment he made a show of examining the palms of his hands. "Well, I haven't started to sprout fur or claws, so perhaps there is hope." He settled back deeper into the soft leather of the wing chair and rearranged the knitted throw that covered his legs. Then he picked up the slim volume of poetry he had set aside earlier and found his place. "You needn't hover over me," he murmured from behind the pages. "If I am about to expire, I will let you know."

When Sykes poked his head into the room a short while later, he was greeted by a most unusual sight. The book had slipped from the marquess's fingers, and his chin had fallen down to rest on the folds of his cravat. The easy rise and fall of his breathing gave further testimony to the fact that he had actually fallen asleep. His valet carefully slipped a pillow behind the marquess's head and straightened the blanket as he regarded Sterling's face, the tension ebbing away with every restful moment.

"Thank you, milady," he whispered as he extinguished the candle.

When the marquess awoke, light was streaming in through the tall mullioned windows. Disoriented for a moment, he jerked upright. To his surprise, the sudden movement caused only a minimal twinge in his leg. He got up gingerly to find that he felt better than he had in ages.

"Awake, are you? Thought you might stay here snoring the whole morning. How do you feel?"

Sterling rubbed at the stubble on his chin. "You are a bloody miracle worker, Sykes. I owe you yet another debt of gratitude."

Sykes lingered at the door for a moment. "There is hot water upstairs for your shave when you are ready, guv. Oh, and it's not me you should thank, guv. It's your wife."

As he left Sterling standing with his mouth agape, a slight smile crossed his grizzled face.

Chapter Six

Sterling tethered his stallion to the branch of a live oak and slowly made his way to the crest of the ridge. The wind kicked up a bit, ruffling his hair with a lick of dampness that hinted at rain to come. He stood for a moment and savored its coolness. It felt welcome after nearly a whole day in the saddle on what had turned out to be a fruitless search along the western border. Now, as the sun sank closer to the rugged hills beyond the pasture, he was content merely to gaze out at the play of light, the smudges of cool pinks and mauves so different from the sunbaked hues of the Peninsula.

It was a pretty vista. He took another few steps over to where a ledge of rock allowed an even better vantage point, as well as a spot for him to relieve the weight from his bad leg. High above, a goshawk floated in the crosscurrents, then beat a lazy retreat toward the moors. There was little sound, save for the rustling of young leaves and the occasional distant hoot of an owl.

And something else. At first he wasn't sure if it was aught but his imagination, then it came again. Low and plaintive, it might almost have been taken for the cry of a wounded bird. Puzzled, he got up and moved quietly in the direction of the odd sound. A fringe of moss on the weathered stone muffled the scrape of his boots as he slid around the outcropping of tumbled granite. The marquess drew in his breath sharply at the sight that appeared before him. Sitting there, knees drawn up to her chin, head buried in her arms, was Miranda.

He fell back a step, uncertain of whether to interrupt her private grief or retreat before she became aware of his presence. Her head jerked up as he stumbled over a loose stone.

"Oh!" She scrambled to her feet and looked around wildly for somewhere to flee, but the only way off the ledge was blocked by Sterling.

"I'm sorry," he stammered. "I didn't mean to . . . intrude. I heard a strange noise and came to invest—" As he caught sight of her tearstained face, he stopped abruptly. "Why, you're frightfully upset. What is wrong?"

Miranda swiped her sleeve over her cheek. "Nothing!" she cried. "Now, kindly step aside, sir, and let me pass." She tried to dodge around him, but his hand on her shoulder prevented her from slipping by.

"Nothing? You have never been one to throw a fit of vapors over nothing, Miranda." His mouth crooked in a rueful half smile. "What you mean is, it is nothing you wish to share with me."

"You . . . wouldn't understand, my lord."

His face was mere inches from hers. "Why don't you try me?"

Miranda became very still.

"Come," he said gently. He took her hand and led her around to where he had been watching the sun sink into the gathering clouds. She sat down stiffly, taking great care to avoid his eyes. The marquess followed the direction of her gaze.

"The wilderness has a great beauty, does it not?" he remarked, taking a seat beside her. He removed a heavy silk handkerchief from his pocket and placed it on her lap.

She nodded.

"I find myself coming here often—to watch the day end . . . and to think."

She fingered the thick embroidered crest in the corner of the square for some time before speaking. "I want to do the right thing for Justin."

"Judging from what I have observed, it would seem you have precious little to fear on that score."

She slanted him a quick look that betrayed her surprise.

"I meant what I said before, Miranda," he said quietly. "It is clear you have been a wonderful mother."

A heavy sigh escaped her lips. "I had expected that certain decisions might be put off until he was older. But now that you are here. . . ." She trailed off.

Sterling didn't press her.

After a long silence she went on. "I'm . . . afraid. Afraid that I may be tempted to choose what is best for me, rather than what is best for Justin. But you see, I'm not sure I can bear to lose him"—her voice broke—"for he's all I have."

To her consternation, the tears had welled up again. Angry and embarrassed at having given way to such weakness, she muttered an oath under her breath and made to brush them away. But before she could do any such thing, she found her cheek buried in the fine Melton wool of the marquess's riding jacket.

"You never have to fear that you will lose Justin," he whispered as his long fingers crept up to stroke the top of her hair. "As for the other things—well, we'll find a way to manage."

It was the scent that undid her—bay rum, a woodsy undernote and the hint of his own exertion. It was still so achingly familiar, even after all the years. Instead of pulling away, as she meant to do, she gave vent to another sob. Then another, and another.

Sterling held her until at last her shoulders ceased to heave and she was able to lift her head from his shoulder.

"Oh, dear, I'm never such a watering pot," she said rather shakily. Essaying a weak smile, she added, "I fear your coat, sir, will soon be in ruins, what with the ill-treatment it has seen of late."

"The devil take my coat." He regarded her with concern. "Better?"

Miranda took a deep breath. "Yes. Thank you."

"You know," he said after a brief hesitation. "There is no need for you to face all of these things on your own anymore."

Her head came up sharply. "No?"

"What I mean is, you may count on my support from now on. Together we may—"

"Don't be absurd!" she cried unsteadily, turning away. "Why, even if we weren't—" She stopped in search for words. "That is, it is quite the most ridiculous notion to suggest that I might come to depend on your help. Just how long will it be before you return to London?"

When he didn't answer, her mouth twitched in a grim smile. "So, there. You see."

Sterling jammed his hands into the pockets of his coat and stared out at the setting sun. It was some time before he finally spoke again. "I'll have you know I have already sent word to my man of affairs to have the papers drawn up recognizing Justin as my legal heir."

"That is certainly . . . magnanimous of you, sir."

"Magnanimous?" he repeated incredulously. "Why, it is the only right thing to do! He is my son." His eyes flicked toward her. "Of that, I have no doubt."

Some flash of emotion crossed her face. "It may be, as you say, the right thing, but have you truly considered the ramifications of such action?"

He looked at her in confusion.

She drew in a deep breath. "When you remarry, sir, your new wife will not be best pleased to learn that her firstborn son will not be the future Marquess of Sterling. It is a serious matter, and one that your man of affairs will no doubt suggest you think about very carefully. I imagine his advice—and that of many of your friends— will be to leave things as they are."

"You think me so easily led by the nose that I should choose that which is expedient rather than that which is right?" he asked with a touch of bitterness.

She avoided his eyes.

"Besides," he added in a low voice. "I have no plans to remarry."

"But what about the Incomparable Miss Wiltshire?" The words were out of her mouth before she realized what she was saying. "I had thought the *ton* expected an announcement of the upcoming nuptials any day now."

The marquess looked startled.

"Aunt Sophia receives the London papers," she said in response to his expression, mortified to find her cheeks were beginning to burn with color. "I may have lost my name and my looks, but I have not lost my ability to read."

Sterling shot her an indecipherable look before replying. "There is no understanding between the young lady and myself," he growled. "Regardless of what the gossips may speculate."

Miranda's hands remained clasped tightly in her lap. "It is said the young lady is beyond beautiful," she said softly. "And entirely beyond reproach, which must be an even greater attraction for you, considering . . . the past."

Sterling's brow creased momentarily at her words. He shifted his seat uncomfortably. "I have made no offer— to Miss Wiltshire or to anyone." For a moment his gaze seemed to linger on the tips of his polished Hessians. "What of you, Miranda?" he asked in a halting voice. "Have you no plans to remarry?"

A harsh laugh burst from her lips. "I imagine it is very gratifying to be able to mock me thus, my lord. Rest assured I need no reminder from you of the differences in our future prospects."

"Mock?" he repeated slowly. "Is that what you think I was doing?"

Her profile was to him, her eyes intent on following the peregrinations of the distant hawk. "No doubt you wish to be paid back for the humiliation you suffered because of the scandal." She raised her chin a fraction. "I am well aware of the fact that no man would waste a glance at me—"

A spasm of emotion crossed the marquess's features. His hand came out to cover her wrist. "Of that you are very wrong," he whispered. "You have, if anything, grown even more beautiful, Miranda."

She pulled away from him in some confusion. "You may cease such teasing, sir. I look in the mirror each day and have no illusions of how I appear. Not that it matters, for I have no intention of putting myself at the mercy of some man's whim ever again."

Sterling opened his mouth as if to speak.

"And even if I did, what man on earth would wish to offer for a female thrown off as a . . . whore?" There was a catch in her voice as she spoke the last, awful word. With a jerk of her skirts, she jumped to her feet and hurried away back down the path.

The marquess was too shocked to react. He watched in stunned silence as her willowy figure melded into the lengthening shadows. A covering of clouds had leached the colors from the setting sun, casting a pall of grey over the weathered granite and windswept pines. For some reason his spirits suddenly felt as leaden as his surroundings.

His mouth compressed in a tight line as he tried to make some sense out of it all. In some ways, Miranda's accusations were not far from the truth. More times than he cared to admit, he had lain awake at night imagining a meeting between them, one where he would take great satisfaction in seeing her humbled and hurt before his own eyes. He had thought that somehow it would serve to assuage his own pain.

But in reality he found that what he felt was neither triumph nor righteousness, only a strange, aching emptiness. If what had just occurred was in any sense a moral victory for himself, it was a bitter one indeed. Why, it was only when she was in his arms and he had shared her pain, rather than reveled in it, that it had felt the least bit right inside.

Perhaps it was because a part of him cringed when he

thought about the past. Seven long years of war had taught him that precious few people made no mistakes. Who had he, a green youth, been to judge so harshly? His eyes pressed tightly closed as he considered all the foolish blunders he had made in his first years on the Peninsula. How easily he could have been broken in spirit had his commanding officer been a rigid martinet rather than a man of compassion as well as discipline. He couldn't shake the feeling that maybe he wasn't quite as blameless in what had happened as he had been wont to think.

Sterling buried his head in his hands as her last words echoed in his ears. A moment later a violent oath rent the still air as his fist slammed into the cracked stone with such force that the knuckles were left bruised and bleeding. Jamming the damaged hand into his pocket, he stumbled to his feet and rushed toward where he had left his horse.

He caught up with her not far from the boundary of her aunt's lands.

"Miranda, a word if you will," he called as he slid down from the saddle.

She had turned at the sound of an approaching rider, then quickened her step on seeing who it was.

"Miranda!" Sterling sought to match her stride. In the near darkness his boot caught in a rut of the rough cart track, and he fell heavily to the ground.

The sound caused her to glance around. With a small cry, she rushed back and knelt by his side. "Ju—sir, are you all right?" Her hand was already moving gently down over his thigh, seeking to ascertain whether there was any new damage to his knee.

He muttered an oath of frustration under his breath. "Yes, yes. Just stupid clumsiness—" There was a sharp intake of breath as Miranda's fingers pressed a jagged lump to one side of his kneecap.

Her eyes widened in concern. "Why, there is still a

good deal of shrapnel in your leg. Cannot a surgeon do anything to remove the fragments?"

"No bloody sawbones will ever get near me," he said through gritted teeth. "It will be fine in just a minute." With a slight grimace, he made to get up.

"Come, then, let me help you over to where you may sit down, sir."

As she spoke, she slipped her arm around his waist. The linen of his shirt had been tugged about in some disarray, and her fingers brushed up against bare skin. To add to his overall embarrassment, her touch started to evoke a decidedly masculine reaction. He managed to stagger over to the low stone wall she had indicated, then slumped against the mossy surface. Her hand fell away from the hard planes of his stomach, only to begin massaging once again at the tender area around his injured knee.

He sat watching her in rigid silence until he had his emotions under tight rein. "I hardly meant to force your attention in such a pitiable manner," he said in a low voice. "But now that you are here, perhaps you will do me the favor of listening to what I came to say."

Miranda's eyes came up hesitantly to meet his.

"I . . . I never thought you a"—he swallowed hard before being able to continue—"a whore. Never."

She wrenched her gaze away. "No? Yet you cast me off as if I were nothing more than . . . a soiled shirt."

"I was hurt, Miranda." His voice was raw with pain. "I—I had thought we shared a. . . ." His words trailed off.

"It was you, sir, who began to spend every night out carousing with your friends."

A tremor ran through Sterling's jaw. "I would much rather have been with you," he admitted. "But the teasings—I did not wish to appear a man-milliner. I was counseled that it wasn't at all the thing to dance attendance on one's new bride, lest one be considered under the cat's paw."

"Ah, the advice of your estimable friends," she said with a cutting edge to her voice. "No doubt they had only your best interest in mind, especially—" She couldn't bring herself to say the name.

His head jerked around. "What do you mean by that?"

Miranda didn't answer but merely shook her head sadly. "Perhaps you should have trusted your own feelings."

He took a deep breath. "If you must know, I still couldn't quite believe that you had accepted my suit over all the others that sought your hand. You were so beautiful and so self-assured, while I was awkward and shy. . . ."

The frank admission left her speechless. She had failed to realize how he had viewed himself. Why, in her eyes, the handsome young viscount had been reserved rather than awkward, quiet rather than shy. And it was those qualities—along with his keen intelligence and sharp wit—that had attracted her to him.

Her nails dug into her palms as the thought washed over her that perhaps she had not been as perceptive as she wished to believe.

"I worried that I had not the graces to keep your attention. Averill used to tease me about how—"

Her body went very rigid at the mention of the marquess's good friend.

"I'm sorry," he said haltingly. "That was extremely cowhanded of me. I did not mean to mention his name." He cleared his throat. "I understand how you would naturally hold it against him for being the one to come to me, but he took no pleasure in it. He told me over and over that only his strict code of honor as a gentleman forced him to—"

"You understand nothing!" she cried.

"But—"

The sound of pounding hooves interrupted the marquess's reply. Sykes materialized from out of the twilight and reined his mount to halt next to the riderless Zeus.

"Guv!" he shouted, standing in his stirrups to search in all directions. His hand began to reach for the pistol in his coat pocket.

"Hell and damnation," muttered Sterling under his breath before answering his valet's urgent hail.

The look of concern on Sykes's face eased on catching sight of the marquess. It changed, however, to one of contrition on seeing Miranda seated close at his side.

"Er, sorry." His eyes flicked from one tense face to the other. "I heard several shots a while back, and as darkness was beginning to set in and you hadn't returned, guv, I thought I'd best have a look around. Then I saw Zeus here, standing all alone, and, well—I didn't mean to come thundering in like a banshee and all . . ."

Miranda rose hastily. "I'm sure his lordship appreciates your concern, Mr. Sykes. I am afraid it is I who has caused his delay. As you say, it is getting late, and I should return home—" Her words stopped short as she noticed his palm still resting on the butt of his pistol. A furrow came to her brow. "You are armed, Mr. Sykes. What cause have you for such measures here in Hingham? Why would you think his lordship is in any sort of danger?"

Sykes coughed as he looked to Sterling for help. Miranda turned her gaze on him as well.

"There is no danger," he replied quickly. "Sykes is merely being cautious. It's a . . . habit from the Peninsula."

Her frown deepened, betraying the fact that his rushed assurance had not fooled her in the least. "Does your being here have anything to do with the recent unrest in the area?"

It was a moment before he answered. "I am having a look around for a friend in the Home Office. There is reason to believe that the current troubles are being stirred up by—"

Sykes coughed again, this time even louder. "Here, now, guv. You sure you want to be telling Mrs. Ransford about that?" he asked as he dismounted and went to lead Zeus over to Sterling's side.

The marquess directed an icy look at his valet. "I believe Lady Miranda can be trusted with such knowledge."

"What I meant was, are you sure that in knowing what you are up to, she won't be put in danger herself?"

Sterling pursed his lips, but before he could answer, Miranda spoke up.

"I believe I am capable of making that decision for myself, Mr. Sykes." She turned back to the marquess. "My lord, I would prefer to know what it is you suspect."

"Whitehall fears the trouble is being instigated by an outsider—one with ties abroad. Unrest here in the north, especially if it spills into Scotland, could greatly hinder our efforts on the Continent."

"That would be a serious matter, indeed." She paused to consider the import of his words. "From what I have seen, the people around here are good, decent folk, but times are very hard, and when one's family has no food, men can be stirred to do desperate things. Still, I cannot believe they would be a party to treason."

"Not knowingly." Sterling's expression turned grim as he got to his feet. "I have seen how difficult things are with my own eyes. You may rest assured that no family on any land of mine shall worry about going hungry."

"I have heard of your generosity," said Miranda softly. "That is very good of you, sir." Her hands twitched at the folds of her gown in some agitation. "I will keep my eyes and ears open on my visits to the surrounding farms, and make some discreet inquiries. Perhaps I may hear something of use to you. But now, I really must go, before Aunt Sophia begins to wonder what has become of me. Good night, my lord. Good night, Mr. Sykes." There was a slight hesitation. "Have a care. Both of you."

Sterling placed a hand on her arm. "I will see you home, Miranda."

"That's hardly necessary, sir. I have no reason to fear any harm."

"It is not safe to be out alone after dark, not with the current situation and prospect of strangers in the area."

Before she could argue, his hands came around her waist and lifted her up across his saddle. His boot found the stirrup, and he swung up behind her, settling her close to his chest. The big stallion set off at an easy canter, with Sykes bringing up the rear. Sterling made no attempt to pick up the threads of their earlier conversation. It would be hard enough later to unravel his feelings about this newest confrontation concerning the past, but at the moment, he was content just to feel the soft curves of her body close to his and take in the faint perfume of fresh lavender in her hair. After the initial shock of such intimate contact, she had slowly relaxed against his chest, the warmth of her body seeping in through his coat, her breath feathering against the upturned corners of his shirt points. For some unaccountable reason, a ghost of a smile flitted across his lips as his arms tightened ever so slightly.

It was way past dark when the two horses came to a halt before the steps of the small manor house. The heavy oak door swung open at the sound of the hooves on the stones, and Lady Thornton came to the top step, her face wreathed in concern.

"Miranda!" she exclaimed as Sykes jumped down and assisted her niece down from the marquess's arms. "I had begun to grow worried about you, my dear." Her eyes rose to meet her nephew's. "Thank you, Julian. I must say, I do not like the idea of her out unescorted after dark."

"Aunt Sophia, I am known here, and besides, there is precious little reason for anyone to accost me, as they can well see. I have nothing of value to take."

Her aunt merely frowned at that. "You are not as well-known as around Loch Lomand, my dear, and the situation is, well, different. You must have a care."

"Miranda has promised me that she will not go out alone at night anymore," replied the marquess.

"Sir, I have done no such—" She fell silent on catching the intense look in his eye. "Very well," she sighed. "If it will put to rest your fears, Aunt Sophia, I will not venture out after sunset without Angus to accompany me."

"I should like it if you would not venture out at all," growled the marquess. "at least, not until things are more settled."

"There are times that I must. I shall, however, exercise due caution."

Sterling's mouth compressed in a tight line, but he said nothing more, knowing he would have to be satisfied with that.

"Will you come in for a glass of sherry?" asked Lady Thornton.

"I thank you for the invitation, but Sykes and I must be off. I shall see you both on the morrow when I come for Justin." He inclined his head a fraction. "Good night, Aunt Sophia. Good night, Miranda."

"Good night, my lord," murmured Miranda before she turned and hurried into the house. Though her face was mostly in shadows, her aunt caught a glimpse of her expression as she rushed by.

A thoughtful look spread over her features as Lady Thornton turned to regard her nephew. Sterling's expression was indecipherable as he watched Miranda disappear inside.

"Good night, Julian, and Godspeed. Perhaps you will join us for supper on Sunday night?"

"Yes—yes, I should like that very much, Aunt Sophia."

Miranda realized that another stitch had slipped from her needle. If she did not start paying attention, the sock would soon be a hopeless mess! With a sigh, she set the darning down in her lap and stared at the flickering pattern of light on the stone hearth. It was difficult, however, to order her thoughts. No matter how hard she tried, it seemed impossible to banish those piercing blue eyes and chiseled planes of an all too familiar face from her mind.

She bit her lip. No good could come of dwelling on such disquieting things. The past loomed as dark and forbidding between them as the granite hills outside her doors. She had a right to be bitter and angry, she reminded herself. Why, without such emotions to cling to, she would be perilously close to. . . . To what?

That was hardly a question she dared face. She forced her fingers back to work. One thing was certain. The less she saw of the marquess, the better it would—

"Miranda?"

Her head came up with a start.

Lady Thornton's brows arched in amusement. "I fear you haven't heard a word I was saying."

A faint blush of color rose to Miranda's cheeks. "I'm sorry. I . . . I must have been wool-gathering," she stammered.

"So it would seem, my dear," observed the other lady dryly. "I suggest you put aside that sock, lest you wish to add another several inches to its length."

"Oh!" She stared down at the tangle of stitches. After a moment both of them began to laugh. "I suppose you are right," continued Miranda as she placed her things back in the sewing basket.

"Is there something on your mind?"

To Miranda's consternation, her cheeks grew even hotter. "No—that is, did you know that Mrs. Harton's father-in-law has come down with a nasty inflammation of the throat, and I must be sure to brew a special tisane for him and deliver it first thing in the morning. And Mr. Alford's wife is nearing the time of her confinement." She stopped to catch her breath. "And—pray, what was it you asked me?"

Lady Thornton, casually turned another page in the book she was reading. "Oh, I merely mentioned that I invited Julian to dine with us on Sunday." She regarded her niece from under her lashes. "Do you mind? I should not like to cause you any distress."

Miranda's gaze returned to the dancing patterns of light and dark. "It would be most unfair of me if I sought to deny you the pleasure of your nephew's company," she replied slowly. Her hands tightened in her lap. "Besides, his lordship and I are, after all, mature adults. It appears that when we set our minds to it, we are both capable of acting civil in each other's presence."

"How very reasonable. I am glad to hear it," Lady Thornton bent back down over her volume of Lord Byron's latest epic in order that her niece would not see the slight smile on her lips.

Chapter Seven

The marquess put his feet up and swirled the amber contents slowly in his glass. "It's damnably frustrating. I have ridden nearly the entire breadth of the shire and seen no sign of imminent unrest. Except, of course, for the grinding poverty." His lips compressed. "If the government would see fit to ensure that our own people had enough to eat and that our returning soldiers had honest work, perhaps we would not have to worry about trouble in our own backyard."

Sykes sank back a bit deeper in the wing chair and took a small sip of spirits. "Well, we both knew it would not be easy gaining any acceptance among these folk. I have been slipping out to have a pint at the local tavern for quite some time." He paused to rub at his jaw, a slight smile coming to his lips. "Unfortunately, you now have a reputation for being a rather ill-tempered employer, as well as having a penchant for constantly complaining and working me quite to the bone, but I had to appear as one of them, you know. Wouldn't have done at all to be seen to be too cozy with my august employer."

Sterling gave a dry chuckle. "Do I beat you as well? Or do I limit myself to administering just a verbal lashing?"

"Hmmm," mused his valet. "That's an idea. Perhaps I should consider darkening one of my deadlights for added sympathy."

"I doubt you need take it that far. But have you learned anything that may be of import?"

"I overheard one of the men at a nearby table mumble

something about a gathering the night after the morrow. He was quickly hushed by two of his friends, but I pretended as if I hadn't taken note of his words. They left soon after, but later I made a point of being very vocal with my own drinking companions about my dissatisfaction with how the government is treating us ex-soldiers, and how unfair the proposed Corn Laws are. The groom from Squire Darwood's estate let slip that the fellows were strangers in the area, but he didn't know much else. I'll just have to keep spending your blunt to keep my new set of friends well lubricated and see if any other information turns up."

The marquess nodded grimly. "I suppose there is little else to do but that for the moment, but it's a sore trial that I cannot be involved at this point."

"There's no help for it, guv. Nobody would think of breathing a word with the likes of you around. We both agreed this is the only way to find out what is going on. Once I learn anything of substance, you can move into action. There's really little danger in my role right now—and I am well able to look after myself." He gazed into his drink. "And, besides, you have enough to engage your thoughts for the time being."

Sterling gave a grunt. "My personal affairs are naught next to this."

Sykes got up to refill the marquess's glass. "I regret I have not yet had the chance to make the acquaintance of Master Justin."

"He's quite an amazing little fellow." The marquess's lips curved in a fond smile. "I should like very much for you to meet him, but I do not wish to appear to press things. Miran—his mother is concerned about how much contact he has with me and any of my household. She is worried that he may become . . . confused about it all." His eyes became clouded. "I hardly wish to argue. She has done such a wonderful job of raising him, under what must have been . . . difficult circumstances."

His valet looked away into the fire, his expression

thoughtful until his brows drew together. "I don't mean to pry, guv, but it appears that your wi—Mrs. Ransford is living with nary a penny to her name. I should have thought that a lady. . . ." He let the words die away.

Sterling raked a hand through his locks. "Her parents cast her out as a stain on the family name. Her considerable dowry stayed in my hands. I never knew." His mouth quirked in a grimace. "No, I am being too kind to myself. I never gave it a thought. Can you imagine, a female has no rights at all to any property, not even that which she brought to a marriage. Why, the courts would find me entirely within my rights to tear Justin from her bosom, though I have had nothing to do with his care or upbringing. There is much injustice in the world. I have come to realize that women do not have an easy lot. And then I look around here and see what our laws and tariffs have done to the working people." He shook his head slowly. "Good Lord, how could I have been so blind that I never saw any of the suffering and hardship before?"

"Don't be too hard on yourself. Most people in your position wouldn't see it in a lifetime."

The marquess pursed his lips and looked as if he took little solace in that thought.

A solid blow from an ax smashed the rest of the loom. The shattered wood was tossed by several men onto the large bonfire, whose licking flames cast an eerie glow that made the proceedings appear even more sinister. Another group of men, hardly more than shadowy figures, hurled rocks through the windows of the brick building while others hauled the remains of the overseer's desk toward the plume of smoke. Makeshift clubs knocked the gears from the last bit of machinery within the walls, then, at the sound of a shrill whistle, the figures disappeared into the moonless night.

From his vantage point in a copse of elm, McTavish watched the men melt away into the darkness with a sense of smug triumph. He had been particularly skillful in inciting the men who had gathered covertly in the clearing near the main road, not that much encouragement had been needed. The ragged band had been quickly sparked to a righteous anger by his fiery words on the injustice and the tyranny of the Regent and his cronies who were bleeding the country dry with their wars and their excesses. The nearby mill was reduced to a smoking wreck in short order.

Scofield and Gibbs made their way through the trees and removed the hooded black masks from their sooty faces.

"A pretty piece of work tonight was," said McTavish with a grunt of satisfaction. "Things are going well. The men are getting bolder, and a few new ones have joined in the past week. We should have no trouble striking again soon."

His two companions wiped at the sweat on their brows. "Things are going according to plan, aren't they?" ventured Gibbs. "We're going to get paid a pretty penny for this un', ain't we?"

McTavish bounced a heavy leather purse in his palm. "We already have. And if we succeed in knocking off the one in Sillton, we shall see an even bigger bonus."

The clink of gold caused both of the other men to wet their lips.

"Oh, we'll succeed right enough. The men have little choice now but to follow us until you pay 'em off and allow 'em ta slink home. And ain't nobody gonna find our hiding place. Even if any of the locals has seen anything, they ain't gonna spill it to the authorities," said Scofield, his eye glued on the bulging sack of coins. "I been keeping an ear open to what's being said in the taverns."

McTavish slid the purse back into his coat pocket. "Nothing of note?"

Scofield shook his head, but Gibbs cleared his throat, drawing a sharp look from the leader. "Well?"

There was a nervous shuffling of feet before the other man replied. "It's just that, well, didn't we overhear a bit about how that Mrs. Ransford was asking some questions about such things as no female should be concerned with."

Scofield spat on the ground. "She ain't nothing to worry about. Poor widow who spends her time nursing the sick in the area."

"Aye, but I've also spotted that flash cove hanging around her and her son," continued Gibbs.

"The marquess?" asked McTavish quickly.

Gibbs nodded, his expression betraying his satisfaction to having dug up a nugget of useful information over-looked by his cohort.

Scofield gave a snort. "She lives with the marquess's aunt—some sort of poor relation. It ain't anything to worry on." His lips curled into a slight leer. "There don't seem to be a Mr. Ransford around. He's no doubt just trying to turn the widow up sweet in order to get her in his bed. She's a rare beauty, she is. Wouldn't mind a poke—"

"Shut up," snarled McTavish. He turned to stare out at the wreath of smoke curling up from the river, his hand running over his stubbled chin. "Get moving. It's time to meet up with the men," he said after a few moments of silence. But as he followed the other two, his eyes remained narrowed in thought. He, too, had not failed to notice the dark-haired young widow on her solitary walks through the fields. It seemed there was now more than one reason to keep a careful eye on her.

Sterling gave a last pat to the flank of the chestnut pony. The polished metal gleamed bright against the new leather of the saddle and bridle as he tossed the reins up to Sykes.

"A fine animal," remarked his valet. "The boy will be ecstatic over him." He shot a look at the other horse, a spirited grey filly with lovely lines. "A prime one, too," he murmured. "You sure you don't want to take them over to Lady Thornton's yourself?"

The marquess shook his head. "I would rather you deliver them."

"Whatever you say, guv." Sykes took hold of the filly's reins as well and spurred his own mount into an easy trot.

The stable yard was empty as he rode into Lady Thornton's estate. He dismounted and was about to go in search of one of the grooms when Miranda came out from a small shed behind the paddock.

"Good morning, Mr. Sykes. What brings you to—" She stopped short at the sight of the two horses tethered next to his.

He tipped his cap. "Good morning, ma'am. Guv asked me to bring by this pony for his—for Master Justin."

"I see." Her brow knitted in confusion as her gaze shifted to the dancing grey. "But there are two animals tied over there. What is that other horse for?" As she spoke, there was a flash of admiration in her eyes as she took in the finer points of the magnificent filly.

"Well, er, he said as it was for you, ma'am. So that you may accompany Master Justin on his rides."

Miranda's eyes widened in surprise, then wrenched away from the horse. "I'm sorry, Mr. Sykes, but you will have to bring her back to his lordship. I . . . I cannot accept it."

"Can't."

"Can't what?" she demanded.

"Can't take her back." As Miranda made to argue, he added, "I've a number of matters to attend to in Hingham, so I'll just have to leave her here for the time being." He untied the two horses and began to stroke the grey's velvet nose. "A shame, she's a prime goer," he murmured, then began to lead them toward the stable.

"But, Mr. Sykes . . ."

Sykes ignored her feeble protest and disappeared inside.

Angus laid aside his hammer and drew his large hands across his leather apron as Sykes halted in front of him.

"Morning to you." His voice was full of good cheer as he extended his hand. "I'm William Sykes."

Angus made no effort to take it. "You his lordship's man?"

When Sykes nodded, the other man said nothing, but turned his head and spat into the hay.

Sykes hid his surprise as he held out the reins. "I'll leave these two in your care. They belong here now."

Angus ran an appraising eye over them. "Knows his horseflesh at least. They look to be fine animals."

"The best."

He grunted and took hold of the horses. "I'll see to them," he said curtly.

Sykes shrugged and headed back outside, puzzling over the groom's decidedly cold demeanor. His musings were interrupted by the shout of excitement.

"Mama, Mama, I saw the man bring a pony! Major said he was going to give me one of my very own. Is it for me?" The little boy pulled up breathless with anticipation. At the look in Miranda's eye, his face took on a slightly guilty look. "Miss MacKenzie said I might take a short break from my lessons to come down and see."

Miranda smiled in spite of her efforts to look stern. "Yes, love. The major has sent your pony, and a lovely one he is." She took Justin's hand and turned to Sykes. "You must thank Mr. Sykes for bringing him to you."

The boy turned his blue eyes upward, and the marquess's valet drew in a sharp breath at the striking resemblance between father and son. "Thank you ever so much for bringing me my pony," said Justin earnestly. He suddenly tugged at his mother's hand, and as she bent down, he whispered something in her ear.

"No," she answered, an amused look stealing to her face. "You need not make a bow, dear. Mr. Sykes is not a marquess, too. Not even an earl."

Sykes gave a chuckle as he crouched down on his

haunches. "Nor even a lowly baron," he added as he held out his hand. "Just plain Sykes I am, and pleased to make your acquaintance, lad."

"This is my son, Justin, Mr. Sykes," said Miranda as the boy shyly reached out to accept the greeting.

"Mama, now that I have minded my manners, may I go see my pony?" he asked with barely contained impatience.

She slowly released his hand. "Mind you, only for a bit, and then you must finish your lessons before you may have a ride."

"Yes, Mama," he promised.

"What a fine lad," said Sykes quietly as the two of them watched Justin race off toward the stable. "Why, he looks very much like—" He broke off in some embarrassment.

"Like his father," finished Miranda. "Yes, he does." Her mouth quirked in a thin line. "For that I imagine I should be most grateful." Her hands caught at the edges of her gown. "You must excuse me now, Mr. Sykes, I have things I must attend to." There was a fraction of a pause. "Kindly ask his lordship to come fetch his property at his earliest convenience."

"Why?" he asked impulsively.

She went rather pale and stood silent for a moment. "Because," she answered slowly, "a female does not accept gifts from a gentleman who is not related to her unless she is a . . ." Her voice struggled with the last word. ". . . unless she is a whore, Mr. Sykes."

"Hell's teeth," swore the marquess as Sykes reluctantly repeated Miranda's words to him. He slammed his pen down onto the desk and without further words, got up and left the library. Grabbing up his gloves and crop from the side table, he stalked from the manor house, calling out a brusque order for his stallion to be brought around without delay.

He rode into Lady Thornton's, his mount well lathered

from a prolonged gallop. Ignoring the fact that it was not his appointed day to visit, he slid down from the saddle and looked about the yard. Jem was by the side of the paddock, mending a split rail in the fence.

"Is Lady Miranda down here?" demanded Sterling.

The young groom looked as though he might like to refuse to answer, but then he nodded and pointed at the stable.

The marquess marched toward the open door, confident that he was well prepared to deal her. On the ride over, he had rehearsed an eloquent speech designed to counter any argument she cared to throw out. The sound of his steps on the earthen floor caused her head to come up from the task of sorting through a basket of dried roots. She set it aside and stood up, absently wiping her hands on the worn apron around her waist.

"I'm glad to see Mr. Sykes can be counted on to deliver messages to you without delay. The filly, sir, is in the second stall, and the tack is hanging on the door." A lock of hair had escaped her simple chignon and fell across her cheek as she spoke.

All his carefully constructed words seemed to desert him as he noted once again what an indescribable shade of green her eyes were, and how haunting the exact curve of her lips. Without thinking, he took another step forward and brought his gloved hand up to tuck the errant curl behind her ear. "Keep the horse, Miranda," he whispered hoarsely. "You love to ride."

She turned away sharply. "I cannot."

"Because you think it brands you as . . . less than respectable? What utter fustian! You imagine I would think any less of you for accepting what should be yours in the first place?"

Miranda gave a harsh laugh. "Think any less of me? Why, no, my lord, I don't imagine that is possible, for you could hardly think any less of me than you already do."

He had to fight the sudden urge to pull her close and

soothe away the look of hurt in her eyes, to cover those expressive lips with his own. . . . Slightly dazed by the intensity of his own emotions, he managed to stammer out a reply. "That is far from true."

She stared at him in wary disbelief.

"I have been thinking—" His words were interrupted by the high trill of Justin's excited cries.

"Mama! My lessons are done. May we go for a ride now?" As he barreled around the corner, his eyes lit up at the sight of Sterling. "Major! Oh, thank you! I love my pony—he is quite the best one in the whole world."

"I am glad you like him, lad."

Justin looked up expectantly at his mother. "Are you thanking Major, too? Angus says that the other horse is a present for you." A look of delight spread across his face. "Now that Major is here, we can all go together, and both of you can watch me gallop!"

"Run along and help Angus to saddle your pony, love," replied Miranda rather sharply. As soon as he was out of earshot, she turned back to the marquess. "And I shall thank you to stop trying to manipulate me through my son, sir!" she snapped.

It took Sterling a moment to recover from the harsh accusation. "That was hardly my intention," he said in a low voice.

Miranda was surprised to see the look on his face was not one of anger, rather one of hurt mingled with disappointment, and something else she couldn't quite fathom.

He gave vent to a sigh of frustration. "I shall send Sykes to fetch the filly in the morning," he continued, then turned on his heel and started to walk away.

"Wait!"

He stopped.

"What I said—I'm sorry. That was unjust."

His back was still toward her, his wounded feelings evident in the rigid set of his shoulders. "And I am sorry if I have created an awkward situation for you with Justin by appearing at other than my allotted time. You may tell him—oh, hell and damnation, tell him whatever you want to explain my absence." He began moving toward the door.

"Please stay. He would be so disappointed if you do not."

Sterling turned around slowly. "I do not wish to cause you a problem. You are sure?"

She nodded.

His fingers tightened around the filigreed silver butt of his crop. "And what do you plan to do?"

Miranda bit her lip as she considered the dilemma. "I suppose it will do no great harm if I borrow your filly this once." She looked down at her old gown with ill-concealed dismay. "Even if I am hardly dressed properly for the occasion."

"It matters not," murmured the marquess. "You will like her—she moves as smoothly as silk."

Her mouth crooked upward. "I would be less than honest if I did not admit I am dying to put her through her paces, for I vow, I have never seen such a magnificent animal."

"Well, then, let us fetch Justin and be off."

It took little time for the grey filly to be saddled along with Justin's pony, and soon the three of them were headed off down the winding drive. Sterling led the way, keeping his stallion reined in at an easy trot to make sure the little boy had no difficulty keeping his seat. Miranda brought up the rear. The marquess had little opportunity to see how she was taking to the spirited horse. A few surreptitious glances were all that he could manage as they swung off onto a well-used cart path that bordered a wide expanse of pastureland, but it appeared that she had things well in hand.

As the fields opened up before them, Justin dug his heels into his pony's flanks, sending it off at a canter. As it seemed the boy was in no danger of falling off, Sterling paused to follow his progress over the gently rolling field. A rush of pride swelled his breast as he watched his young son handle his mount with fearless pluck and no little skill. Justin finally slowed the pony to a walk and turned to wave.

"You have taught him well, Miranda," he said softly as she came up beside him.

Her eyes were locked on Justin as well. She waved in return and motioned for him to remain where he was. "I can hardly claim credit. Even at this young age, he is a natural in the saddle."

"Like his mother."

She didn't answer.

Sterling ventured a sideways glance. "How do you find the grey?"

A slight pressure on the reins was all that Miranda needed to control the spirited filly's impatience to be off after the pony. "She is a dream, sir. I've never ridden such a responsive animal, or one with such spirit." Her hand patted the horse's muscled neck. "I venture she has stamina, and can run like the wind as well."

The marquess arched one eyebrow as a faint smile came to his lips. "Care to test that assumption? Say, to the crest of the hill where Justin is awaiting us?"

She eyed the larger stallion, who was also chafing at the bit. "Hmmm. That's hardly fair, sir," she countered. "Not without a headstart to allow for your stallion's greater size and strength."

Sterling's smile broadened. "Two lengths."

Miranda gathered her reins and, with a murmur of encouragement, spurred her horse forward. The filly fairly shot off the mark. With Miranda bent low over her mane, she lengthened her stride, hooves flying over the close-cut stubble. It wasn't until halfway up the gentle slope that the stallion drew even. Even then, the smaller horse responded to the challenge by laying her ears back and straining every muscle to hold him off. It was only by little more than a nose that the marquess's mount reached the top of the hill first.

The wind had whipped the color to Miranda's cheeks,

and her eyes danced with the exhilaration of it all. "Oh!" she exclaimed, stroking the filly's lathered neck as she slowed to a trot. "What a magnificent run!"

Sterling drew in his big stallion as well. "What say you, Zeus?" he said with a grin. "We nearly met our match today."

Miranda broke into an answering smile. "Lucky for you, sir, that there was a hill. On flat ground I'm not sure the two of you would have caught us."

Their eyes met, and for an instant it was as if all the anger and hurt of the past melted away in the warmth of their shared laughter. Just as suddenly, Miranda's features stiffened, and she jerked her gaze away.

Sterling felt a sting of disappointment at seeing the guarded expression return to her face. It was, he realized, the first time she had laughed—truly laughed—in his presence. The sparkle in her eye, the set of her smile had nearly taken his breath away in those few moments. Good Lord, it made absolutely no sense, he reasoned with himself. Countless ladies had smiled at him in much more alluring ways over the last few months, trying to excite his attention. Every one of them had left him feeling indifferent, so why was it that right now, a heat was coursing through him that he could not understand, much less control?

He turned abruptly and urged his stallion forward to where Miranda stood chatting with Justin. She had dismounted and was making a small adjustment to the length of his stirrup.

"Major! Major," called the little boy. "You won, but then Zeus is bigger than Mama's horse."

Despite his agitated emotions, Sterling couldn't help but smile at the boy's simple reasoning. Before he could answer, Justin went on.

"Look, Mama, she already likes you!" Indeed, the filly had come up from behind and was nuzzling her velvety nose against Miranda's windblown tresses. "What are you going to name your new horse?"

Miranda began to stutter in confusion.

"I know!" continued Justin. "You should name her Hera."

She went pale at the impulsive words—in his innocence, her son had suggested naming the filly after Zeus' wife. "I . . . that is, love, I fear you have misunderstood Angus. I am merely borrowing her for the day. She belongs to his lordship and so is not mine to name."

"Oh." He looked a bit crestfallen.

"An excellent suggestion, lad," said Sterling, careful to avoid meeting Miranda's eyes. "Hera she shall be." He reached down to ruffle the boy's already tousled locks. "You did remarkably well today, lad. No doubt you will soon be leaving both your mama and me in the dust."

Justin beamed with pleasure.

"I'm afraid I must take my leave of you here. I depend on you to see your mama home safely."

"But, sir, your horse—"

Ignoring Miranda's startled protest, he spurred Zeus forward and rode off without a backward glance.

Chapter Eight

Miranda gave up on trying to sleep and threw back the covers. Reaching for her faded wrapper, she pulled it on, then lit the single taper by her bedside and made her way downstairs. In the kitchen she stirred the few remaining coals in the stove to life and brewed a cup of chamomile tea. Rather than return to her own chamber, she wandered into her aunt's cozy study and curled up on the comfortable sofa that faced the shelves of books. Despite the soothing warmth of the herbal brew, she couldn't seem to banish whatever it was that disturbed her peace.

Try as she might, she couldn't deny that she had an inkling of what it was that had sparked the warring emotions within her breast. With a heavy sigh, she took another sip and tried not to think about the past afternoon. Another few encounters like that, and she would find herself totally lost!

How was it that a simple smile could be so devastating?

Good Lord, she would have thought that seven years— each and every day punctuating the wrongs she had suffered—would be enough to inure her to the mere superficial charms of a handsome face. Surely she was not so foolish as to imagine there was any real warmth behind the fleeting expression. And surely she wasn't so foolish as to allow any flame to rekindle in her own breast. She would only end up badly burned once again.

Still, she couldn't help but think on vignettes of her erstwhile husband and their son. He appeared to truly care for the boy, and of that she was inordinately happy. They made a touching picture together—the dark locks, the shape of the chin, the color of the eyes, one so reminiscent of the other. She had feared ever having to share Justin with him, but rather than feel diminished in any way, she found it only brought her great satisfaction. And there was no doubt it was the best thing for their son.

But what of her? Was this reacquaintance the best thing for her?

There was no question that the Marquess of Sterling had thrown her emotions into a welter. She must learn to steady her resolve and not let his presence affect her so.

Yet even with that admonition, she found she could not tear her thoughts away from him quite so easily. His recent behavior had been so . . . confusing. Though she knew it could not be so, it was almost as if there still existed a shred of tenderness toward her. At times, he had seemed to truly care—about her well-being, her hopes, her fears, her future.

Nonsense! she cajoled herself. She mustn't mistake a sense of duty for anything more meaningful. He would feel honor bound to see his son cared for properly, and if that meant he must evince a concern for her, he would do so, no matter how onerous he found it. The past afternoon had made that only too clear. He had pressed such a generous gift as the grey filly on her so that Justin would be sure to have proper supervision in his rides. If he had seemed hurt by her refusal to accept the magnificent animal, it was only because his pride was wounded, not his heart. She could be sure of it because that was a feeling she knew all too well.

She shook her head, as if such action could banish the lurking image of that brief, fleeting smile. Now what could explain that? Her lips curled upward in self-mockery. Mere illusion, she answered herself. She was simply giving way to flights of fancy to imagine there was any special meaning there.

After all, he had certainly not found it difficult to take his leave of them. She couldn't stop from wondering why he had rushed off so abruptly. Had he an engagement for which he must not be late? Perhaps he was entertaining guests for the evening? Her mind drifted off, imagining the trill of laughter over dinner, the clink of crystal, the shimmer of silk and jewels in candlelight. And the tilt of a lovely face, hanging on his every word. Despite his denial, she couldn't imagine that he wouldn't remarry. She read the papers from London and was not so far removed from Society that she couldn't decipher what was said between the lines. He was considered one of the most eligible bachelors in the realm and could have his pick of any lady he wished.

What possible reason could he have for not choosing a bride from among them?

And why did the notion of it make her feel so—

"Miranda?"

A candle glimmered near the open door, and Lady Thornton stepped softly into the room. "Is something wrong, child?"

Miranda gave a wan smile. "Only the fact that I am a bigger fool than I imagined," she murmured.

Her aunt took a seat in the facing wing chair. "And why is that?" she asked slowly, her keen eyes taking in the hint of wetness on her niece's cheeks.

"I . . . I fear that of late I cannot help but let thoughts of . . . his lordship disturb my sleep. I had thought I was well over such foolishness."

It was some moments before she made any reply. "I can't help but find myself agreeing with your first assessment—but not for the reasons you think."

It was most definitely not the answer Miranda had expected. Her head shot up in shocked surprise. "Whatever do you mean?"

Again, there was a long silence before Lady Thornton spoke. "I think, my dear, that perhaps it is best if I leave it to you to puzzle out my meaning. You seem to be doing a good amount of thinking on the matter already, and I have no doubt that your innate good sense will eventually win out."

"But—"

Lady Thornton raised her hand. "You know quite well my feelings about meddling in another's personal life. I vowed from the beginning I would not seek to influence your feelings. I have always felt that it must be you, and you alone, who decides what is right for you. And much as it has been difficult at times, I have abided by that promise to myself. I see no reason to change now."

Miranda looked rather dazed. "But—you truly think me a fool?"

Lady Thornton relented only enough to say one last thing. "I think it foolish to refuse to consider that things are not always as they seem. I also think it foolish to mistake stubborn pride for reason." She gathered her heavy silk wrapper closer to her frail form and rose from the chair. "And now if you will excuse me, this foolish old lady is feeling very sleepy. I shall see you in the morning."

It was quite some time before Miranda rose and made her way back to bed.

There was no clink of crystal, only that of cut glass, and the light caught only muslin and the simple chain of garnets at Lady Thornton's throat rather than figured silk and cut emeralds. Miranda almost smiled to herself as she took a sip of wine and regarded the marquess from across the simple pine table as he conversed with his aunt. No doubt the evening was as different from those he had become used to as chalk was to cheese, but he seemed to be keeping any dismay he might have felt at the simple surroundings well hidden. She, too, had managed to mask her own unsettled emotions enough to appear outwardly unaffected by his presence at the supper table.

If truth be told, she was not as indifferent as she

seemed. Despite all efforts to convince herself otherwise, she had found herself actually looking forward to his visit. The sound of his stallion's hooves on the drive had only echoed the quickening of her own heart. Why, she could not begin to explain. With all thought she had given to dissecting the marquess's true feelings, she had studiously avoided probing her own.

A ghost of a smile flitted across her lips at the irony of it. Perhaps it was because she was afraid of what she might discover. And perhaps that was part of what her aunt had meant by—

"—isn't that so, Miranda?"

Her eyes came up from where they had been locked, unseeing, on the glass of claret by her fingertips, and a tinge of color rose to her cheeks. "I'm sorry, I fear I haven't been attending to you, Aunt Sophia," she apologized.

Lady Thornton repeated the question, and as Miranda struggled to overcome her embarrassment, she noted that the marquess's expression was not one of rebuke but rather one of gentle amusement.

"I hope that we are not proving to be such sad company that you wish yourself elsewhere." The tone indicated that he meant exactly what he said—there was no trace of sarcasm or barbed teasing.

She colored even more. "Not at all, sir."

There it was. That smile again.

"I am glad to hear it," he said in return.

Somehow, Miranda managed to make a coherent answer to her aunt's question. Then to her relief, Lady Thornton launched into a long, amusing anecdote that allowed her a chance to recover some measure of composure. The marquess seemed to be engrossed in the story, which involved a hard-of-hearing Scottish shepherd trying to make sense of Lady Thornton's London accent. Yet every so often, his gaze would cross with Miranda's, and the smile playing on his lips would soften even more.

She looked away, trying to suppress the little lurch she

felt inside. Why, if she didn't know better, she would think he was . . . enjoying her company.

As the two elderly servants cleared the soup plates and brought out the simple roast fowl and accompanying side dishes, there was a lull in the conversation. It was the marquess who steered the talk in a new direction. To Miranda's surprise, he asked her opinion as to the work of a poet much lauded in Town during the past year. In the past, they had much enjoyed discussing the merits of various verses. That he remembered—or cared—of her interest in such things took her aback.

She hesitated, wondering if perhaps he meant to make sport her feelings. But when she ventured a tentative reply, he only nodded in friendly encouragement and voiced a similar sentiment. Lady Thornton was quick to join in, and soon a lively discussion was under way, all lingering reserve brushed aside by the exchange of opinions.

Sterling drew in his breath at the sparkle in Miranda's eyes as she laughed softly at the pithy observation just finished by her aunt. Good Lord, he thought, had she any idea how damnably attractive she was, despite the sack of a gown? He longed to see the arch of her neck, the creamy expanse of skin that he could picture so clearly when his lids pressed closed, and the graceful curve of her shoulders. It was only through rigid self-control that he repressed an audible sigh. No amount of discipline could cool the heat running through his veins or control the tightening in his groin.

As Miranda listened to another of Lady Thornton's observations, he couldn't help but wonder what she had been thinking of earlier, what had caused the quicksilver changes of expression to pass across her lovely features. Was she thinking of . . . him? He wished he could believe it so, for he had to admit he was finding it difficult to force his mind to attend to anything other than her.

His throat went dry as it slowly dawned on him what

was happening. Here he was, with his choice of nearly any lady in the realm, and the one he was slowly falling in love with all over again was . . . his erstwhile wife.

The one person he could not have.

He supposed it would have been funny if it didn't hurt so much.

Wrenching his attention back to the conversation, Sterling forced himself to join in, as if nothing untoward had occurred. Yet the realization had left him rather shaken. Lady Thornton lifted one eyebrow in slight question as he reached for his glass of wine with a fumbling hand, then just as discreetly turned away, as if she hadn't caught the awkward moment.

As he took a long swallow of the rich claret, he realized the meal was over. He didn't remember having eaten a bite.

"We should leave you to your port, Julian," said Lady Thornton with a twinkle in her eye. "But I fear it would be sadly dull for you to sit here alone. Would you care to take it in the sitting room with us?"

"By all means, Aunt Sophia." He rose with alacrity and came around to offer her his arm. Impulsively, he held out his other one to Miranda. There was the barest of hesitations before her lips quirked upward and she laid her hand on his sleeve.

The talk shifted to the latest gothic novel, which all of them confessed to having read. With more than an occasional laugh, they skewered the actions of the widget of a heroine and her equally flighty hero even while admitting that their candles burned long into the night ere any of them could lay the volume aside. Sterling chuckled over his spirits while the ladies sipped their coffee. Much too soon for his taste, the clock on the mantle chimed the hour.

"Good heavens," remarked Lady Thornton with a start. "I hadn't realized it was so late."

Sterling rose reluctantly. "Forgive me for keeping you

up, Aunt Sophia. I shall take myself home, but thank you for a most pleasant evening."

"You must come again soon," she replied as he bent over her hand.

"I should like that very much," he murmured.

"Miranda, will you please ring for Joseph so that he may go to the stable and ask Angus to bring around Julian's horse." She smiled in apology. "You must forgive us that things take a little longer here—we are a small household."

"Please, you needn't bother—I'm perfectly able to see myself to the stable." He gave a quick smile. "Besides, I've caused enough extra work for the poor fellow. He looked as if reaching the kitchen were a tough enough ordeal. I should hate to think of him having to trek to the stable as well."

"Oh, dear." Lady Thornton was torn between being practical and being less than hospitable. "I don't feel right about making you— "

"I shall see his lordship to the stable, if he truly doesn't mind saddling his horse. Or, I can wake Angus—"

"I don't mind at all."

Lady Thornton flashed Miranda a smile of gratitude. "Thank you, my dear."

"I'll just fetch a lantern, and have Maggie bring you your coat, sir."

The two of them started down the path in silence, each seeming unsure as to how to recapture the easy tone of their earlier words. Caught up in his own thoughts, the marquess failed to notice the paving stones give way to a simple dirt path, and his toe caught on a rut, causing him to stumble forward.

Miranda's hand came around his elbow as she swung the light to his feet. "Have a care, sir. The way becomes rather rough here."

He brought his arm in close by his side, so that her hand would remain where it was. "Thank you." After a moment he added with some vehemence. "Sorry—I'm naught but a clumsy . . . fool these days."

Her hand tightened its hold.

On reaching the stable, Sterling slid the door open and stepped aside for Miranda to lead the way inside. She went to hang the lantern on a peg protruding from one of the thick oak beams.

"I can find my way back without it. You'll need it to saddle Zeus. Remember to blow out the flame when you leave."

He reached out as she made to pass.

She stopped as his hand came to rest on her shoulder.

"I . . . I enjoyed the evening very much, Miranda."

Her chin came up slowly. "As did I, sir."

The look in her eyes tore through his heart.

"Good Lord, I've missed you," he blurted out.

Surprise and some other emotion swept across her pale face. As she started to speak, he lowered his head and took her lips in a gentle kiss.

She went rigid with shock, then slowly relaxed into his arms. His fingers entwined themselves in her silky hair, pulling her closer. To his elation, her mouth softened under the pressure from his—for a few ethereal moments she was returning the kiss. Then, just as suddenly, she wrenched away and fell back a step with a low cry.

"I'm sorry," he stammered, half dazed with the fierceness of his own emotion. "I didn't mean. . . ."

Miranda's hand came up to brush over her lips, as if in disbelief at what had taken place. "I imagine I know very well what you meant," she replied shakily. "No doubt you have passed more time than you are accustomed to without the benefits of your expensive mistresses or other willing ladies—and there is precious little choice of females around here." There was a catch in her voice. "But despite what you think, sir, I do not tumble into bed with a man who is not my husband."

She turned and fled, but not before Sterling caught a glint of a tear in the light of the lantern.

"Miranda!" he cried hoarsely. He made to rush after her but somehow one of the pitchforks leaning against the wall became dislodged and fell between his legs, causing him to stumble awkwardly against a large bin of grain. By the time he recovered his footing, she had disappeared into the black void of the night.

A string of curses fell from the marquess's lips as his fist slammed into the rough wood. With a harried sigh, he gave up any thought of pursuing her and turned around toward the stalls. A slight movement in the flickering shadows caught his eye. A figure standing near the wall was barely discernible in the dim light, but despite the darkness, a smirk of grim satisfaction was evident on the massive groom's face. Without a word, Angus made to go by him. As he drew even, he paused, his lips curled upward in contempt. Slowly, deliberately, he cleared his throat, then spit onto Sterling's well-polished Hessians.

All the anger, frustration, and longing exploded within him. With a grunt of rage, Sterling launched himself at the other man, sending both of them crashing into the side of an empty stall. They wrestled for a moment before Angus, the larger and heavier of the two, managed to control the marquess's flailing arms and thrust him away.

Sterling regained a modicum of self-control, although his chest was still heaving with pent-up fury. "Come on, then," he growled, stripping off his elegant coat of midnight-blue superfine. "You want me, you shall have me."

Angus gave a derisive laugh. "And be transported for thrashing your titled hide? It's tempting, but not worth it."

"You'll suffer no consequences—you have my word of honor."

The other man hesitated.

"I assure you, a gentleman is bound by his word. You have nothing to fear, except being knocked on your arse," added the marquess.

Angus gave another bark of laughter. "Not bloody

likely." He shook his head slowly as he appeared to consider the matter. "Nay, it's hardly fair—I'm not in the habit of darkening the deadlights of a cripple."

Sterling's face paled. "There is nothing wrong with my fists, you lumbering oaf."

The big groom's eyes narrowed. "Very well, then." He took off his own frayed jacket and rolled up his sleeves. "And a rare pleasure it will be, too," he snarled under his breath.

"Angus!" came an apprehensive voice from the shadows. "Ye must be daft to consider risking such a thing! You'll end up—"

"Stay out of this, Jem. This is between this bloody bastard and meself."

The two men warily circled each other in the pool of light cast from the lantern. Each threw a few quick jabs, measuring the other's reactions, then the blows began to fly in earnest. While Angus had the edge in size and strength, Sterling countered with savvy and quickness. Amid the parrying and feinting, both of them were able to land a number of hard punches. In a short time, the groom's left eye was swelling considerably and a trickle of blood was oozing from the marquess's mouth.

A hard right caught Sterling on the chin, but he responded with a shot to the body that drove Angus back on his heels. A look of grudging respect crept across the groom's angry face as the marquess refused to buckle under to a flurry of blows to the head. It was clear he hadn't expected an elegant gentleman to put up any sort of a fight. Keeping his guard up, he slid quickly to the left, seeking an opening.

Sterling moved to cover the other man's position, but as he did, his bad leg caught on the uneven earthen floor, knocking him off balance. His arms dropped for just an instant, and at the same time, Angus let go with a vicious swing. The full force of it connected with the marquess's unprotected ribs. There was a sickening crunch as Sterling doubled over and crumpled to the ground.

"Lord in heaven, you've got to flee! He'll see you hung for this!" cried Jem. He regarded the motionless form before him and added in a frightened whisper. "Do you think he's. . . ."

Angus stared at his bruised knuckles as a flash of uncertainty crossed his own features. "I . . ." he began.

His words were interrupted by a weak voice. "You've naught to fear," said Sterling through clenched teeth. "I don't . . . go . . . back on my word." Though in obvious pain, he levered himself up from the dirt, then staggered to his feet. His hand sought hold of the heavy post for support, but after several deep breaths, he took up his coat from where it hung over the bin of grain and began to limp toward the stall where his horse was waiting.

Jem and Angus exchanged worried glances.

"Here, now," said Angus. "You had best let us see you up to the manor house. You ain't in any condition to ride."

Sterling made no reply but took up his saddle and managed to lift it across the stallion's back. With a few labored movements he tightened the girth and adjusted the reins. His boot, however, could not catch the stirrup. A grunt of pain sounded in his throat as he tried again. Then the effort was simply too much to bear. He sank to his knees and was suddenly, violently sick.

The two grooms hurried to his side. When his retching had subsided, they helped him up.

"We'll see you to the manor house," repeated Angus.

Sterling shook off their hold and fell back against the edge of the water trough. "No!"

"Well, we ain't giving ye any choice. Ye ain't riding out of here tonight. A fine lot of good yer promises would do me if you're lying dead in some ditch come morning. I'd be clapped in irons faster than a merlin snatches a sparrow."

Sterling's lips twitched in humor. "Ah, I appreciate your concern for my person." His eyes fell on the ample pile of straw in an empty stall. "I'll stay here, then."

Angus looked at him in disbelief. "You? In the stable? Hah!"

"I've dossed in far worse places on the Peninsula."

Jem's eyes grew wide. "You . . . you was really in the army?"

The marquess nodded.

"Didn't think a marquess would ever have to sleep in aught but silk sheets," muttered Angus.

Sterling gave a faint smile. "I wasn't a marquess then, just plain Major Grosvenor."

"Major Grosvenor!" Jem darted a startled look at Angus. "Why, my cousin served under you, sir. He said there weren't no braver or fairer officer in Wellington's army than you."

Sterling made a wry face, then leaned over to immerse his head in the tub of brackish water. As the two of them stared at him in some confusion, he ran his fingers through his sodden locks and wiped at the dirt and blood running down his face with the sleeve of his shirt. The slight movement drew a grimace.

"Have you a length of cloth?" he asked quietly. "Or anything that might serve as a bandage? I think several ribs are broken, and I should prefer they don't puncture a lung." His mouth quirked upward. "I would use mine, but it might raise rather embarrassing questions if I were to make my way home bare chested."

Angus spoke a few words in Jem's ear, and the young groom hurried off toward the rear of the stable. He stood in awkward silence for a bit, scuffing at some wisps of straw with his toe.

"I'll have you know I didn't mean fer ta strike ye when ye couldn't defend yerself," he said haltingly. "It was too late to pull up."

Sterling cut him off. "No need to apologize. I didn't expect or want any special quarter. You laid me out fair and square." He rubbed absently at the bruise on his cheek and winced. "Hell's teeth, you can throw a punch near as well as Gentleman Jackson. Sometime I should like you to show me that slide step to the left—it's a fine piece of footwork."

Angus nodded slowly as he gingerly touched his black eye. "Well, ye ain't so bad with yer fives, either. And ye've more bottom than I expected from. . . ." His words trailed off into an incoherent mumble as he recalled to whom he was speaking.

"From a toff," added Sterling with a lopsided grin.

A hint of an answering grin cracked the big groom's normally impassive features. "Aye, from a toff," he agreed.

Jem returned with a roll of moderately clean linen and a stoneware jug. Angus removed the cork and passed it to the marquess.

"You might want some of this first."

Sterling took a long swallow and pulled a face. "What in the devil is this you're poisoning me with—horse piss?"

That drew a bark of laughter from the two grooms. "It's good Scottish whiskey. We brought it with us from home," piped up Jem.

"I knew there were none but heathens up north," quipped the marquess as he took another swig. "I shall stick with good French brandy—this is truly awful." Nonetheless, he took several more pulls before handing it back. With a resigned sigh, he decided there was little point in putting off the unpleasant task of seeing to his new injury. His fingers began to work at the buttons of his shirt, a rueful expression tugging at the corners of his mouth as he regarded the once spotless linen, now streaked with sweat and bloodstains, a large rent marring one of the sleeves.

As the front fell open, Jem's mouth dropped in shock at the sight of the thick red slash that ran from the marquess's left collarbone down to the center of his chest. "Is . . . is that from a saber?" he asked in a hushed tone.

Sterling's mouth compressed as he gave a curt nod.

"And your leg, sir. . . . Was that—"

"Shrapnel."

The young groom regarded him with something akin to awe. "Which battle—"

"Jem! Leave off pestering him. I'm sure he ain't in no mood to talk about being sliced or shot." Angus turned to Sterling with a shrug of apology. "The lad's army-mad." His tone made it evident he did not approve at all.

Ignoring the pointed rebuke, the young groom went on. "Cor, you must have been a real hero, leading cavalry charges, storming—"

"No, just young and rather stupid, lad."

Jem looked slightly bewildered.

"'Tis nothing to wish for, to see the suffering and torments men inflict on each other during war," said the marquess wearily. "There are precious few heroes—we all find that merely to survive the heat, the hunger, the fatigue, and the terror of battle is a daunting enough task." He shifted his weight off his bad leg. "And there is nothing terribly romantic about being a maimed cripple," he added in a grim voice.

"Oh." The young groom swallowed hard. "That's . . . that's what my cousin said, but I thought mayhap you—this is, mayhap he . . . was wrong."

Sterling's eyes pressed closed for a moment. "No, lad, he was not." He held out his hand for the roll of linen only to find Angus regarding him intently. The other man had ceased throwing daggers with every glance. In fact, there was a flash of gratitude in his eyes for not glorifying the military, as well as a touch of respect and something else that was not as easy to decipher.

"Here, I suppose it would be easier if I was ta give ye a hand with that," he said gruffly.

The marquess finished removing his shirt. "Thank you."

"There's hardly call to thank me—ye ain't going to enjoy this. Now, take a deep breath so I can get it good and tight."

Sterling gritted his teeth as Angus began winding the

cloth snugly around his injured middle. The big groom paused once or twice to work the ribs back in place, drawing an involuntary grunt.

"Give me fair warning if ye are going to cast up yer accounts again," he muttered, still poking at the marquess's side. "I don't have another clean shirt until wash day."

"I shall try—though, I imagine that vile stuff you fed me comes up a great deal easier than it went down."

Angus gave another slight grin as he finished tying off the end of the linen. "Aye, but it served its purpose."

Sterling was indeed feeling a bit light-headed, and the pain seemed to have dulled slightly.

The other man straightened up. "You are sure ye do not wish ta go on up to the manor house?"

"No, I've made enough of a cake of myself for one night," he replied in a voice barely above a whisper.

Angus's head jerked in the direction of the back of the barn. "Well, ye might as well come along with us, then. There's an extra cot in our room."

The marquess hesitated. "You needn't put yourselves out. The straw is quite fine."

A decided glint of humor flashed in the groom's eyes. "Aye, but there's another jug of whiskey in the back."

"Ah, well, in that case, lead on."

Chapter Nine

The thin horsehair mattress felt as luxurious as the finest eiderdown to Sterling's bruised body. He sat on the edge of the cot, his long legs stretched out before him, while Jem searched for an extra blanket.

"This is all we have." There was a tinge of embarrassment in his voice, for a brisk shake of the folded bedding had sent a shower dust and bits of hay wafting through the air. "You are welcome to mine instead," he added shyly. "But I fear it's not in much better condition, your . . . your lordship."

The marquess wished to allay any awkwardness over his sharing their humble quarters. "You can stubble the fancy titles and such rot, lad. Sterling is fine, if you wish to call me anything at all." His mouth quirked in a self-deprecating smile. "After all, you've seen I can be knocked on my arse as easily as any other man."

Jem looked quite relieved, as if he had half expected the marquess to climb up on a high horse now that tempers had cooled.

"And the blanket is more than adequate." He glanced over at Angus. "I trust your offer of another jug still stands?"

After the whiskey had made several rounds, the mood had loosened considerably, as had their tongues. Jem soon lost his initial reticence and began to pepper the marquess with questions about his stallion and whether he had ever attended the races at Newmarket, for as well as being army-mad, the lad was even keener on horses.

Sterling was more than happy to oblige with a detailed description of things that had the young groom's eyes glazed with longing.

"If you like," he added, "perhaps I might arrange with my aunt for you to visit my estate during race week. My man Sykes attends near every day, and would be happy to show you the sights."

Jem stammered a near incoherent thanks at the generous offer. Then, emboldened by a good deal more whiskey than he was used to imbibing, he regarded his own stockinged feet, then the marquess's polished Hessians, now slightly the worse for wear, and ventured another sort of question. "Ain't you going to take off your boots to sleep, or does Quality always wear 'em to bed?"

Sterling turned away and appeared to be studying the knots in the rough pine walls by his side. "I can't," he finally answered in a tight voice.

The young groom turned crimson at realizing his unwitting gaffe, and his eyes made a mute appeal to Angus for what to do. Without a word, Angus put aside the jug and went over to the marquess's side, where it took him no more than a few moments to gently ease first one then the other boot off. He placed them side by side next to the cot and returned to his own place, coolly taking up the jug as if nothing had happened. Before Sterling could say a thing, he asked a quick question about the grey filly's lineage, and the awkward moment was past.

As Sterling was in the middle of his explanation, a sharp rap came at the door.

All three heads jerked around.

"Angus? Jem? Are you there?" demanded a female voice. "Is something wrong?"

Sterling's eyes pressed closed. "Hell's teeth," he muttered.

"The marquess's horse is saddled but is still in its stall," continued Miranda. "What has happened to his lordship?"

Angus looked at Sterling and lifted his brows in question.

"Angus!"

The big groom quickly gestured for Jem to answer the knock.

"Me!" he squeaked in surprise. "But—"

"Go on!" whispered Angus. He pointed to his black-ened eye. "Mayhap ye can convince her there's naught to be concerned about."

"Not bloody likely," swore the marquess under his breath.

They exchanged baleful looks as Jem scurried to the door and opened it just a crack.

"What is going on—"

"N . . . n . . . nothing, milady. Everything is, ah, just fine. No need for concern," stammered the young groom.

Miranda tried to peer around him into the darkened room. "Is his lordship in there?"

"Er, well, yes."

Her brows came together. "Why?"

"Why?" he repeated nervously.

"Yes, that is what I said, Jem. Why?"

"Ah . . ."

"Please stand aside. I am coming in."

To his credit, the lad tried to stave her off. "Well, er, there's been a slight mishap. The marquess finds he . . . he has ta stay here tonight."

There was an ominous pause. "What sort of mishap?"

Jem swallowed. "It seems that one—well, maybe two—ribs are broken, but Angus was able—"

She sailed past him as if he weren't there and headed for the two figures seated toward the back of the room.

"How in the name of heaven did—"

At that moment the light from her candle flickered over her groom's face. Though he ducked his head and brought his hand up to rub at his brow, he couldn't hide the swelling eye and several bruises that were already beginning to turn an ugly shade of purple. She stared at him in utter silence for what seemed to be an age, then turned and slowly moved the candle toward Sterling. He studiously avoided meeting her gaze as she studied his split lip and mottled cheek. Her eyes then fell to his torn and bloodied shirt.

"Perhaps one of you would care to explain this . . . this . . ." She gave up trying to find the appropriate word and simply placed one hand on her hip.

There was no response.

Her eyes narrowed, and she thrust the candle hard by Angus's nose. "I expect an answer from *you*. What happened?"

Angus drew in a long breath. "Well—"

"Don't rake the fellow over the coals. It was my fault," interrupted the marquess. "We had a difference of opinion over a . . . certain matter, and I suggested we settle it as gentlemen would, in, er, a sporting manner."

"Gentlemen!" Her tone made them both wince. "Look at the two of you—more like unruly schoolboys I should say." She gave a harried sigh. "Just what caused this . . . squabble."

Sterling caught the groom's eye. "Horses," he said quickly.

"Aye, horses," agreed Angus.

Miranda's face betrayed her skepticism. But instead of pursuing the matter, she turned her attention back to her groom. "Have you gone entirely mad, Angus?" she demanded. "Surely you are aware you could be shipped off to the Antipodes for striking—"

"I should hope you would not think me so lacking in honor that I would strike a man who wasn't free to strike back," said Sterling in a tight voice. "Of course he had my word there would be no such consequences."

"I would not think *you* were so lacking in sense—or decorum—than to be found scrabbling in the dirt with my groom—"

"That's not entirely fair, milady. I provoked him," piped up Angus in defense of the marquess.

Miranda looked nonplussed at the show of unexpected support from that quarter. "Men," she muttered under her breath, causing each of them to look even more abashed. Her brow furrowed in exasperation as she continued to regard the two of them in deafening silence. But when finally she spoke again, her tone had softened considerably. "That eye needs some attention," she said, bending to have a closer look at her groom's face.

"Oh, it's really naught ta worry on, milady," he mumbled. "I've weathered far worse scrapes."

"I shall decide on that," she answered in a voice that brooked no argument. "Neither of you are to stir. Jem—"

The young groom jumped.

"You will come with me. I shall return shortly."

She marched off, leaving the two of them alone with their thoughts. The marquess slumped forward, threading his fingers through his disheveled locks, while Angus threw himself back on his cot and contemplated the low beams above his head.

"I trust you will not be made to suffer in any way for this," murmured Sterling after a bit.

The groom pulled a face. "Nay. Lady Miranda is much too kind ta mete out any punishment. She doesn't have ta—it's bad enough to know I've disappointed her."

The marquess made a sound in his throat, then lapsed into a moody silence.

Angus continued staring at the ceiling. "And I'm sorry if I've caused ye trouble with the lady. But ye see, none of us here takes kindly to anyone who might . . . hurt her."

Sterling's features hardened. "I have no intention of doing any such thing."

"No?" There was a note of challenge in the reply. "Then, what exactly *are* your intentions?"

The words struck him like another blow to the midriff. What indeed? Good Lord, his emotions were in such a state of confusion that he couldn't possibly begin to fathom his feelings, much less explain them to a stranger.

His jaw tightened and eyes dropped to the floor, as if the answer could be found anywhere but within himself.

Lady Miranda soon returned carrying a large basket filled with assorted medical supplies, Jem trailing in her wake bearing a steaming pot of hot water. She knelt beside Angus, extracted a small compress from her things, and pressed it over his swelling eye. Brushing aside his feeble protests, she took up a soft cloth and, after dipping it in the hot water, began to clean the other cuts and bruises.

"You must hold this in place for a bit longer," she said, placing his fingers up to the compress. After applying several dabs of salve to the broken skin, she gathered up her basket and moved on to the marquess.

"Miranda—" he began in a near whisper.

His words died in his throat as her thumb drew across the corner of his mouth. "Your lip is cut," she said softly. A clean cloth came up to gently wipe away the dried blood and caked dirt. Her fingers touched the mottling on his cheek, lingering there for just an instant, then brushed back the tumbled locks from his forehead. "And you've a nasty scrape here. And here."

He let his eyes fall closed as she tended to his injuries. The closeness of her face, the subtle scent of lilac mingling with the sharp herbal whiff of her medicinals, caused him to suck in his breath.

"I shall have a look at those ribs now."

His eyes flew open. "No! I—"

Her fingers were already working at the buttons of his shirt.

"That is, I should rather you didn't."

She paused for a fraction. "I am afraid I must, sir. If they are not properly wrapped, they might cause serious damage—" The shirt front fell open, and her eyes dropped to his bare chest.

An involuntary cry escaped her lips. "Oh, Jul—sir!" she whispered.

"Yes, I know." He tried to pull away. "Hardly a pretty sight."

Miranda looked away quickly to compose her features, but not before Angus caught the look of anguish on her face. In an instant, however, she recovered and managed to school her emotions enough to speak in a normal voice.

"That still looks rather raw. I have a salve that may help. I shall send it to Mr. Sykes on the morrow." Her fingers began to run mechanically over the rough twist of bandage, though her gaze remained riveted on the deep scar cutting across his breast. Sterling's face remained averted from her, its expression hidden in the shadows. Even so, the rigid set of his shoulders gave hint as to the state of his emotions.

"This seems adequate for the moment," she allowed after a bit. Leaning back, she closed up his shirt and made a show of straightening up her supplies. "Come along, now, sir."

That caused his head to jerk around in surprise. "What?"

Miranda looked taken aback. "Why, you can't think I would allow you to stay here."

"Why not?"

"Because you would be a good deal more comfortable in one of Aunt Sophia's guest rooms."

It was a most reasonable answer, but his mouth took on a mulish set as his eyes dropped to the floor. "I prefer to remain where I am."

All of a sudden she seemed to sense that more than his body had taken a beating. Her expression took on a pensive look as she thought for a moment. "Please, sir, it is *I* who would feel a good deal more comfortable if you come with me. I should not wish to think of you out here in the chill with naught but a thin blanket and a hard cot. Besides," she added as she watched the warring between wounded pride and common sense on his face, "what if there arises a problem with those ribs?" She shook her head slowly. "No, if you insist on remaining here, then I shall have to stay close by as well. I imagine Jem can fetch a chair so that I may sit outside the door."

Sterling let out a sigh of resignation. "Very well," he growled. However, his brow creased slightly as his eyes darted from his stockinged feet to his boots.

"Jem, help Lady Miranda gather her things, while I give his lordship a hand with his coat—no doubt those ribs make it nigh impossible to lift an arm," said Angus, rising quickly to his feet.

The young groom jumped to obey his words, and amid the bustle, Angus made short work of slipping the marquess's Hessians back on. As he assisted Sterling up and helped him don his outer garment, their eyes met, and the marquess gave a slight nod of gratitude. The other man merely blinked then stepped aside as Miranda came around to take hold of Sterling's elbow.

She lifted the lantern and smiled warmly at her two grooms. "I trust the night will pass with no further mishaps. I shall fetch the basket in the morning." With that, she turned and nudged the marquess into a slow shuffle toward the door.

As the single candle bobbed in slow progress through the darkness, Jem thrust his hands into the pockets of his breeches. He slanted a sideways look at his companion.

"It's strange—he don't appear to be half so bad as we figured."

Angus didn't answer for a bit, his eyes still following the two silhouettes in the flickering light. "Hmmm," he murmured. "Strange, indeed."

Jem scratched thoughtfully at his chin. "I don't rightly understand—he treated Lady Miranda so cruelly in the past, yet he seems to . . . to—"

Angus cut off his musings with a stern look. "Well, it ain't none of yer business ta be mulling on yer betters," he chided. "Nor mine. It's best ye leave off thinking on it." But the purse of his lips showed he was far from ready to heed his own advice.

* * *

Sterling muffled a groan as he lowered himself onto the edge of the soft mattress. His whole being was overcome with a numbing weariness, and all he wanted was to sink into the oblivion of a deep sleep. His body ached, and his head was still slightly fuzzed with the effects of the whiskey. But not enough to drown the knowledge that he had made a complete cake of himself.

Miranda eyed him with concern. "I shall get you a draught for the pain as soon as I see you settled."

He leaned forward, taking his head in his hands. "If you wish to do me a kindness, you will simply leave me be, Miranda. I have no need of draughts or salves or potions. I merely want to try and get some sleep." His mouth quirked in a rueful grimace. "And try to forget about what a bloody fool I must appear."

Miranda couldn't repress a slight smile. "Well, if it is any consolation, you actually seem to have won over a new admirer. Jem was quite impressed with your showing. He couldn't stop rattling on about how he hadn't seen anyone stand up to Angus in a mill, and that the outcome was rather in doubt until you had the misfortune to slip." She knelt down as she was speaking and began to ease the coat from his shoulders. "Horses," she said softly. "What fustian! However, I do wonder what on earth could spark such a quarrel between you and Angus." Her brow rose in question.

Sterling clamped his jaw shut.

"Men," she muttered again, tossing aside the finely tailored garment. "I've laid out a clean shirt that I borrowed from Wells." Without pause, she began gently working off his boots.

"Miranda—"

The boots fell to the floor with a clatter. Her fingers started with the lacing at the knees of his riding breeches.

"Miranda!" There was a note of rising panic in his voice. "Don't—"

It was too late. She had already peeled back the soft buckskin to expose the injury to his leg.

There was an audible gasp as her hands froze for an instant. "Dear God," she murmured, ducking low to hide the film of tears in her eyes.

A wash of color flooded his face as he tried to push her away. "Yes, I warned you," he said savagely. "It's quite sickening, isn't it. Now, kindly allow me to cover myself."

Miranda looked up at him, puzzled. "Why, you are . . . you are embarrassed."

"Yes!" he exploded. "Of course I am—I'm a damn cripple." He drew in a ragged breath. "More so that you once knew me . . . in a more admirable state," he added in a near whisper.

He flinched as her fingers began massaging the lumpy scars around his knee, but she refused to be brushed away. "You think," she said slowly, "that you are in any way diminished by the fact that your flesh is torn or that you walk with a limp?"

Sterling hung his head.

"Good heavens." She smiled sadly. "You *are* a fool."

His eyes came up, filled with a poignant uncertainty. "But I see the look of revulsion on the faces of the ladies as I pass—"

"Then they are even bigger fools than you."

She rose to leave. "Good night, sir. You have only to ring if you need anything during the night." Her gaze strayed to his bruised face. "You may change your mind about draughts and potions on the morrow. I fear that you are going to feel quite the worse for this evening's activities come morning."

That, he thought with a grimace, was rather an understatement.

A considerably agitated Sykes appeared on Lady Thornton's front steps far earlier than proper manners allowed.

"Oh, heavens," exclaimed Miranda as Wells opened

the door with some reluctance in answer to the urgent rapping. "How remiss of me—we should have sent word to you that the marquess was spending the night here."

A spasm of relief crossed the valet's weathered face before it was replaced by a look that could only be described as miffed. "Well, his lordship might have saved me a good deal of worry if he had seen fit to share such plans with me."

Miranda repressed a smile at the man's injured tone. "I don't believe he began the evening with such a thing in mind. However, there was a slight mishap. . . ."

Sykes's eyebrows shot up.

"The result was several broken ribs, which prevented him from venturing forth on horseback. So you see, he had little choice but to remain here."

"Now, how in the dev—er, deuce did that happen?"

"Ah, I imagine his lordship might prefer to make the explanation himself."

"Which you shall no doubt pester out of me, but not before I have some breakfast." Sterling moved stiffly into the entrance hall. Miranda had sent Wells up to his room earlier so that he was freshly shaved and the worst of the dirt had been brushed from his breeches and boots. Even so, he hardly cut a dashing appearance, what with the bruises spreading over his cheek and a borrowed shirt that hung a good deal too short at the sleeves and a good deal too wide at the midriff.

Sykes had noticed that the big groom was sporting a wicked shiner and put two and two together. A bark of laughter escaped from his lips. "Good Lord, guv! A mite rusty with your fives? I'm afraid it looks like you may have taken the worst of it."

"I'm touched by your concern," replied the marquess dryly. "Perhaps when you have finished expressing your opinion, you might find it in your heart to take Zeus home and return with the carriage. And perhaps some clean linen."

His valet wiped the grin off his face. "Sorry. No doubt

you are hardly in the mood for banter." A flash of concern came to his eyes, and he took a step closer to Sterling. "How are the ribs feeling?" he asked in a low voice.

"As well as can be expected, I suppose," replied Sterling. "But I would like to be on my way home as soon as possible." He muttered a few more instructions in the other man's ear, then Sykes took himself off without further ado.

Miranda had followed the exchange between them with great interest. "Well, I see you were not quizzing me when you said he was not the sort of valet to fall into a fit of vapors over a wrinkled sleeve," she murmured, a flash of amusement evident in her eyes.

He gave her back a rueful grin. "No," he agreed. "And I can assure you, he shall not let me hear the end of this for quite some time."

She slipped her hand around his arm and started off down the hall. "Come, I've had Cook prepare an ample breakfast." She hesitated a fraction. "You still prefer coffee?"

He nodded.

At that moment Lady Thornton burst from the breakfast room and rushed to her nephew.

She made a sympathetic sound in her throat at the sight of his mottled cheek, then reached up to bestow a light kiss on the uninjured one. "Julian, my dear boy. How are you feeling?" Before he could answer, she took hold of his other arm and went on. "I've brought a number of cushions in, and I've ordered a bowl of porridge in case it pains you to chew, and. . . ."

Sterling rolled his eyes, causing Miranda to stifle a smile, then submitted to his aunt's coddling with a resigned sigh.

The smart phaeton rolled up the entrance drive, but before Sykes announced his presence at the main house, he had one errand to attend to. He drew the matched greys to a halt in front of the barn and took up the wooden box on the seat beside him. Pushing open the door to the tack room, he spied the two grooms at work cleaning the cart harness.

Angus turned around at the sound of footsteps. Even in the muted light, his blackened eye was quite noticeable, along with several other marks of Sterling's prowess with his fists. At the sight of the marquess's valet, he gave a slight nod.

Sykes returned the acknowledgment with a cheerful greeting. "Morning, Dagleish." A slow grin spread over his face as he regarded the other man's appearance with obvious interest. "Hmmmm." He stroked his chin. " 'Tis hard to choose."

There was a twitch of Angus's lips. "What is?"

"Which of you looks the worse for it." He seemed to consider the matter for a bit longer before adding. "But seeing as it is the marquess who's suffering the broken ribs, I must assume it is you who came out on top."

Angus rubbed at a brass buckle for several moments. "If he hadn't slipped, I'd not have cared to bet on the outcome," he said gruffly. "Your man fights fair. He ain't lacking in bottom, either."

"No," agreed Sykes. "Come to think of it, I've never found him lacking in any meaningful regard."

The other man gave a low grunt. "Except maybe the sense to recognize a bald-faced lie when he hears one."

The valet's brows drew together at the enigmatic comment, but he let it pass. Instead, he placed the wooden box on the rough-hewn worktable with a thump. "Compliments of his lordship. He says as your choice of piss would sicken a horse with regular use, he begs you to allow him to add this to your stock." As he lofted one of the bottles of fine French brandy up for inspection, he gave a broad wink. "I assure you, this is most definitely *not* horse piss."

That finally brought a real smile to the groom's lips.

Sykes tipped his cap. "Well, I best be off and try to convey the guv home with a minimum of jostling to his

battered bones." With that, he turned and started toward
the door.

"Sykes."

The valet looked around.

"Tell him . . . thanks."

"Aye. I shall be happy to."

Sterling winced as the light carriage hit another rut.
"Would you prefer that I take over the ribbons? Or have
I displeased you in some way recently, that you are seek-
ing to take a suitable revenge?" he drawled.

"Sorry, sir," muttered Sykes, trying to avoid a large
stone. "These country roads are devilishly rough going."
He shot a sideways glance at the marquess and noted
with some concern that his features were pale beneath
the bruises and that his jaw was set in a clench. "I take
it you're feeling poorly."

"I am feeling as if some hulking giant planted his fist
in my gut!"

The valet tried to suppress a chuckle. The marquess's
lips twitched as well, then both of them started to laugh.
Sterling's mirth was cut off by a sharp intake of breath
as the horses veered around a curve. "Damnation," he
muttered as he shifted uncomfortably in his seat.

"Nearly there." Sykes urged the team into a faster
pace as the way became smoother. "Well, at least you
haven't lost your sense of humor, guv."

The marquess made some sort of sound in his throat.
"I suppose it had some elements of the absurd, but rest
assured, I was hardly in the mood for laughter last night."

Sykes cocked an eyebrow and waited expectantly. But
instead of going on, Sterling lapsed into a moody silence
for the rest of the journey. A groom rushed to lead away
the lathered team while the marquess's butler whipped
open the front door before a knock could be sounded,
his craggy face betraying nary a hint of surprise at seeing
the bedraggled appearance of his employer. The sympathetic clucking of the housekeeper was cut short by a

glare from Sykes as he assisted Sterling up the winding staircase and on to his bedchamber.

Sterling sunk down on the edge of his immense four-poster bed and allowed the other man to strip off his soiled garments and wrap a heavy silk dressing gown around his shoulders.

"I imagine you'd not be averse to a long, hot soak before sliding between the sheets." Sykes gestured to the screen set up in the corner of the room. "So I took the liberty of ordering up a hot bath."

"That," murmured the marquess, "more than earns you forgiveness for the torture inflicted on me earlier. You are a man of many talents, but driving is not one of them."

Leaning heavily on Sykes's shoulder, he limped over to the tub. With a long sigh of relief, he slid into the hot, sudsy water, and his eyes fell closed. Sykes quietly moved away, rearranging the items on the inlaid dressing table, then pausing to inspect the buckskin breeches and tailored riding coat for any permanent damage. After a time he returned to the bath with a thick towel in hand and perched himself on the edge of the rim.

"So?"

Sterling pried one lid open. "What?" he asked reluctantly, although he was well enough acquainted with his valet to know exactly what was meant.

"It's still puzzling me what could cause you to end up in a bout of fisticuffs with your aunt's groom. Care to fill me in on what the devil happened last night?"

"No."

Sykes picked at a thread on his cuff.

"But no doubt you will find a way to make my life intolerable if I do not," he added with a grumble.

"Aye." A mischievous grin stole to the valet's face. "I could offer to handle the ribbons for the entire journey back to London."

Sterling made a mock grimace. "Well," he began after a short pause. "I, er, took exception to Dagleish interfering with a . . . conversation I was having with Lady Miranda in the barn—"

"A conversation? In the barn?"

Sterling colored slightly. "Yes, well, as it was rather late, she offered to light the way instead of asking my aunt's butler. He's rather elderly, you know."

"Now, I may be a bit of a slowtop here, guv, but I fail to see why the groom would, er, take it upon himself to interfere. He ain't exactly been the friendly sort, but he ain't a candidate for Bedlam, either."

The marquess gave a slight cough. "I believe he was under the notion he was . . . protecting the lady."

The valet looked at him rather strangely. "What would have given him that idea?"

"Bloody hell, you are not making this any easier," muttered Sterling. "I'm afraid that Lady Miranda misinterpreted my . . . embrace, and as I was seeking to follow her out of the barn to, er, explain, Dagleish caused me to loose my footing. After a brief exchange of words, I suggested we settle the matter with our fists. I'll also have you know," he added defensively, "I was more than holding my own, until my cursed leg gave out at the wrong moment."

"So I heard from Dagleish." The other man tugged at his chin. "A most interesting evening, I would say."

"Oh, that isn't the half of it. Lady Miranda came back to investigate why she hadn't heard Zeus leave, only to find the two of us—I believe the phrase she used was, looking worse than unruly schoolboys."

Sykes burst out laughing.

"You would think, with my exalted position, I could expect a modicum of respect in my own house," grumbled Sterling under his breath.

The other man continued grinning for a bit, then his expression sobered considerably.

Sterling shifted uncomfortably as he regarded the other man's furrowed brow. He stood up and began to dry off. "Now what?" he finally demanded as his valet helped him into his dressing gown.

Sykes merely shrugged.

"Out with it, man—I would rather that than have to regard that disapproving mug of yours."

There was a lengthy silence. "It's not my place to give advice, guv, but I hope you know what you are about. Lady Miranda is—" He hesitated, as if aware that perhaps he was going too far. Their eyes met, and though the marquess's shoulders went rigid, he nodded almost imperceptibly.

"Go on."

"Well," Sykes continued slowly, "despite whatever happened in the past, she appears to be a very good sort of person. It doesn't seem that she deserves to be . . . hurt."

Sterling knotted the sash of the heavy silk dressing gown with great deliberation. "No," he whispered hoarsely. "She does not."

His valet eyed him with something akin to sympathy. "Have a care, guv. Seems you could be in danger of falling into deep water if you are not careful."

The marquess made no answer.

It was a bit too late for warnings—he feared he had already been pulled under by the swirling currents.

Chapter Ten

McTavish eased himself up over the last tumble of weathered stone and slipped into the makeshift camp. Squatting down near the opening to the shallow cave in the rocks that served as his shelter from the elements, he signaled for Gibbs and Scofield to join him.

"Did everything go according te plan?" Scofield couldn't contain his impatience as McTavish took his time in coaxing a flame to life in the remains of the morning's fire.

Putting his flint away, the other man straightened. "Bring me some whiskey."

Gibbs scurried to fetch the earthenware jug. McTavish took several long pulls on it before leaning back with a grunt. "Things are going more than well." The jangle of a purse in his pocket emphasized his words, spoken low enough so that none of the ragged men huddled around the main fire could hear. "He just paid fer us to take care of the mill in Sillton next week. Then we're te scatter this band of raghearts and slip back across the border to enjoy the blunt we've earned fer a while." He gave a snort of contempt as his eyes strayed over the rest of his band. "I'll be glad to see these lot gone. A sorrier lot of lily-livered coves I ain't never seen. No stomach fer this sort of work." He paused to take another swig. "But it don't matter. After the militia rushes over here, all in a lather, he'll have us move way east in a few weeks, over near the coast, to raise up another gang to strike again."

Scofield and Gibbs broke into wide grins.

His voice dropped even lower. "I been thinking, though. We wouldn't want anyone to interfere with our plans now, would we?"

Both faces fell.

Scofield gnawed at his lip. "Who could do that?"

"That damned Ransford woman, if she keeps asking too many prying questions."

"You want we should take care of her? It wouldn't be a hard task to see she slips off some steep path, or such."

McTavish bared his teeth in a wolfish smile. "That's not quite what I had in mind. No, I have a better plan to get her out of the way until we've finished our work here." He leaned in closer to his cronies and winked. "After all, why take a risk fer no reward? And what I've got in mind fer Mrs. Ransford will, shall we say, prove most profitable."

"Ye don't think messing with her is asking fer trouble?" ventured Scofield. "I mean, what with her being friendly with the marquess—"

McTavish shot him a withering look. "Ye's seen the man. He's a bloody cripple. Ye think he's gonna cause us any trouble when the whole damn militia can't lay a finger us? And, besides, that's just what I'm counting on, her being friendly with the marquess."

Gibbs rubbed at the stubble on his jaw. "Well, ye ain't ever been wrong yet." His eyes took on a gleam nearly as bright as the pieces of gold he was imagining. "Tell us what ye have in mind."

"Don't worry. I've got it all planned out. Now, listen closely. . . ."

Miranda arranged the last few items in her basket, then with a slight smile, added the ample packet that Cook had prepared. It was far more than she and her son could consume, but as she planned a visit to one of the sick children she was tending to, the extra food would be a welcome addition to the family's meager table. She paused, then slid the thin canvas roll containing her medical implements into the pocket of her gown as well. The boil on the child's foot had been of some concern to her on the last visit. There was a chance that this time it may have to be lanced.

"It appears that you expect to be gone for the rest of the day," remarked Lady Thornton as she entered the kitchen and caught sight of the well-stocked basket.

Miranda nodded. "I have need to replenish my supply of St. John's wort, and then I must look in on Mrs. White's daughter. And since Justin wishes to come along, too, I've given leave for his lessons to end early." A smile stole to her lips. "It seems he has need to add to his menagerie."

Lady Thornton rolled her eyes. "What is it to be this time?"

"You don't want to know."

"Oh, dear, whatever it is, let us hope it does not find its way into Miss MacKenzie's bed, like the toad."

Miranda nodded in agreement. "This would be infinitely worse, I'm afraid." In answer to her aunt's questioning look, she added, "He is looking for a snake—a garter snake."

The other lady shuddered.

"Mama, my lessons are finished!" Justin came scampering into the room. "Are we ready to leave?"

"Yes, love," she answered, bending down to do up the buttons of her son's jacket.

Lady Thornton regarded the lad's empty hands. "Just how do you plan to carry the, er, intended addition to your pets? I'm sure your mama does not plan to allow such a creature in her basket."

"Oh, I'll just put it in my shirt," explained Justin. "That way it will stay nice and warm. They like warm places."

"I think I shall return to the library," she said faintly, "and put *out* the fire."

*   *   *

"Well, well, well. It appears we are finally in luck today."

McTavish edged his way off the ledge and snapped the brass spyglass shut with a smirk of satisfaction. The small group of ill-clad men sitting in the lee of the tumbled rocks eyed him with some wariness.

"Mrs. Ransford is heading for the high pasture, along with her brat as well." His expression turned calculating. "Here is the plan. We're gonna nab the widow, before she goes asking too many more nosy questions. When it's time fer us te leave, the marquess can have her back—that is, if he's willing to cough up the blunt for her ransom. But he'll pay. A gentleman of his sort don't like his bed to be empty for long, and no doubt a piece as fine as the widow keeps his sheets more than warm."

"Hear, now. I didn't agree to nothing like this, McTavish," ventured one of the men. "It's one thing to bust up a mill or two for blunt your man pays us—we ain't got no choice if we don't wish our families to starve. But kidnapping . . ." He shook his head. "That's going too far."

Several of the others began to murmur in agreement, but McTavish cut them off with an abrupt laugh. "A little late to be getting a conscience, Davies." With a flick of his head, he made a signal to his two cronies. They got to their feet and began to tap their thick cudgels against their palms. "Or do you fancy explaining to the local magistrate your part in what's been going on here lately?" continued McTavish. He let the veiled threat sink in for a moment or two before going on, his voice dripping with mock concern. "Think they will feel much in charity with ye? A pity what would happen to your wife and children if you was to be arrested and hung."

Davies dropped his eyes, and the other men fell silent as well.

Satisfied that he had squashed any show of dissent. McTavish slowly removed the brace of pistols from his belt and made a show of checking the priming. "Well, now that we are all full in agreement, let's move into action."

Justin made a swift lunge into the tall grass. "Look! I got it."

Miranda repressed a grimace at the sight of the wriggling creature in her son's hand. It was harmless, she reminded herself with a swallow as she watched it disappear between the buttons of his shirt. And on regarding the look of delight on his face, she hadn't the heart to order him to turn it loose. No doubt Angus could build a tall enough box to keep the creature from throwing the household into an uproar.

"How nice. But remember, one is enough," she answered. "And don't stray too far, love. I'm nearly finished, and then we must be off to look in on Mrs. White's daughter." She turned back to the tangle of roots at her knees and began to carefully separate them with her trowel. As she worked, she couldn't keep her thoughts from straying to the marquess, as they had been doing all too frequently of late. Though it had been over a week since their last encounter, she still felt the heat rise to her cheeks at the memory of his embrace, and her own response to it. She still could not fathom the meaning of it—any of it. Nothing made any sense, unless. . . .

No. She wouldn't allow herself to imagine such a thing. Just because she couldn't hide anymore from the realization that her own feelings were not nearly so hardened as she might have wished did not mean that he—

"Mama?" Justin's voice interrupted her reverie. "Who are those men coming toward us?"

Miranda's head jerked around. Three figures were already halfway across the field. A glance to either side revealed several others making their way through the gorse and brambles to cut off any line of retreat.

Her hand came around her son's arm. "Justin, listen to me and do exactly as I say," she said in a low voice. "When I tell you to, you must run and not let those men catch you. Do you understand? Take the way through the woods and don't stop for anything until you are safely home."

"But, Mama—"

"Please, love. You must do as I say." She hugged him hard. "I shall be fine, I promise. Now, *run!*"

To Miranda's immense relief, Justin obeyed and bolted toward the copse of gnarled hawthorns that fringed the deep forest. But then her breath caught in her throat as one of the men rushed to cut him off. The little boy saw the danger and veered sharply away to his left. His strides, however, were no match for those of his much larger pursuer.

"Here, now, imp. Hold up if you know what's good fer ye," cried the man as he grabbed hold of Justin's sleeve. Both of them skittered to a near halt on the precarious footing of fallen leaves and tangled roots. The man reached out his other hand to take a firmer grasp on the boy. All at once he gave a sudden scream and staggered backward, releasing his hold and jerking both arms heavenward. A small, wriggling shape flew through the air and fell into a thicket of brambles. Justin quickly darted out of his reach and disappeared into the shadows of the trees.

Seeing that he was safely away, Miranda rose and calmly stood her ground as the men approached.

As the one with the evil-looking pistols thrust through his belt drew close, it became clear he was the leader. Eyes narrowed, he snarled a heated rebuke at the member of his band who had allowed Justin to elude capture.

"You bloody idiot—I wanted the brat as well!"

"A snake! A bloody snake came out of the imp's sleeve—I swear it!"

A snort of disbelief was the only reply. His angry gaze came back to rake over Miranda. She met it without flinching, and indeed, her coolness seemed to goad his temper even more. "You'll have to do," he said with a sneer, then licked his lips. "And you'll do very nicely, indeed. You had better hope the blunt comes quickly, else we'll be forced to take out payment in other ways."

Miranda paled slightly, but her voice remained steady. "Is that what you expect? A ransom? My aunt is not wealthy—"

McTavish gave a nasty laugh. "Oh, it's not your aunt we're thinking of, it's yer fancy man, the marquess. No doubt he'll be willing to pay extra to keep getting a roll in the hay."

A slight smile came to her lips. "I fear you are sadly mistaken if you think the marquess will pay a farthing to secure my release."

"Of course he will! I've seen him hanging around your skirts." A note of uncertainty caused his voice to ring even harsher. "It's clear you're his doxie, and I mean to see that he pays us well if he wishes to continue having you warm his sheets." He spat on the ground. "He can well afford it."

She shook her head doggedly. "You are wrong. I am nothing to his lordship."

There was a nervous shuffling among several of the men. "The boy will raise the alarm," muttered one of them. "Perhaps it would be best to have done with this and leave her be—especially if she's telling the truth. I've heard the locals talk about her, and she doesn't seem that sort—"

"Shut up!" The leader glared at them, then turned back to Miranda and dealt her a stinging blow across the cheek. "You, too."

He removed a good-sized rock from his coat, around which was tied a note. After hefting from one hand to the other, he tossed it to one of the men. "You know what to do—heave it right through the window I showed you. And be quick about it." There was a slight pause. "Don't go getting any clever ideas, either. I promise you, the authorities would have precious little sympathy for any tale from the likes of you. You'll only end up swinging from the gibbet, and then what would happen to your family?"

The other man pocketed the ransom note without a word and set off.

The leader signaled for Scofield to take hold of Miranda's arm. "Come on, then. Let's get her back to the camp before the brat spreads the word on what has happened."

Sterling urged his stallion into a brisk gallop, enjoying the feel of the wind in his face again after what had seemed like an interminable confinement.

"Easy, now, guv," cautioned Sykes after the marquess's mount had cleared the low stone wall at full speed.

"Oh, stubble it, man," he called with a grin as he reined the big animal to a walk. "Good Lord, you've been acting worse than a damn nursemaid over a few bruised ribs."

Sykes rolled his eyes. "Someone here has to exercise a little common sense," he grumbled.

Sterling laughed outright. "Come now, it's too nice a day to brangle." He thought of the small package he had tied at the back of his saddle and turned in the direction of his aunt's property. "Let us ride to Lady Thornton's. The book I ordered from London for Justin arrived yesterday, and I wish to give it to him." A fond smile played on his lips. "I think he shall like the pictures of the animals."

That there was also a fine edition of a rare herbal for Miranda he didn't feel the need to mention. The truth was, he felt a bit like a nervous schoolboy as he wondered whether she would accept it. Somehow, it mattered a great deal. A sigh slipped out as he thought of all the other things he would like her to have as well. Along with the books, several large trunks had also arrived from London. Though his man of affairs must have been thoroughly perplexed by the orders he had received, he had carried them out to the letter. Sterling now had a full wardrobe of exquisite gowns and sundries made by Miranda's former modiste, still considered the most exclusive in Town. He had no doubt that colors and styles selected by that most discerning lady would be perfect. Now, if only he could convince Miranda to—

His stallion shied sharply to one side, nearly unseating him. "Behave yourself, Zeus," he grumbled. "I know you've been sadly neglected over the past week, but you needn't toss me on my ear over it."

He looked up to see that Sykes had drawn his mount to a halt, and his hand was moving toward the brace of pistols at his saddle. In answer to Sterling's questioning gesture, the valet pointed at the stand of thick scotch pine trees flanking the narrow trail just ahead. There was a quick movement in among the boughs, then utter stillness. The two exchanged glances and slowly drew their weapons.

"Whoever is there, come out and show yourself, else risk a bellyful of lead," called Sykes in a menacing voice.

There was no answer.

The valet cocked one pistol, the ominous click echoing like a shot through the surrounding woods. Suddenly a small figure appeared from the sheltering shadows.

"M-Major?"

"My God, it's Justin!" Sterling jammed his pistols back in the holsters, spurred forward, and swooped the little boy up into his arms. "Steady, lad," he said softly as Justin began to sob against his shoulder. "Good Lord, tell me what's wrong."

"Mama said I was to run home and not stop for anything." He brushed away a tear. "But I got lost in the woods, and . . ."

"You've been very brave and done very well, but if I am to help, I must know exactly what has happened."

"W-we were gathering herbs up in the field near old shepherd McDuff's cottage when some . . . men came out of the woods toward us. That was when Mama told me I was to do just as she said and run."

Sykes had drawn alongside the marquess. His brows came together as the soldier in him began to assess the situation. "How many men were there, Justin?"

The boy thought for a moment. "There were three in the field. And two more were by the trees. Then one other tried to catch me, but I got away."

"So, at least six." The valet's brows came together, and he slanted a look at Sterling. "Squire Hawkins is the local magistrate, and he isn't above twenty minutes ride from here. It shouldn't take long to raise an armed party. Have you any idea where this McDuff's cottage is?"

"Aye, I know the place."

Justin swallowed hard. "Nothing is going to happen to Mama, is it?" he asked in a small voice.

Sterling hugged the boy hard to his chest. "No, lad. I promise." He tousled the boy's hair, then abruptly thrust him into his valet's arms. "See him safely to my aunt's."

"But, guv!"

"Then ride on to the magistrate and raise the alarm."

Sykes opened his mouth to protest again, but Sterling cut him off. "There's no time to waste on arguments."

"Surely you can't mean to go after them by yourself!"

The marquess's face was grim. "That's exactly what I mean to do."

The other man swore under his breath as Sterling's big stallion took off at full gallop and disappeared around the bend. But then another snuffle from the small figure in his arms reminded him of his duty. Tucking the little boy firmly to his chest, he spurred his own mount forward.

Angus put down his pitchfork and poked his head out of the barn at the sound of pounding hooves. His expression changed to one of alarm at the sight of the lathered horse and the figure of Justin clinging to Sykes's neck. He raced out to intercept them.

"Has there been an accident?" he demanded. "Has the bairn been hurt? And where is Lady—"

Sykes tersely explained what had happened, drawing a muttered oath from the big groom. "Let me see Justin settled with Lady Thornton. Find Jem, then we must move, and quickly. I cannot like the odds of the marquess going up after them by himself."

Angus gave a curt nod, then disappeared back into the barn.

When Sykes returned, he found the two grooms already saddling the grey filly and Justin's pony.

Jem cast a pained look at the smaller animal and lifted his shoulders in apology. "He ain't exactly fit for our size, but there's little choice other than poor old Thistle."

"He'll stand up to your weight long enough for you to reach Squire Hawkins," said Angus. "Up you go."

Jem's face took on a mutinous look. "But I want to go with you and—"

"Now!"

His lower lip thrust out, but he climbed into the saddle without further argument. The other two watched him set off, legs dangling perilously close to the ground, as fast as the pony could manage. Sykes turned and held up the grubby piece of paper that Lady Thornton had just handed to him.

"This is what came crashing through the parlor window not ten minutes ago."

The groom's eyes narrowed as he read the rough scrawl. "Bloody bastards," he growled.

Sykes nodded as he checked the priming on his pistols. "Aye. Now, if you will ride over to the marquess's estate and alert—"

"The hell I will. I'm coming with you."

The valet looked up in surprise.

"If his lordship has gone after Lady Miranda, then I figure we had best go after his lordship, to make sure that both of 'em get out of this coil unhurt. Somehow I think she would take it greatly amiss if anything were ta happen to him, and I would hate ta see milady disappointed." As he spoke, he slowly unwrapped the thick bundle of canvas in his hands, revealing a long barreled pistol. "I keep it around just fer emergencies," he added. The gun went into his coat pocket.

A slow grin had spread across Sykes's face. "Your company would be most welcome, Dagleish. Though I doubt the guv intends to let anything stop him from seeing that no harm comes to his wife, our assistance might come in handy."

Angus joined the valet in taking to the saddle. "She ain't his wife, Sykes. It seems ta me that it don't do either of them any good to forget that fact."

"We shall see," murmured the valet as he set his heels into his horse's flanks.

The two men rode hard and quickly reached the point where the road turned into a rough cart track and began to wind its way up between the rugged pastures toward a thick stand of forest, then on to the craggy moors. Sykes reined to a walk. Shading his eyes, he surveyed the wild surroundings with an increasingly long face.

"Any idea where these men might be holed up?" His voice did not indicate he held out much hope for that.

The big groom remained silent. After a bit his brows furrowed, and he suddenly turned his mount around. "Wait here."

Sykes opened his mouth to argue. Angus cut off his protest with a jerk of his head. "Ye noticed that we passed some laborers fixing a gap in the stone wall?"

The valet grunted an impatient reply.

"Times are very hard here, Sykes," explained Angus. "The locals may not have any doings with such a bad lot, but they also ain't likely ta bark ta the authorities about what they know. There's a chance one of those men back there has seen or heard something that may be of use ta us."

Sykes looked dubious. "Why would they tell you, then?"

"Because Lady Miranda has already made herself well

liked and respected round these parts. They won't abide by that sort of violence against her. Besides," he growled, "they hold anything back, and I'll thrash 'em within an inch of their bloody lives." He trotted off, leaving Sykes no doubt that if there was information to be had, the big groom would have it out of them with no argument.

Sure enough, he returned shortly with a grim smile on his lips. "A bit of smoke, even far up in these hills, doesn't go unnoticed." He indicated a direction that led up into the most forbidding part of the moors. "Follow me."

Though Sykes did not like above half the idea of leaving the marquess on his own, he had to agree that the groom's plan seemed to make the most sense. With a reluctant sigh, he fell in behind the grey filly.

Sterling reached the stone cottage and turned his stallion into the adjoining pasture. He approached the clearing near the trees with great caution, his pistols loosened in their holsters, his gaze sweeping the surroundings with a practiced scrutiny. It took little time to pick the signs of recent disturbance—the scuffed earth, the bent grasses, the snapped twigs. A clear trail had been left by the numerous footsteps. It skirted the edge of the forest and led into the higher grazing lands. The marquess had no trouble discerning the direction they had taken, even on horseback, for the group had made no effort to hide their tracks.

That was cause for some concern. The fact that they had little worry of being followed boasted of a certain brash overconfidence. Whoever the leader of this band of ruffians was, he had lost all fear of being caught. No doubt his continued success at eluding the authorities had imbued him with a sense of invincibility.

And that made him a very dangerous fellow. Very dangerous indeed.

Sterling felt a knot form in the pit of his stomach as he thought of Miranda at the mercy of such a man. He urged his stallion to a faster pace while his eyes raked the way ahead for any sign of movement. Surely he must be cutting into their lead, he told himself. And surely he would reach them before any harm could befall her. His mouth thinned in a determined line, and his spurs dug into his horse's flanks yet again.

He had no intention of losing her for a second time.

Chapter Eleven

McTavish glanced back down the rocky slope, then turned away, smugly satisfied that no one would be able to follow their trail over the rugged terrain. Hurrying ahead, he caught Miranda hard by the arm and took charge of leading her over the short distance that remained. As they entered the small clearing surrounded by tumbled boulders and thin, windswept pines, the four men left behind looked up from the blazing campfire. Their expressions of surprise quickly turned into ones of thinly veiled disapproval. The rest of the band straggled into the camp, and though no words were spoken, the mutinous air was suddenly thick enough that Scofield and Gibbs loosened the pistols at their belts and cast warning looks all around.

With deliberate roughness, McTavish shoved Miranda forward with enough force that she stumbled and fell to her knees. She merely looked up at him with icy calmness, then began to slowly brush the dirt from her hem. Her failure to weep and carry on seemed to pique his anger to greater heat.

"Get up, you doxie," he snarled, dragging her up to her feet.

"Here, now, McTavish. Have a care," cautioned one of the men who had participated in the kidnapping. "If the marquess pays the blunt, he ain't gonna want to see her marked up."

"Keep yer mummer closed, if you know what's good fer ye." He gave Miranda a shake. "And you, you better hope the bloody marquess comes up with the money." A nasty leer spread across his swarthy features. "Because I don't intend to go unrewarded for the risk I have taken."

Miranda was more frightened than she allowed herself to appear. She doubted that McTavish's threats were idle ones. He looked thoroughly capable of any sort of violence, and the fact that his own men seemed cowed by him only heightened the feeling that she was in real danger. Why, even if the marquess went along with the ransom demands—no sure thing—she was not entirely convinced the man was going to release her. After all, she had seen his face, knew his name. She dropped her eyes to the ground, hoping that McTavish would not see her growing apprehension.

To her great relief, he released his hold with a muttered oath and stalked over to the earthenware jug sitting near the fire. Lifting it to his mouth, he took a long swig, then passed it to his two cronies. Ignored, the other men drifted over to sit around the crackling logs and wait in sullen silence for a pot of water to boil. Miranda ventured to sit as well, hoping to escape further attention. She had no idea what the ransom demands entailed, but as she watched the sun move ever closer to the horizon, she felt her own spirits sinking as well. It seemed likely that she would be forced to spend the night here among these men. A shudder ran through her at the thought. At least Justin was out of their clutches. Surely he must be home now, safely enfolded in the arms of Lady Thornton.

Her eyes pressed closed at the thought of home, and she bit her lip to hold back the tears. Her aunt would be dreadfully worried about her, of that she had no doubt. And what of the marquess? What would he be feeling? She forced herself to put questions of that nature out of her mind. No matter what he felt, it at least seemed likely that a sense of duty would impel him to alert the authorities to what had happened. She bucked up her flagging courage by telling herself that she was not entirely without hope of rescue, that even now, the magistrate must be gathering a party to begin a search for her.

As she looked up, her gaze fell on one of the men across the dancing flames, and she realized with a start that she had seen him before, several years ago, while treating a sick child. For a moment their eyes locked, and he flashed a fleeting look of sympathy before turning back to his steaming cup. The ragged fellow next to her made a bit of room nearer the fire and nudged a battered mug of tea in her direction, all while taking care not to give so much as a glance in her direction. Not daring to speak any thanks, she took a furtive sip or two, feeling much better as the strong brew spread its warmth within her. After all, she had faced down fear in the past and had found the strength to overcome it. She would keep a cool head and do the same now.

But any hope that McTavish might have reined in his belligerence soon ebbed away. The jug had only fueled his volatile mood, and as his voice rose another notch, it became clear trouble was brewing. The comments, mostly about her, became bolder and bawdier, encouraged by the snickers of his two cronies. After one more swig, he lapsed into an ominous silence, then started toward her.

Sterling began to understand why the band he was following showed little fear of being followed. As the trail twisted up into the forbidding moors, their tracks had all but disappeared into the steep slopes of flinty scree and weathered rock. McTavish and his band had not, however, reckoned with the marquess's years of experience in the hardscrabble terrain of the Peninsula. His keen eye had little difficulty in picking out the subtle signs that marked their passage.

He had to stop for a moment, both to catch his breath and to allow the searing pain in his leg to ease just a bit.

The unstable footing and rocky outcroppings had forced him to abandon his horse some way back, so that his progress had slowed considerably, though not through lack of effort. Sweat had soaked his once crisp linen shirt, and several times he had nearly lost his footing and taken a nasty spill. Eyes narrowed, he surveyed the way ahead, noting with grim satisfaction that he was nearing the top of the crag.

A narrow ledge was the only way around a slide of large boulders. Sterling took several cautious steps, straining to hear any sound from the other side. His boots inched slowly over the uneven stone until he could manage a glimpse of what lay beyond. There was no sign of Miranda and her captors, only a ghost of a path that threaded back through a stand of scraggly pines and up into a series of narrow ravines. Before the trees, however, lay a short traverse over flat ground, completely exposed on all sides. It was risky, but there was no other choice. He would simply have to move quickly, he thought grimly as another twinge shot through his knee.

As he picked his way ahead, a shard of stone broke loose from the ledge. Sterling fought to regain his balance, but his bad leg twisted, then buckled completely under his weight. The marquess pitched forward, then felt himself tumbling over the edge. The drop was precipitous, with nothing to break his fall but the litter of rocks over one hundred feet below. As his leg smashed into the side of the cliff, he grabbed desperately for any hold. His fingers managed to lodge in a narrow crevasse, though the force of his momentum nearly wrenched his shoulder from its socket. Stifling a groan, he began to pull himself back to the lip of the ledge. Finally, his hands raw and bleeding from the effort, he was able to twist up to safety.

Although muzzy with pain, Sterling remained alert to the danger of being seen. With barely a pause, he forced himself to crawl forward to what little shelter the windswept pines afforded. Once there, his weary limbs gave way, and he rolled onto his back, gasping for breath. His heart felt as if it might burst through his chest, and as the rush of adrenaline receded, his muscles felt as limp as wet felt. It took several long minutes before he could begin to assess the extent of his injuries. The scrapes and bruises were hardly cause for concern, but the blow to his already weakened leg had caused some damage. By craning his neck, he could make out a small stain of crimson slowly seeping through his breeches just above the boot, and an attempt at flexing the knee nearly brought on a wave of nausea.

The marquess's jaw tightened like a vise as he stared up at the scudding clouds. Was he to lay there in ignominious defeat, in need of rescue as well? Such a thought was made even more bitter to swallow by the fact that he couldn't repress the uneasy feeling that somehow it was not the first time he was failing Miranda in a time of need. His hands slowly felt at the pockets of his coat. The pistols were still there.

That was all there was to it—he would go on if he had to do it on his hands and knees.

As he took in another lungful of air, he noticed a thin white plume of smoke wafting up against the darker grey of the sky. Surely it must mean Miranda and her captors were close by. Spurred on by that encouraging sign, he found the strength to haul himself to his feet and push onward.

"Get up!" ordered McTavish.

When Miranda hesitated for just a fraction, he grabbed her arm and yanked her to her feet. "When I give an order, you will jump to obey it!"

She said nothing, but the rise of her chin and the flare of defiance in her eyes spoke loud enough.

His hand came across her cheek again, this time hard enough to raise an ugly red welt. A low murmur ran through the group of men seated around the fire. McTav-

ish spun around, his grip still locked on Miranda's arm.
"Any of you looking for the same?"

The sound died away.

"You see—no hero is going to jump up to yer rescue,"
he sneered. "So I suggest you find your manners and
begin to act sweet with me." His hand began to snake
its way up her arm. "Just like you do with his lordship."

Miranda tried to pull away.

"Oh, no, you don't. Perhaps he likes a show of spirit
in his doxies, but me, I prefer my females obedient—
very obedient."

The laugh that followed sent a frisson of real fear
through her. It became more than a mere shiver as he
released her and removed the belt from his rough breeches.
He slapped the thick leather against his meaty palm.
"Now, come here and show me how you kiss the
bloody swells."

She looked for any way of retreat, but Scofield and
Gibbs had already moved in closer on either side, their
leering expressions leaving no doubt that they expected
some entertainment. Scofield licked his lips. "How about
a taste for us as well, McTavish?"

The leader spit on the ground. "Perhaps when I'm
finished—but that won't be for a while." He took a step
closer to Miranda and snapped the belt in the air. "I
said, come here!" But unlike earlier, he made no effort
to grab her. It was clear he was enjoying himself. Though
she had her outward emotions under rigid control, he
must have sensed some sign of her mounting terror and
was taking pleasure in prolonging it. "Think on it, my
pretty one. If I have to come get you, you'll soon feel
the strap on that milky skin of yours. I only want what
you're giving all too freely to your fancy man."

The other two snickered and murmured rude encouragements.

"Yes," continued McTavish. "Just a few sweet kisses."
One hand dropped down to fiddle suggestively with the

fastening of his breeches. "Then you will toss up your skirts and let me have a ride."

A sound of disgust caught in Miranda's throat.

His face turned dark with anger. "I think it's time for you to start learning how to act proper with a man. Maybe his lordship will even thank me for breaking you to the saddle."

"Why don't you ask him yourself?" said Sterling quietly as he stepped from behind the largest fall of rocks. His two pistols were leveled at McTavish's chest.

For an instant the leader's jaw went slack with surprise, then he quickly recovered his wits, his eyes narrowing as they flicked from the marquess to Miranda to his underlings.

"My lor—" Miranda cut off her cry of surprise, sensing that any display of emotion might only serve to distract the marquess.

Scofield and Gibbs fell back a step or two in confusion, but managed to catch sight of McTavish's unspoken order and jerked their own weapons up to cover Sterling. The men around the fire sat in stunned silence, their expressions ranging from blank shock to disbelief to outright terror at the prospect of capture. Not one of them so much as twitched a muscle.

Sterling started to advance, but stumbled slightly, giving McTavish just the opportunity he had been watching for. The leader whirled to his right, snatched a pistol from the belt of the startled Scofield, and brought it to bear on Miranda in one rapid motion.

"Drop your guns, or I'll kill her!"

"Will you, now?" replied the marquess in a calm voice. His lips curled in a grim smile. "In that case, I shall also be forced to pull the trigger."

"And my men will drop you like a dog."

Sterling's brow arched upward. "Really? The hue and cry over your present activities would be nothing compared to that for the murder of a gentleman of my rank. They would be hunted down like curs, no matter where they tried to flee. I wonder that they would stick their necks out in such a manner for a man already dead." He shifted one of his weapons to cover Scofield. "Besides, I think I'll take my chances. Their hands look rather shaky to me. Perhaps they are unused to aiming at people who can aim back." The smile became more pronounced. "I assure you, after my years of fighting on the Peninsula, I have no lack of experience in such a thing. And *my* aim is accorded to be very good."

Scofield swallowed hard. Indeed, his hand was trembling perceptibly, and Gibbs appeared to be in no better shape. McTavish shot them both a look of contempt, then turned back to Sterling. His face revealed a seething anger, just waiting to boil over as soon as he had figured out how to turn the situation back to his favor. But despite such emotion, there remained a glint of cunning in his narrowed eyes.

"The Peninsula?" he repeated with a shuffling of feet designed to distract the marquess's attention. At the same time he sought to edge within arm's reach of Miranda, seeing that if he could grab her to use as a shield, he would immediately regain the upper hand.

The hammer of Sterling's pistol came back with an audible click. "That's quite far enough. One more movement of any kind and it is you, and not the lady, who will be meeting his Maker."

"You wouldn't dare. My men would kill both of you in an instant." McTavish's words came out in a rush of bravado, but an edge of uncertainty had crept into his voice.

Sterling twitched another ghost of a smile. "You are welcome to test my nerve."

The other man clenched his fist in frustration, but he remained still. "You'll not have her, not until I get my blunt. You make a move forward, and I'll kill her, I swear."

"Well, then, it seems we have a standoff," remarked the marquess after several moments of tense silence.

McTavish growled something unintelligible.

"There may, however, be a way to resolve it."

A calculating look came to the leader's face. "What do you mean?"

"Take me in exchange for the lady. I imagine you planned to send directions on how to deliver the ransom to my estate. My valet is not a fool. He will know how to handle the exchange."

A gasp escaped Miranda's lips. "You cannot mean—"

Again, she swallowed her words at the pointed look Sterling flashed her.

Someone around the fire emitted a low whistle, followed by several coughs as the men shifted uncomfortably in their places. It was clear that the idea of holding a titled lord hostage was even less palatable than that of snatching Miranda in the first place. McTavish snarled a curse, and sounds died away.

His tongue came out to run over his lower lip. "Take you instead?" An ugly grin began to spread over his face. "I expect the price would be considerably higher than it would be for a slut."

It was only with great effort that Sterling refrained from pulling the trigger.

"But maybe I'll just keep the both of you—"

The marquess spoke softly, yet his words slashed through the chill air with all the force of a saber. "What you will do is lower your pistol and allow my—Mrs. Ransford to join me here by the time I count to three, or you are a dead man. And don't think of so much as a blink, or the consequence will be the same."

McTavish shot him a murderous look.

"One."

He wet his lips as his features betrayed his inner struggle.

"Two."

"How do I know you'll keep your end of the bargain?"

"Because I am a gentleman, and my word is binding, even to a piece of gutter slime like you."

McTavish's face twisted into a scowl that made it clear he intended the marquess to pay for such a remark, but after a slight hesitation, he slowly lowered his weapon.

Miranda crossed quickly to where Sterling was standing. She hadn't failed to notice the patch of crimson seeping through the knee of his buckskins or the pallor of his skin under the sweat and grime.

"You're hurt," she exclaimed in a murmur low enough that only he could hear. "I'm not going to leave you with that cur. Keep your pistols up—we'll both go. You needn't honor any pledge made to that sort of man. The men by the fire will not try to stop us. They wish themselves well out of this, and he and his two underlings hold them here only out of fear and force."

"No. Now, go!" he whispered, not taking his eyes off of McTavish. "And quickly!"

"But—"

"Please don't argue." His voice was tight with concern. "It's no good—I'd never manage the climb back. Justin found us. Sykes knows what's happened. He'll see to things." A spasm of pain crossed his face. "Besides, there is no real cause for worry. If he murders me, there would be such a reaction from London that the authorities would be forced to tear these hills apart searching for the culprit. Whatever else, he doesn't appear to be a total fool. Besides, he wants the money too badly, and he knows he'll have to produce me in one piece."

Sterling raised his voice to address McTavish. "I'm going to give the lady one of my pistols. The other one will remain aimed at your heart until she is well away." His mouth quirked in a dry smile. "Then I will submit to your hospitality until satisfactory arrangements can be made. But don't forget, my man is a rather cautious sort of fellow and will demand to see the merchandise before he pays for it." Though his words retained their steely edge, the marquess couldn't keep from swaying slightly as he finished.

Miranda's hand came up instinctively to rest on his sleeve.

"Julian!"

It was the first time she had uttered his name. Sterling felt a lurch in his throat as his eyes fell away to regard her pale features. He wanted nothing more than to gather her in his arms and beg her to say it again. And again. "It's all right," he whispered, then his gaze swung back to the leader.

It was too late.

McTavish hadn't taken his eyes from the marquess. At the momentary lapse in attention, he was ready to take the advantage. The pistol was still dangling in his hand. In one quick motion, he hurled the heavy weapon at Sterling's injured leg while dodging to one side to avoid any answering shot. It caught the marquess flush on the knee. Stifling a groan, he dropped to the ground where he lay in stunned agony.

"Julian!" cried Miranda as she dropped down to the ground next to him.

"Cover them, you idiots!" screamed McTavish.

Scofield and Gibbs managed to recover their wits enough to train their weapons on the two figures in the dirt.

"Well, well," sneered McTavish as he sauntered toward them. "Isn't this an interesting turn of events?" He tossed one of the marquess's pistols to one of his two cohorts and stuck the other in the waistband of his pants.

"Think on it," Sterling warned. He managed to push himself up to a sitting position. "You'll get not a farthing if, as I said, the merchandise isn't in one piece."

An ugly laugh rent the chill air. "Oh, the merchandise will be in one piece. It will just be a bit . . . used." His expression turned even uglier as his gaze strayed to Miranda and then back to the marquess. "Perhaps you'd like to watch."

Sterling went absolutely rigid. His tone remained low, but the words cut through the air with all the steely force of a saber. "You so much as lay a finger on my wife," he said very slowly, "and I will rip your heart out of your chest with my bare hands."

A murmur of shock and surprise ran through the men around the fire.

"Shut up," snarled McTavish, but it was clear he, too, was taken aback by the force as well as the import of Sterling's words. It was one thing to take advantage of some poor widow of dubious morals, but even he had to think twice about forcing himself on the wife of a marquess.

"Wife? She ain't your wife," he said uncertainly. "It's a hum."

"It's no hum."

"Look at her gown! It's naught but a rag. And she don't live with you." He was beginning to regain his bravado. "I tell you, it's a hum." He took another step forward.

"The reasons for our current arrangements are of no concern to the likes of you, but rest assured, the lady is my wife, and if you touch her, you—and your underlings—are dead men."

Scofield swallowed convulsively while Gibbs shuffled nervously from foot to foot. "Maybe we should talk things over," said Scofield. "There's still plenty left in the jug, and besides, they ain't going nowhere."

Seeing that his support was in danger of ebbing away, McTavish allowed himself to be convinced. "Very well, but I'll see them tied up in any case. You!" He pointed to one of the men at the edge of the fire. "Fetch some rope and bind their hands."

The fellow rose reluctantly and returned with a length of rough hemp. After cutting it into two lengths with one of the cooking knives, he did as he was told.

"Bring them over here." McTavish pointed to a place hard up against a slab of rock and some distance from the warmth of the fire. Miranda was able to walk on her own, but Sterling didn't have the strength to get to his feet. The man had to drag him over to the spot.

"Rip out my heart," said McTavish as he glowered over the marquess's prostrate form. "Why, you don't look so mighty now, your bloody lordship." As he finished, he took back his booted foot and delivered a vicious kick to the injured leg.

Sterling bit back a scream. His head spun in a haze of pain, then everything went black.

Chapter Twelve

Miranda also bit back a cry, one of outrage rather than pain. She realized she must keep both her wits and her emotions together if she was to find some way to extricate the two of them from this nightmare. She bit her lip as she ran her eyes over Sterling. He had clearly lost consciousness, and his labored breathing sounded too shallow for her liking. Worse, the patch of blood on his breeches was spreading noticeably. She could hardly bear imagining what lay beneath the torn buckskin.

Tears welled up, but she forced herself not to dwell on how badly he was hurt. What mattered now was to find a way to get him the help he needed. She twisted her hands behind her. At least she had a start, she thought grimly. The man who had bound her wrists had whispered a caution not to struggle so that he could leave the bonds as badly tied as possible. Indeed, they were loose. Loose enough for her to work the skirts of her gown around so that her fingers could just about reach into one of the pockets. They fumbled for the canvas packet and were finally able to extract it on the third try. She got the strings undone and searched within the folds for the thin scalpel. The razor sharp blade cut through the knots in a trice.

As the rope fell away, she studied how things were. It was impossible to slip away unnoticed, even if she wished to. Rocks hemmed her in from behind and on both sides. Straight ahead was the fire, with the group of men now finishing a meager meal and exchanging muted conversation. Beyond them, in a small group to themselves, were McTavish and his two underlings. The jug had indeed reappeared, and it was passed around with increasing frequency.

Her mouth tightened. There seemed precious little she could do, despite her freedom. Then her eyes fell on the pistol that McTavish had flung at the marquess's leg. It lay unretrieved in the shadows, not ten feet from where she sat. Her gaze darted back to the leader's group. They appeared to be arguing, though McTavish was doing most of the talking. His gestures became more and more animated, and she was aware of the rise in his voice, though she couldn't make out the words.

Slowly, she inched sideways just a bit.

When nobody noticed, she began a stealthy crawl toward the forgotten weapon. It was nearly in reach when her half boot dislodged a stone. She froze as it fell with what sounded like a resounding crash to her ears. The sound must have been faint, for only one of the men turned slightly to the noise. With a quick glance, he took in her position, the pistol on the ground, and then their eyes locked. After only the briefest hesitation, he merely blinked and went back to the contents of his battered tin plate.

Miranda let out the breath she was holding. She moved another few feet and began to reach out for the gun. To her horror, McTavish suddenly lurched to his feet and, with a loud oath, started to walk toward where the marquess lay motionless. It took a moment, but he registered that something was not quite right.

"Where is she?" he roared, yanking his own weapon from the waistband of his pants and breaking into a run.

Miranda snatched up the pistol, praying that the priming had not been jarred loose. "Stay where you are!" she warned. "I know how to use this."

He spun around. "You meddlesome female. I'll get more than enough blunt for the marquess alone and be well away into Scotland before they find your corpse."

His pistol started to draw a bead. "Though, when I get through with him, he's going to wish he were dead."

She gritted her teeth and pulled the trigger.

Nothing.

McTavish threw back his head and began to laugh. His pistol came up higher. The laughter turned into a scream as a shot echoed among the rocks. He staggered forward several steps, staring in wild disbelief at the spreading circle of red on his shirt, then collapsed facedown in the dirt.

Sykes stepped from behind a boulder. "In the future, milady, you must remember to check your flint."

Scofield and Gibbs, slowed by the copious amounts of liquor they had consumed to drown their growing anxiety, made no pretense of resistance when Angus appeared and motioned for them to throw down their weapons. The big groom quickly gathered them up and turned his attention to the group of frightened men by the fire.

"You've naught to worry from them," said Miranda quickly. "They wanted nothing to do with this. Couldn't we allow them to simply slip away? I'm sure they have learned their lesson about where a life of crime can lead."

"You've too soft a heart," murmured Angus, but on regarding the ragged fellows before him, he had to agree they hardly looked like a bunch of hardened criminals, just a sad lot of hungry, desperate men.

"You are free to go, but those of you who truly wish an honest job may stay and count that the marquess will provide you and your family with work, as well as food and shelter," she said, addressing the men. "We are going to need some help in getting his lordship down from here."

Hope slowly replaced fear in many of the faces. One man stepped forward, twisting a corner of his tattered jacket in his hands. "What would you have us do, milady?"

"We shall need a litter. Perhaps some of you can find two trees and a blanket and rope—"

"Aye, ma'am. I know what you mean, I'll see to it." The fellow who spoke jerked his head at two of his companions, and they hurried off.

"Somebody put on a pot of water to boil. And torches. We shall need a number of torches so we may light the way."

Several others nodded and set to work.

"And someone should go ahead of us and make sure a carriage is ready below," she continued. Her brow furrowed. "Though, I confess, I'm not quite sure how we will manage to get Julian down parts of that trail."

"There is another way down," piped up a voice. "It's shorter, too, and not nearly as steep, though it leads down the other side of the moor, close to Leadton."

Miranda gave a sigh of relief. "It doesn't matter where, so long as there is a road."

"I'll go, ma'am. The others can show you how to go." He hesitated before adding in an unsteady voice. "The authorities . . . they won't put me in jail, will they?"

Sykes dug deep in his pocket. "Take this." He pressed a gold button engraved with the marquess's crest into the man's hand. "It fell off one of the guv's jackets, and I hadn't gotten around to replacing it. Just tell them you are one of the marquess's men, and you won't have any trouble." He shot a menacing look at the cowering Scofield and Gibbs. "Make sure a magistrate is there as well."

The man set off at a trot.

Miranda was already at Sterling's side, smoothing the tangled dark locks from his streaked brow.

"How is he?" Sykes knelt down next to her.

She could barely control the tremor in her voice. "I fear he's badly hurt. I need to treat that leg before we can think of moving him."

The valet's expression became very grim, and he mut-

tered an oath. "It would nigh on kill him if he should
lose his leg."

Miranda took a deep breath. "Julian is *not* going to
lose his leg, Mr. Sykes. Now, help me get him nearer the
fire. Then find as clean a cloth as you can and start making some bandages."

He looked at his own soiled shirt and looked dubious.
She thought for a moment. "Please avert your eyes."
Lifting her skirt she tore off a large section of her chemise. "This should do." She thrust it into his hands, then
felt around on the ground until she found her scalpel
and the rest of her instruments. "Come, let's hurry."

Sykes waved two of the others over to help him, and
together they carried Sterling toward the crackling
flames.

"Build the fire higher," she ordered as she folded the
few blankets she could find into some sort of cushioning
from the hard ground. "And is there anything left in
that jug?"

Angus brought it over and poured the rest of the contents into a tin cup. She sniffed at it. "Is it strong?"

That brought a ghost of a grin to his face. "Aye, milady. That it is."

"Good. Then, help me get it down his throat." She
arranged a spare jacket over Sterling's chest. He stirred
slightly, and his eyes fluttered open. "Lord, he feels
cold." Her hand gently lifted his head. "Julian, please,
you must drink this." She put the cup to his lips and
forced him to take a swallow. Most of it went down,
though he coughed and tried to push it away.

To her relief, the alcohol had some effect. His dis-
jointed muttering ceased, and he fell back into a haze of
unconsciousness. She turned to Sykes and Angus. "I
need you to hold his leg as still as possible. If he stays
like this, it will be easier, but if he wakes. . . ."

They nodded their understanding.

"Mr. Sykes, please remove his boot."

She signaled for the pot bubbling over the fire. After

plunging her scalpel into the scalding water, she started to cut away the bloodied buckskins.

Angus sucked in his breath while Sykes had to look away for a moment. Miranda felt her own hands begin to tremble at the sight of the torn flesh and the jagged pieces of metal ripping through the skin. She clenched her teeth to steady her nerves and set to work. Slowly, with great skill, she made several small incisions. Reaching for the tweezers she used to extract the occasional splinter from one of her patients, she methodically began to remove the bits of shrapnel from the open wound. Every so often, she stopped to clean away the blood and check that the bleeding had not become too severe.

None of them spoke. It seemed the slivers of twisted metal would never come to an end. Finally, satisfied that she had found them all, she leaned back and wiped the beads of perspiration from her pale forehead with an audible sigh. Angus and Sykes looked drained as well. Next, she probed gently into the tissue and muscle surrounding the lacerations, looking for any further damage. One or two more fragments came out before she laid the medical instruments aside. Looping a length of black silk thread through a large needle, she set to stitching the skin together as neatly as possible.

When that was done, she sprinkled a small packet of basilicum powder over the wound. A large pad of folded material went over it, followed by a wrapping of the bandages Sykes had fashioned from her chemise.

"I fear that must do until we get him where he can be looked after properly." She looked up. "The last thing we need is two straight stout sticks, to serve as a splint of sorts, so his leg won't be jostled too badly in the journey."

When those had been tied in place, she got shakily to her feet. Her own limbs were so numb that on trying to take a step, she stumbled and would have tumbled headfirst had not Sykes reached out to catch her.

"Your pardon, Mr. Sy—" she started to stammer, but

the rest of the words caught in her throat, and all that came out was a strangled sob. A tear spilled onto her cheek, then another and another. She tried to brush them away. "S-Sorry. I don't know what's come over me. I'm not usually—"

Somehow she found her nose buried in the rough wool of the valet's coat, his calloused hand awkwardly patting the back of her head. He was not nearly as large as the marquess or Angus, but his shoulder felt just as reassuringly solid.

"Here, now, Lady Miranda, the worst of it is over."

When finally she regained a modicum of control over her emotions, she lifted her tearstained face and took a deep breath. "You must think me nothing more than an hysterical female," she murmured. "But truly, I am not usually prone to throwing a fit of vapors."

"Think you an hysterical female?" repeated Sykes as his brows rose in amazement. "Why, what I think is you've shown more courage than most seasoned soldiers, not to speak of being a dab hand at organizing your troops with more skill than any general I've ever seen." Unused to speaking so plainly to a lady, he shuffled his feet in embarrassment. "And, no doubt, you've saved the guv's leg."

Miranda's fingers fumbled with the folds of her skirt. "You are being more than kind." Then her head jerked up. "But nothing is assured yet. We must get his lordship down from here as quickly as possible." She looked around. "Is everything ready?"

"Aye, ma'am."

Angus had already tested the litter and assigned each man a place, taking one of the front positions for himself. A number of torches had been fashioned out of rags torn up from the spare clothing and bedding. At the big groom's signal, the marquess was gently lifted from the ground. Miranda carefully tucked another blanket around his unconscious form, and the small party headed off.

Sykes armed several of the remaining men and appointed them the task of trussing up the whining Scofield and Gibbs. "Keep a close guard on them until we can hand the miserable varmints over to the authorities."

The men smiled in grim pleasure. "You may count on us, Mr. Sykes. These two won't be slipping away."

The other trail was indeed easier, though there were stretches that made some rough going. In places the steepness caused the footing to become perilous while at times the narrowness made it tricky to maneuver. Slipping, sweating, straining, the men took great pains not to jostle their heavy burden. It was hard work, and every so often a stop would be made so that the torchbearers could exchange places with the men carrying the marquess.

Each time, Miranda would check that his leg had not begun to bleed through the bandages and to coax some water down his throat. Though he stirred occasionally under the thin blankets, he had yet to waken fully.

It was perhaps a blessing that he had not, she thought grimly, as she straightened the covers and motioned for the men to start up again. The pain would be intense, and she had no laudanum to help ease it. She could only hope that the man sent ahead would be able to marshal a proper doctor and a carriage.

As the trail pinched in, she was forced to fall back behind the litter. Close to exhaustion herself, Miranda found her steps faltering over a patch of treacherous scree. A hand came around her elbow and guided her to firmer ground.

"Come, walk with me for a bit, milady," said Sykes, who was bringing up the rear, the marquess's own pistols tucked at the ready in his belt. He took note of the dark smudges under her eyes and the slump in her shoulders, and kept a firm grip on her arm. "Just lean into my shoulder—why the guv would pin my ears back if I was to let you take a tumble and twist your ankle after all this."

Miranda managed a wan smile. "Somehow I doubt very much that you tremble at the prospect of any set-down from his lordship."

He grinned. "We have our understanding, the guv and me. I suppose that comes from pulling each other's irons out of the fire on more than one occasion."

"Mmmm."

They walked on for a bit in silence before Miranda spoke again. "I'm . . . glad that he had you to look after him during all those years," she said haltingly.

The valet's leathery cheeks reddened in embarrassed pleasure.

"Tell me how his leg was injured."

Sykes slanted a sideways glance at her. "You are sure you want to hear it? It is not, well, not a very pretty story."

She nodded. "I doubt that anything about war is very pretty, but, yes, I am sure."

He drew in a breath and told her of the battle. As he described the murderous havoc played by the Spanish battery sweeping the panicking foot soldiers, the desperate cavalry charge, and how it was repulsed, he could feel her whole body go rigid.

"No, go on," she said when he stopped, an expression of concern etched on his face. "I want to know."

He regarded her intently, then finished without further pause.

"And the saber scars he bears on his chest and arms. How did that happen?"

Sykes pursed his lips. "I'm . . . I'm not sure the guv would want me to be upsetting you with such—"

"Please, Mr. Sykes! Tell me about how he was hurt, how the two of you lived, how—oh, everything!" There was such a look of poignant need in her eyes that he heaved a sigh and shrugged in reluctant surrender. "No doubt he really will pin back my ears for this," he muttered, but went ahead anyway. The former batman told of the arduous campaigns, the boredom of camp life, the factions within Wellington's staff, leaving out mention, however, of the several dark-haired Spanish beauties who had come and gone in the marquess's life.

The sky was just beginning to show a graze of color at the horizon when Miranda had finally exhausted all her questions. And, in truth, by now she was so weary that she could barely put one foot in front of the other, let alone carry on a coherent conversation. Sykes, sensing how close she was to the limits of her endurance, kept a gentle grip on her elbow and fell in with the companionable silence. The faint trail had left the harsh terrain of the steep moor, leveling into a more discernible path through a woodland of live oak and beech. An occasional cart rut gave hint that they were nearly out of the wilds.

Sure enough, the trees soon gave way to a pasture hemmed in by a thick stone wall. Up ahead, several carriages along with an assortment of carts were drawn to a halt on the edge of a road, and a number of well-armed men milled around in obvious impatience. A shout went up as someone caught sight of the ragged band emerging from the swirling mists. Fresh hands came up to relieve the ones rubbed raw and bloody from the rough journey. While several of the local squires formed a belated escort around the marquess's litter, a doctor edged his way to Sterling's side and regarded his ashen face with a cluck of concern.

"Put his lordship into Lord Everleigh's carriage immediately," he shouted. "We must get him to Highcroft Manor as soon as possible." He looked around at the cluster of tired faces. "Can any of you men tell me what sort of injuries he has sustained?"

Sykes made his way to the front of the group. "Aye. It's his leg. He's taken a severe blow to an old war injury, and the fragments of shrapnel have torn it up something terrible. Mrs. Ransford"—he looked around for Miranda, but she had chosen to hang back—"Mrs. Ransford has tended to it—"

The doctor glanced at her, then pulled a face to show

what good he thought that would amount to. "Good Lord, man, let's not waste time in long-winded explanations. Are you part of his lordship's household?"

"His valet."

"Come with me, then." He took Sykes by the arm, then motioned for the men to load the litter into the head carriage.

Baron Ansley and Lord Everleigh began bellowing orders to the others who had been mustered in response to the alarm. Not to be outdone, the local magistrate piped in with his own demands to hear a full account of things. In all the jostling and shouting, Miranda was pushed even farther out of the way, a forlorn picture with her bedraggled hair, smudged face, and tattered gown. It was Angus who ploughed through the knot of the men and slipped his brawny arm around her shoulders. "Come, milady. Let me take you home."

Her eyes followed the litter until it disappeared into the elegant carriage. As Sykes climbed in after it, he managed a backward glance at her and gave a quick nod, as if to assure her that all would be well. Then he was gone, too.

She made no protest as Angus led her toward the other carriages and carts gathered along the verge. "Mrs. Ransford needs a ride home as well. To Lady Thornton's," he demanded in a deep voice, straightened up to his full height. "The marquess's aunt," he reminded those close by to add even more weight to his words.

"Ah, yes, of course." Baron Ansley cleared his throat. It was evident he had given not the slightest thought to her. His brow furrowed in impatience as he chewed on a corner of his lip. As a figure moved past them, he brightened and pointed to a modest curricle toward the back of the line. "You, Willsley! Be so kind as to drive Mrs. Ransford home." He gave a curt bow to her and hurried off to deal with the question of the prisoners.

Miranda let out a low sigh. "Yes, Angus. Let's go home."

Chapter Thirteen

"My dear, thank the Lord you are safe!" Lady Thornton crushed Miranda to her frail chest, not bothering in the least to stem the tears of relief that flowed down her cheek. "And Julian?"

"He's been hurt. His leg . . ." Miranda took a ragged breath and blinked away her own tears. "I saw to him as best I could, but . . ." Her lips began to quiver. "A doctor is with him now."

Sensing that her niece was perilously close to collapse, Lady Thornton collected herself and sprang into action. Hot water was ordered for a bath, along with a large glass of brandy.

"Drink it," she ordered, thrusting it into Miranda's trembling hands. "Every drop. And, Wells, see that Angus has a tot as well." She flashed a warm smile at the big groom, still hovering protectively behind Miranda. "As many as he wants."

Under her basilisk eye, Miranda was forced to choke down the contents of the glass. To Lady Thornton's satisfaction, the spirits brought a hint of color back to the pale cheeks. Ignoring the feeble protests from her niece, made even weaker by the effects of the brandy, she took hold of Miranda's arm and marched her to her bedchamber. Every stitch of torn and muddied clothing was stripped away, and her aching body eased beneath the steaming water.

Miranda's eyes drooped shut as fragrant suds came up to her chin. She opened her mouth as if to speak, but the soothing heat of both the bath and the brandy seemed to have melted away the last bit of resistance against the enveloping exhaustion. No words came out, just a funny sound somewhere between a croak and a sob.

"Julian has no doubt weathered far worse in Spain, my dear," whispered Lady Thornton. "He'll come through with flying colors. It is *you* we are concerned with now. You must rest. We'll talk later."

Miranda was scarcely aware of being toweled off, of her nightrail being tugged over her head, of being tucked between the sheets of her own bed. By the time the curtains were drawn, she had already given into a deep, dreamless sleep.

Looking up from her book, Lady Thornton stole a glance at her niece as she ruffled her son's curls and released him from her lap. The dark smudges beneath her eyes had lightened considerably, helped along by a day and a night of uninterrupted rest. Still, the fine lines etched around her mouth revealed that the ordeal was not nearly forgotten.

Justin sprawled on the patterned carpet and opened a wooden box. He, at least, seemed not a whit affected by the nasty ordeal he had experienced. His stubby fingers extracted a miniature cavalry officer, resplendid in full-dress uniform, from the tangle of toys. He galloped it over a series of imaginary hills. "It's Major," he announced. "Riding to Mama's rescue." His rich blue eyes, so like those of another, came up. "You see, I wasn't worried at all. I knew you were going to be safe because Major promised." A cloud seemed to darken the boy's soft features. "Major is going to be all right, isn't he?"

Miranda bit her lip, wondering how it was that little ears always managed to hear everything. "Yes, love, he will be fine, though it may be some time before he can come ride with you again."

"I wish he could be here now," said Justin as he took out a platoon of foot soldiers out of the box and positioned them behind the mounted figure. "He's a great gun. I wish he could be here *all* the time."

Miranda was saved from having to make any reply by the entrance of their butler, who handed Lady Thornton a sealed sheet of paper. Her chest tightened as she watched her aunt slowly unfold it and scan its contents.

"You see, my dear. It appears there is no reason for worry." Lady Thornton at last put down the note and removed her delicate gold spectacles. "Sykes writes that Julian has spent a restful night, and there is no sign of fever or infection."

It suddenly became less difficult to breathe. "It is still too early to tell," she replied as she watched Justin maneuver his band of lead soldiers across the parlor floor. "And I don't like that the doctor insists on keeping him dosed so heavily with laudanum that he hasn't regained consciousness."

"Well, at least he did not find fault with your efforts. Sykes says that the man had to admit that no more skillful job could have been done on Julian's injuries." A small smile stole across her aunt's features. "Though, our friend adds, it was obvious it pained him greatly to admit it."

Miranda made a face. "I have a distillation of willow bark and extracts I find quite effective for preventing fever," she continued. "And a salve for the wound that helps stave off any sort of infection." Her lips tightened. "Though I doubt the doctor would pay any attention to my suggestions."

"Perhaps not, but I have no doubt that Sykes would be more than willing to do whatever you asked. By the tone of the note here, he seems very . . . impressed with your abilities."

"Jul—his lordship is lucky to have such a good man about him," she murmured.

Lady Thornton appeared to ignore the fumbling of words. Her face came alight. "Yes, that's a splendid idea," she mused aloud. "We shall just have to deliver your medicines to Highcroft Manor so we may rest assured that Julian is receiving the proper treatment. I had planned to visit in any case." There was a fraction of a pause. "Do you care to come as well? Sykes may need some guidance in what to do."

Miranda's face betrayed the warring of her emotions. "I . . . I think not," she finally answered. Her eyes couldn't keep from straying to her son, still engrossed in his games of make-believe. She, however, had no such childish illusions. "I don't belong at Highcroft Manor," she added in a low voice. "You will have no trouble explaining my directions to Mr. Sykes." She rose abruptly. "I'll fetch what you'll need from my stores."

"Do that one more time, and I shall be tempted to ram that smile right down your throat," growled Sterling.

Sykes took on an injured expression. "I'm only doing following Lady Miranda's orders, guv. She says that it's important to move the joint a little every day else it will grow together all stiff and tight. And I'm only smiling because we're making progress—your leg is able to bend a good deal more than even two days ago." He gave a sniff. "So don't go ringing a peal over my head."

A sheen of sweat coated the marquess's forehead, and he gritted his teeth against the pain as his valet took hold of his knee and flexed it again.

"I suppose that will do for the day," said Sykes, leaning back from the task and wiping his own brow.

"Don't do me any great favors," muttered the marquess.

His valet shot him another aggrieved look, surprised at his employer's uncharacteristic irritability. "It isn't as if I'm enjoying myself any more than you are, guv. Now, stop squawking, and I'll just unwrap the bandages and have a look at how those flesh wounds are healing."

Sterling had the grace to color. "Your pardon, Sykes. I'm afraid this interminable bed rest has made me snappish as a caged bear." He fell back against the pillow. "And I don't expect you to play the nursemaid to me.

Surely some local girl may be hired to do these tedious tasks."

"You know I don't mind." A true grin split his weathered face. "Besides, when you start jawing at me, I know you're feeling better." The smile faded somewhat as he undid the bandages and regarded the jagged cuts. "I don't like that bit of red there," he murmured, applying a generous dab of salve to the entire area. "It doesn't look quite right."

The marquess craned his neck to see. "Are you sure? Dr. Reynolds noticed nothing amiss this morning."

"Hmmph." The valet's grimace indicated what he thought of the learned doctor's opinion. "I'm not sure that nodcock would notice if you grew scales and sprouted wings, he's so intent on currying your favor."

"You think him a toadeater?"

"I think him a jackass."

That drew a chuckle from Sterling.

"It's no joke, guv. Why, I had to threaten the fellow with bodily harm to stop him from plying you so full of narcotic that it would have been months before your eyes uncrossed. And on top of that, he had the nerve to try and throw away the medicines Lady Miranda made up for you. Called her a quack, he did. A meddlesome, ignorant female." Sykes grew even more heated. "I should have darkened his deadlights right then," he added under his breath.

The marquess bristled. "He called her meddlesome and ignorant?"

"Aye. And her knowing more about healing arts than any sawbones I ever met." He looked down at Sterling's injured leg once more and pursed his lips. "Perhaps I shall ride over to Lady Thornton's today and ask her advice on this."

In truth, the spot in question was, at worse, only a trifle redder than the surrounding areas, but Sykes was not averse to a bit of exaggeration if he could contrive for Miranda to feel compelled to make a visit. For it wasn't mere confinement that was driving the marquess to distraction.

And Sykes felt sure Miranda felt the same. Every few days he had stopped in at Lady Thornton's to keep the two ladies informed on Sterling's condition, and while Miranda had questioned him concerning the injuries and provided medical suggestions with a cool efficiency, she couldn't quite hide the true depths of her emotions from his keen gaze. It was clear she would have liked to hear of more than the medical details, though she held back from asking anything of a personal nature. Still, he noticed how her hands stopped whatever they were doing when he repeated some little anecdote concerning the marquess and how he had passed his day. He gave a mental shake of his head, wondering if ever the erstwhile couple would admit to what was really ailing them.

"Hmmph," remarked Sterling after some thought. "Perhaps it is time to give the good doctor his notice." Another silence followed as Sykes straightened up the marquess's dressing table. "You are going to visit the Hall?"

"I could do with some fresh air—that is, unless there is something you'd rather have me attend to."

"No, not at all," answered the marquess quickly. "You will of course give my regards to my aunt and tell her I look forward to her next visit, though I don't intend to let her win another fortune at cards." He cleared his throat. "My regards to Miranda, too." After a fraction of a pause he added rather self-consciously, "She is . . . well?"

Sykes couldn't resist. Repressing a grin, he turned to rearrange the set of silver-backed brushes. "Your aunt is in fine fettle. I should say she's as sprightly as a lady half her years."

Sterling's face fell ever so slightly.

The valet relented. "Lady Miranda appears quite fine as well, and shows no ill effects from her ordeal." He dusted a bottle of bay rum on his sleeve. "There's a very brave lady, guv. All courage and heart. Why, if you could have seen the way she took aim at that bastard when he threatened to go at you again."

The marquess murmured something unintelligible in reply.

"Well, then, if you're not needing me for anything else, I'll be on my way."

Sykes put down the delicate china teacup with great care and shifted uncomfortably in his chair. "I'm not used to having to act the gentleman," he mumbled, looking around the cozy parlor. "A tin cup is more what I am accustomed to."

The corners of Lady Thornton's lips twitched. "Well, I assure you that you show to better advantage than most fellows who can lay claim to the title, Mr. Sykes. Another cake?"

The valet shook his head and stood up rather awkwardly. "I'd best be heading back, ma'am. I like to keep my eye on the guv, seeing as I don't trust any of the advice given by that Dr. Reynolds. In my humble opinion, he has no notion of what he is about."

Lady Thornton's face pinched in concern. "You don't think my nephew is healing as he ought?"

He gave an eloquent shrug. "Well, I can't rightly tell, having no skill in these things myself."

Miranda rose abruptly. "Come along with me, Mr. Sykes. I'll give you a fresh supply of salve and an herbal tisane that may help his lordship sleep through the night."

Sykes followed her through the kitchen to a small pantry near the scullery door that served to hold her stores.

"You say there is a redness around the sutures? What is the doctor's opinion?" she asked as she began to sort through an array of vials and crocks.

The valet gave a snort. "All he wants to do is shut the windows up tight, claiming it is the night air that causes inflammation."

Miranda's mouth tightened. "Fool," she muttered under her breath. "Is the skin hot to the touch?"

"I, er . . . I'm afraid I can't really say."

For several moments there was only the sound of bottles clinking and jars being uncapped.

"Is there any sign of fever?"

"I don't think so."

Miranda went back to filling a small vial with a viscous ointment the color of deep amber.

"I, er, I don't suppose you might spare the time to look at the leg yourself, ma'am? That way you might tell me what I should do."

Her fingers froze on what she was doing. "It is not a question of time, Mr. Sykes," she said in a voice barely above a whisper. "The matter is a good deal more . . . complicated than that."

"I'm sorry. I had no right to ask you. Besides, surely the doctor must know what he is doing. I mean, there's many who believe that drawing a cup or two of blood from a patient is effective in fighting off an inflammation."

Her head jerked up. "The doctor means to bleed him! Why, that's all wrong! I have never known the practice to be of the least good—indeed, I believe it only does harm."

Sykes gave a pained grimace. "In that case I shall do my best to prevent it."

She bit her lip.

"I daresay the guv won't allow it either, that is, if he's strong enough to argue." Sykes hoped he wasn't doing it a bit too brown. Seeing the look of distress that crossed Miranda's face, he felt a momentary prick of guilt at taking liberties with the truth, but then quickly pushed such feelings aside with the reminder that he was only acting for the higher good. Heaving an exaggerated sigh, he held out his horny palm for her preparations. "Thank you for your trouble, ma'am."

Instead of handing over the medicines, she shoved

them into the pocket of her gown. "Please have Angus saddle the filly while I fetch my cloak, Mr. Sykes."

The valet ducked his head to hide his smile. "Yes, ma'am!"

Nothing seemed to be of the least interest this afternoon, Sterling noted with some dismay. Not history. Not poetry. Not even the Bard was able to keep his attention from straying. By the time he reached the end of even the simplest sentence, the beginning had already eluded him. The elegant printed words stared back at him, as incomprehensible as his own inability to concentrate.

No doubt it was the sheer boredom of confinement that was driving him to distraction. He should be feeling a sense of satisfaction, for he had accomplished what he had set out to do. The ringleader was dead, and with the information supplied by the man's terrified underlings, Lord Atwater was well on the way to tracking down the mastermind of the recent troubles. Yet somehow things did not feel entirely resolved.

With a snort of frustration, he tossed aside the leather-bound volume and stared at the stream of sunlight flooding in through the tall, mullioned windows of his bedchamber. It looked to be a lovely day. He couldn't help but wonder what Miranda was doing. Was she out with Justin, gathering herbs for her healing arts? Or was she perhaps taking him for a ride, the breeze ruffling their hair as they cantered through the fields.

The devil take it, he missed her! He missed the way her eyes turned a shade greener when she laughed, the way her voice could drop to a smoky timbre, the way her lips crooked into a smile. And he missed his son. He wished to be out there as well, wherever they were, sharing the warmth of their laughter.

Teeth set against the stab of pain, Sterling gingerly flexed his leg. Sykes was right. The improvement was noticeable, and the discomfort was lessening with each day. Throwing back the covers, he swung his feet to the ground, cautiously testing the weakened limb. It still hurt like the devil, but the leg would bear his weight.

And there was something else. Missing was the sensation of a knife twisting inside his flesh every time he moved, something he had come to accept would be inexorably part of him for the rest of his days. His valet had told him of what Miranda had done that night, of how she had refused to stitch him up until she had patiently picked out every twisted shard of metal she could find in his ravaged leg. He hardly dared allow himself to hope it would make a difference, but the feeling was . . . different.

Good Lord, he might truly be able to hoist his son in the air without an awkward stumble. He might offer to carry Miranda's basket without fear of falling on his rump. He might even waltz with a lady in his arms without feeling like half a man.

Emboldened, he tried a step.

Only his hand's firm grip on one of the carved posts of his imposing bed saved him from ending in a heap on the floor. With a rueful grimace, he eased himself back onto the soft mattress. It would be a difficult task, almost like being a babe again learning its first steps, but he would start right away. As soon as Sykes returned.

Bloody hell. Where was the fellow? thought the marquess. He had been gone a devil of a long time. No doubt he had been invited to stay and chat with his aunt—and Miranda. Somehow the notion only served to increase his irritation at being confined to bed.

At the sound of footsteps in the hall, Sterling hastily rearranged the sheets and sank back against the pillows with some relief, finding that even so paltry a physical effort had taxed his strength. But at least the return of his valet promised a welcome respite from tedious tomes and chafing silence. A game of chess might serve as a distraction, provided he spotted Sykes a rook and a knight. And perhaps he might even convince the man to allow a thick slab of beefsteak to be sent up instead of that cursed boiled fowl, and a good claret instead of sugared tea.

It was time he set himself to making a full recovery.

Chapter Fourteen

The door opened.

"Bloody well time you got your arse back here," muttered the marquess. A bit of verbal sparring usually served to punch away his flat spirits. When there was not the usual sharp retort, he slowly opened his eyes.

"Miranda!"

She swallowed hard in evident embarrassment. "Mr. Sykes told me . . . that is, he would have had me believe your condition was in danger of becoming very grave, else I should never have thought to . . . intrude on your privacy."

Behind her, the valet gave a strangled cough.

"You certainly do not seem in danger of sticking your spoon into the wall just yet, but from what Mr. Sykes tells me, it appears that doctor has a number of foolish notions, which of course is not surprising, given how set in their ways the medical profession is," she continued in a rush. "They are never able to admit they may be wrong, while in my experience there are any number of local remedies that have proven to be effective in treating injuries such as yours." She knew she was gabbling on like a Bedlamite, but she couldn't seem to stop. Just as she couldn't seem to force her eyes away from a spot below his neck where the unbuttoned top of his nightshirt was exposing a hint of the dark ringlets on his broad chest. To her dismay, she felt her face begin to flame. "Now, since Mr. Sykes seems to believe that certain of my salves are of some help, and since he seems to have little faith in the doctor, either, I—"

"I'm glad you came."

There was no mistaking the sincerity in his voice, or the warmth of the smile that had spread over his face. She stopped in some confusion, still unable to meet his eyes.

Sykes made another sound in his throat. "I had best go check on how Cook is coming with the, er, gruel for your supper, guv."

Miranda spun around. "But, Mr. Sykes—"

He was already gone.

The smile was still on Sterling's lips when she turned back. "Well, now that I am here, sir, I had best have a look at how your leg is healing."

Sterling's mouth crooked at the corners. "Sir?" he repeated softly. "Is it back to 'sir' and 'your lordship'? The last time we spoke, you called me Julian."

Her color deepened. "I . . . wasn't thinking properly."

"Then I should wish your thoughts to remain in a whirl."

There was no fear on that score, she admitted to herself. Had the man any idea how devastatingly handsome he looked when he smiled like that? Good Lord, she knew it was a mistake to come.

"And how is Justin?" he added after a moment.

Grateful for the change of subject, she answered quickly. "He is quite fine, and wishes me to tell you that . . . he misses you."

"I miss him as well." Sterling unaccountably turned to look out the window again. "Tell me, he has no lingering effects from his experience? No nightmares or such? It must have been a very frightening thing for a child to see his mother taken."

Her lips quirked. "On the contrary. He was not afraid at all. He told Aunt Sophia that since you had promised him that you would see me safe, there was no reason to worry."

Sterling found himself blushing like a schoolroom miss just paid her first flowery compliment, and felt nearly as giddy. "Did he?"

Miranda withdrew a square of paper from her pocket, smoothed out its folds, and placed it on his lap. "That is you," she said, pointing at the lopsided stick figure drawn in colored chalk perched atop an odd tan blob. "And that is Zeus, in case you have trouble recognizing your gallant steed, galloping neck and leather to the rescue."

The marquess's jaw worked as he stared at the exuberant scrawls. For a moment he wondered whether he was going to disgrace himself with a rather unmanly show of emotion.

Miranda moved a chair closer to the side of the massive carved bed. "Now, about that leg." She turned down the covers, exposing a good deal of his long, muscled limbs, and hesitantly turned the nightshirt up above his knees.

He sucked in his breath at her gossamer touch. Now he feared the danger might be that he would disgrace himself with a show of emotion that was decidedly *not* unmanly.

With great care, she gently undid the bandages and began to inspect the wound. Her fingers probed along the line of sutures, then ran over the small area of swelling. "Well," she said after a bit. "Mr. Sykes was right to notice the slight inflammation, but it's nothing to be overly concerned about. The salve I have brought should remedy the matter." Her hand remained on his thigh, while she took hold of his knee and bent it slightly. "How does this feel?"

"Hardly a twinge. In fact, I daresay I'm ready to be on my feet again."

"I should not like you to rush things, but I suppose you may be permitted to try a few steps in another day or two." She made to move away but his hand covered hers.

"I haven't had a chance to thank you. Sykes told me

what you did that night. I would have lost my leg, if not my life, were it not for your skill," he said.

"Neither your leg nor your life would have been in danger had you not come after me. It is I who owe the thanks. You needn't have taken such a risk. I . . . I never expected it."

An inscrutable expression flitted across his lean features. "No," he said in a low whisper. "I've given you no reason to think I'd do aught but turn my back on you in a time of need."

The very nearness of him—the heat emanating through the fine cotton fabric, the faint scent of bay rum, the strong touch of his long fingers—along with his strange words had thrown her into a state of even greater confusion. She managed to slip her hand out from under his and stood up abruptly. "That leg must be rebandaged, my lord. Has Mr. Sykes left any linen about?"

Sterling's brows came together slightly at her choice of address. "On the dressing table, I believe."

She went to fetch the roll of soft material, only to stop short at the sight of the neat arrangement of the marquess's things on the burled walnut top. There were the same two silver-backed brushes she had seen every morning of her marriage. Such a trivial little thing, but it was that which was her undoing.

All at once her shoulders began to shake.

"Miranda?"

She refused to turn around.

"Miranda! Please, tell me what's the matter!"

She fought down a rising wave of hysteria. How could she possibly explain?

Her hand brushed angrily at the trickle of tears. "It's nothing. Nothing at all."

There was a thud as his feet hit the floor. He lurched forward, steadying himself on the back of the chair to keep from ending up in a heap at her feet.

"Julian! You mustn't—"

Then she was in his arms, her wet cheek pressed against his shoulder.

"There, you see, I won't fall now," he murmured in her ear. "I have you to support me." He held her even tighter. "Won't you tell me why you are crying?"

"It's so ridiculous." And, in truth, she felt like an utter fool for having turned into the worst sort of watering pot over something so absurd. She tried to raise her head, but his hand prevented her from pulling away.

"Please. Tell me," he urged.

"The brushes," she said haltingly, her body going stiff with embarrassment. "It's such a silly thing, I know. But—"

Sterling's eyes filled with understanding. "We bought them on Bond Street. You had chosen a silver comb and cachepot for your earrings," he whispered. "To tease you, I chose the most extravagant set of brushes I could find. The design is still as hideous as ever, is it not?"

Miranda wasn't sure if she was laughing or crying.

He lifted her chin, and his lips came down upon hers.

The kiss fairly seared her senses. It was hard, possessive, full of need, and this time her response was more than fleeting. She opened her mouth to his demand, and their tongues entwined. A groan rumbled in his throat as he thrust in deeper, drinking in the taste of her. Their bodies arched closer together. Miranda could feel every taut muscle and plane of his body through the thin fabric of his nightshirt, then the hard ridge of his arousal pressed up against her front.

She gave a low cry as he released her mouth to trail a string of kisses along the line of her jaw. Her hands came up to tangle in his long raven locks as she sought out his lips once more.

"I thought the two of you might like some tea." Sykes stepped through the half-opened door with a silver tray in his hands. "Shall I—" The words died in his throat, a look of sheer mortification spreading across his leathery face. "Good Lord, I didn't realize I was . . . interrupting. . . ." He started to edge backward.

Miranda gave a horrified gasp and tried to push away from the marquess's chest. "No! You are not interrupting—that is, it is not exactly what you might think," she stammered. "His lordship was attempting to walk and . . ."

"And making great strides, it appears," quipped Sykes, unable to repress a grin.

Miranda went scarlet, and her head dropped in embarrassment.

The valet looked stricken on realizing what he had unwittingly done. "Please, milady, I shan't forgive myself if I've gone and upset you."

"The fault is not yours, it's mine," she said in a small voice.

Sykes shook his head. "As far as I can see, ma'am, there's no fault at all. I daresay nothing in the least wrong has occurred. When two people—"

"*Everything* wrong has occurred," she interrupted in a voice made shrill by her overwrought emotions. "It's *wrong* that I came to the marquess's residence. It's *wrong* that I should be in his bedchamber, in his arms. And it's most certainly *wrong* that I return his embraces—"

Sterling gently drew her back toward him. "No, my love, it's entirely right. A man may kiss his wife—"

"But I am *not* your wife anymore."

"Perhaps it's time to remedy that," he replied quietly.

Her mouth went very dry.

"Upon my word, guv, you've finally come to your senses! That's the best idea you've had since engaging me as your batman." Sykes rubbed at his chin. "Now, let me see, first off you'll need a special license if you mean to put things right without any more delay."

"It's been in my desk for several weeks."

The valet's face was wreathed in a broad smile. "I always said you was a dab hand at planning. It's still early—shall I fetch the vicar now?"

"Aye. And on your way back, you must stop and bring back my aunt and my son so they may be part of the celebration. Oh, and why not ask Angus and Jem to join us as well." His lips brushed against her forehead. "It may not be St. George's in Hanover Square this time, my love, but we will have the people we care about most with us." He looked back at Sykes. "Tell Cook she will have to outdo herself tonight, for we will be in need of a wedding supper."

Miranda finally found her voice. "Have both of you taken leave of your senses? Mr. Sykes, you will ignore his lordship's orders. I fear he has succumbed to a sudden fever and has lost all reason."

Sterling chuckled. "I may be delirious, but only with happiness, my love. Now, on your way, Sykes."

"Mr. Sykes!"

"Sorry, milady." He gave her a little wink. "But an order is an order, and I dare not disobey."

"Wait!"

The valet hesitated.

The marquess's brows rose in question.

Miranda took a deep breath. Things were happening at a dizzying rate. She needed a moment to collect herself and grasped at the one reason for delay that no man could possibly argue with. "For one thing, surely neither of you could expect a female to consent to being married dressed like *this.*"

Her gesture took in the front of her shabby gown, the frayed cuffs and hem, the discreetly mended tears, and the faded color that now lingered somewhere between smoke and dust. Sykes pursed his lips, unable to think of any reply, but the marquess merely smiled once more.

"Indeed not. Fortunately, there is a trunkful of Madame Celeste's creations freshly arrived from London. Sykes, on your way downstairs, have one of the maids lay them out in the adjoining suite so that Miranda may take her choice. And make sure that she sees that dress"—he indicated the offending garment—"is consigned to the rag bin, where my wife will never have to lay her eyes on it again."

The valet left the forgotten tea tray on top of the marquess's polished bureau and snapped a smart salute as he hurried from the room. The door came firmly shut behind him.

Overcome with confusion, Miranda fell silent and refused to meet Sterling's gaze.

The laughter died from his face. "I'm sorry. Good Lord, I've made a worse mull of things than before. I meant to pay my addresses properly and with polish this time, not stammer them out like some tongue-tied idiot."

She murmured something, in so soft a voice that he had to ask her to repeat the words.

"I never thought of them as idiotic."

"They were those of a callow schoolboy." He gave a crooked smile. "I've composed a countless number of more eloquent speeches these past number of days, but I find all the fine words have suddenly deserted me. Can you bring yourself to accept my proposal of marriage—along with my deepest regret for the pain of the past? I shall endeavor to be a better husband to you in the future."

Miranda looked up in a shock. "*You* are apologizing?"

"Yes. I have come to realize how pompous and foolish I was. We all make mistakes. Instead of trying to understand and work things out, I cast away the thing I loved best in a fit of childish pique. You may not countenance it, but I have suffered perhaps as much as you from it. I have missed you every day of these past seven years."

Her head sank against his shoulder. "Yes, I made a mistake, but not the one you think. I should have come to you and forced you to listen rather than retreat behind a wall of pride. Aunt Sophia has always said I was a fool to have given you up so easily. She might have made me see reason, but then . . . you were gone."

"The past doesn't matter anymore."

"It does, though." She choked down a sob. "Julian, I cannot marry you."

He went very pale. "Why not?"

When she didn't answer right away, he tipped her chin up so that she was forced to look in his eyes. "I had come to believe that you still harbored some regard for me, but perhaps I am wrong. Is your heart engaged elsewhere?"

"No," she whispered. "I shall never love anyone but you."

His face betrayed his relief. "Then, why?"

Still she remained silent. As he made to caress her cheek, his leg buckled slightly, drawing a cry of alarm from Miranda. Her arm came around his waist in support, and she guided him back to the side of the bed, forcing him to take a seat on the plump mattress. To her surprise, he refused to release her and drew her down close beside him.

"I won't be driven away so easily this time, Miranda. I want you here next to me every night. I want to raise our son together. I want to have other sons and daughters with you as well. Good Lord, one lesson I have learned in war is that there are precious few second chances in life, so let us not waste this one."

She buried her face in his shoulder. "That you could offer your forgiveness means more to me than I can ever express, but. . . ." Her voice faltered. "But you would always think, in your heart, that I had been capable of betraying you. I don't think I could bear it, Julian."

It was suddenly very difficult for him to catch his breath, as if her big groom had landed another powerful blow to the middle of his chest. Struggling to recover a semblance of control, he managed a hoarse whisper. "I think it's time you help me understand what happened that night."

"Do you know how many times I have wished that I had heard that request on your lips, rather than see the look of bitter accusation in your eyes?"

"I am asking it now, Miranda. Tell me, and strip the past of the power to hurt us anymore."

She looked up at him, a mixture of hope and fear mingled in her expression.

Hope that he was right, and fear that he may not believe the truth. That was the crux of it, wasn't it, she admitted to herself? She had been too afraid of what his choice would have been when faced with trusting her or another. She wasn't sure she could have survived that sort of rejection, and so she had hidden behind pride and anger. She had survived all the insults and hardships thrown at her by Society—that had seemed almost easy in comparison.

Was she strong enough now to meet the same challenge?

As their eyes met, Sterling gave her hand a gentle squeeze of encouragement. The decision suddenly didn't seem so difficult.

"There was no clandestine meeting in the library with some lover."

Sterling's throat tightened.

"It was. . . ." She nearly choked on the words. ". . . it was Lord Averill. He found me alone and tried to convince me to dally with me."

The marquess's eyes pressed closed as the awful truth began to sink in.

"When I refused, he . . . he forced his attentions on me, just enough to put me in the state you saw." She shuddered at the memory. "I tried to fight back, but he was too strong. After he had humiliated me, he warned me not to speak of it to anyone, lest you be caught up in a scandal. I agreed, thinking it would save you any . . . hurt."

Sterling fought down the urge to be sick.

"And so he left the room, telling me to wait for a bit before I tried to make my way to my room." She shuddered. "What a gudgeon I was to believe he had even a shred of honor. I had heard him mutter that he would see me suffer for thwarting his plans. I just never imagined even he could come up with such a malicious plot."

"Good God. And instead of the support you needed, I gave you only harsh accusations." Sterling's arms fell away from her, and he buried his head in his hands. "I deserve every ounce of your scorn, and more," came his hollow voice. "Averill sought me out in the billiard room, and with a great sigh of regret told me that as a friend and a gentleman he felt obliged to inform me of what he had seen. He claimed that he had gone looking for a book in the library, only to surprise you and a lover . . . in the throes of lovemaking, and quite clearly enjoying it." His jaw worked. "He was always the clever one, and he certainly sensed how vulnerable I was to the suggestion that perhaps I wasn't man enough to hold your esteem. Well, he played me for the fool. And what a fool I was, not to see through his shameless lies."

"Then, you . . . you believe me?"

"My God, how you must hate me," was his only response.

"No." Her hand stroked through his tangled locks. "Oh, I told myself I did because it helped me bear what followed. But I always knew I was only fooling myself." She sighed. "It was unfair—I didn't give you a chance. What else could you think when confronted with such a sight. I should have followed you and forced you to listen! It is only to your credit that you could not conceive of a gentleman making such a mockery of honor."

"You are far too generous in excusing my actions. As your husband, I promised to love and protect you, and I failed miserably. I see now that I don't deserve a second chance."

The marquess raised his head, and to Miranda's shock there were tears on his lean cheeks.

"Oh, Julian."

Cradled in her arms, he wept like a child.

When at last he stopped, she lifted his face and pressed her lips to his salty skin. "We all deserve a second chance," she murmured between kisses. "And I think you are right. That monster, and the past, has held us in his thrall long enough. Let our tears today wash the slate clean. I love you, Julian. I finally understand that is what is important. You. Me. Our son. The future."

He hardly dared hope. "My love, are you saying you might consider—"

"I am saying that if your offer still stands, my answer is yes."

There was no need for further words.

It was some time later that a discreet knock finally interrupted their embraces.

"Er, sorry to disturb you, guv, but the vicar will be arriving shortly, and so will Lady Thornton, who is fairly bursting with curiosity to know what is going on. I barely escaped the thumbscrews and rack as it is."

Sterling gave a soft laugh. "No doubt she is. Well, I suppose I had best allow Sykes in here to make me presentable." He glanced down at his rumpled nightshirt and grinned. "I'm afraid I would cut a sorry picture indeed were I to appear at my nuptials clad only in this."

Miranda looked at her own sadly disheveled dress and smiled, too. "I had better see to myself as well. Aunt Sophia would never forgive me if I didn't rid myself of this gown. Nor can I claim I shall be sorry to see it go."

"There is a ivory-watered silk gown trimmed in a smoky emerald to match your eyes. It occurred to me as soon as I saw it that it would make a splendid wedding dress."

She stood up, but he kept hold of her hand for a moment longer. "Have I told you that you have grown even more beautiful over the years?"

"Perhaps you need spectacles at your advanced age, my dear."

She had gone only a few steps before a sharp exclamation caused her to turn around.

"Dash it all! A ring! The one thing I've forgotten is a ring."

Miranda undid a button at her bodice and drew out a thin filigree chain that hung around her neck. Suspended on its length was a simple gold band. "Perhaps we may give this a second chance as well."

Lady Thornton regarded the marquess and his bride through lowered lashes as she raised her glass of champagne. "My dears, you really must be more careful about subjecting an old lady to such unexpected surprises— why, it's very taxing on the heart, you know. Not that I mind this particular shock," she added. "I don't. In fact, I couldn't be happier over the turn of events."

"Shock—hah!" exclaimed Sterling with a grin. "If Wellington had a general half so clever with planning and strategy, the war would have been over long ago."

Her lips twitched. "Really, Julian, I have no idea what you are talking about."

The marquess gave a chuckle as he shifted in his chair. The late afternoon sunlight flooding the airy drawing room caught a glint of gold on the hand that touched his shoulder. Miranda leaned close to her husband's ear. "You must be careful about letting yourself become too fatigued, Julian. I am not at all convinced it is the best thing for you to be out of bed for so long."

A roguish grin spread over his face. "Neither am I, but we shall rectify that shortly."

Her cheeks became a pretty shade of rose.

"But I fear it would be rag-mannered to desert our guests quite yet."

"Where *are* the rest of our guests?"

"Sykes is introducing Angus and Jem to the delights of champagne while giving them a tour of the stables, and then I believe he was going to take Justin to see the litter of puppies at the kennel."

A chorus of furious barking and yelps of delight confirmed the last statement. The next moment Justin burst into the room, the tail of his shirt hanging out from his muddied pantaloons, a shaggy little creature nipping at his heels. "Mama! Major! Isn't he nice?" He scooped the puppy up into his arms, blissfully unaware of the series of paw prints now tattooed across his chest. "Mr. Sykes said that I could choose the one I liked best—that is, if you say it is all right to keep him." He looked at Miranda with undisguised longing. "Mama, I don't think he will cost very much to feed, and I could always share my own supper with him."

"I don't believe that will be necessary, love. But you must also ask his lordship."

Justin turned an eager face to Sterling.

"I think the expense of a puppy can be managed," he said dryly.

As if to cement the new friendship, the puppy began squirming in Justin's arms and running his pink tongue all over the little boy's face.

"Perhaps you might let Sykes take your new friend into the kitchen for some warm milk," suggested Sterling, noting that the animal's tail was beginning to twitch in a rather ominous manner.

The valet nodded in understanding and quickly whisked the puppy out of the room to the accompaniment of its doleful howls. Fortunately, the accident the marquess had foreseen might happen occurred just out of range of the expensive Oriental carpet.

"Oh, dear, I'm afraid you have no idea how much your peaceable existence is about to change," murmured Miranda.

There was a decided twinkle in Sterling's eyes. "I daresay Sykes and I shall learn to cope with unruly animals and muddy children."

Justin stared in some dismay at the state of his dress. "I didn't mean to—"

The marquess ruffled the little boy's hair. "I imagine I ruined a good deal more clothing in my time than you, lad. Now that I am to look after you and your mama, you needn't worry about that."

Justin's eyes grew wide. "Then, it is true?" he ventured

in a voice tinged with awe. "Mr. Sykes said that Mama and I were to come live with you, but I thought that, well, maybe he was just teasing me."

Sterling reached out and hoisted the boy onto his lap. "No, it was no joke. Does that meet with your approval?"

Justin wound his arms around the marquess's neck, wreaking havoc with the precise folds of his neck cloth. "Oh, I should like it above all things!" There was a brief pause. "Can Aunt Sophia live with us, too? And Angus and Jem?"

"They have all been invited," answered Sterling.

A blissful smile came to his lips as his head nestled against the marquess's shoulder and his eyes drooped half shut. "Why, today has been just like one of the fairy tales you read to me, Mama, where all wishes come true," he said in a sleepy voice.

"Indeed, lad. Indeed." Sterling hugged him closer while exchanging smiles with Miranda.

Lady Thornton put aside her glass and rose. "I think Justin has had quite enough excitement for one day—as have we all! I will take him home and leave the two of you some peace and quiet on your wedding night." A flicker of sly amusement crossed her face. "I leave it to you, Miranda, to see that Julian does not suffer any ill effects from all of the strenuous activities required of him today."

The marquess repressed a chuckle. "You are a marvel, Aunt Sophia."

"Yes, aren't I?"

Sykes came back into the room, followed by Angus and Jem. Seeing that Sterling was about to attempt getting to his feet, the small boy still in his arms, the big groom moved quickly to the marquess's side.

"Here, now, yer lordship, I'll make sure to see the bairn safely home."

Sterling handed over his drowsy son without hesitation. "Yes, I know you will. My thanks, Dagleish. For everything."

Angus bobbed his head in awkward acknowledgment.

"Did you find the stables to your liking?" inquired Sterling after a moment.

Emboldened by the champagne, Jem couldn't keep his own answer from bubbling out. "Cor, I ain't seen such prime horseflesh, and Will—that is, Mr. Sykes—says that they don't begin to hold a candle to what's at Crestwood." The awe in his voice was mirrored in the widened eyes that wandered over the rich carpets, the mahogany furniture and magnificent woodwork of the room.

"Do I take that as an acceptance to come work for me?"

"Oh, yes, sir!" He swallowed hard. "That is, if Lady Thornton don't have need of me."

Lady Thornton smiled. "As I plan to accept my niece and nephew's kind invitation to spend a good part of the year with them, I fear I will have little call for a staff other than Wells and Mrs. Walters to keep up Talney Hall."

Jem let out a sigh of relief.

"And you, Dagleish. What say you?" asked Sterling.

The big groom took a moment to answer. "Well, I suppose I'd best say yes, since someone needs te keep an eye on everyone—and to knock some sense into ye if you ever bring a tear ta the eye of your wife again."

"I assure you, I shall stay in line," murmured the marquess. "Though I would take it kindly that you do not spread the word to the rest of my staff that you are in the habit of giving me a thrashing. Not at all the thing, you see. My other grooms are actually a bit in awe of me."

Angus gave what for him was a broad grin. "I think we can come ta some agreement on that."

Sterling signaled to Sykes. "Have John Coachman bring round the carriage and escort all of our guests home. Oh, and take along several bottles for the ride. It seems our friends have had no difficulty acquiring a taste for champagne."

Lady Thornton raised an eyebrow as the others made rather eagerly for the entrance hall. "Well, that should make for a jolly trip home."

"As well it should be."

"As well it should be," she agreed. She blew a kiss to each of them, then turned to leave herself. On reaching the paneled oak door, she paused, then gave a quick wink before pulling it firmly closed.

Sterling was shaking with repressed laughter.

Miranda grinned as well, but her hand stroked his shoulder in some concern. "Julian, you mustn't tire yourself too much. I think it's time we went upstairs."

He took her hand and brought it to his lips. "Yes, my love, I couldn't agree with you more. It's high time we begin sharing our nights together again."